Veritas Series

CAT'S PAW
KILLING GAME
BROKEN DREAMS

KILLING GAME

A Veritas Novel

Jana Oliver

Published by
MageSpell LLC
Coimbra, Portugal

KILLING GAME

A Veritas Novel

ISBN: 978-1-941527-33-7
2nd Edition

Acknowledgments

An author can write a book, but it takes a village
to see it published.

**Mollie Traver (www.MollieTraver.com) who served as
content advisor, and offered both editorial
and copy-editing expertise.**

Helena Ramos who served as our Portuguese translator.

Lieutenant Colonel Janine Garner, USMC Ret.

**Melanie Fletcher (https://melaniefletcher.com/belaurient-
arts) who created the cover design.**

~ Jana Oliver
August 2025

In an effort to make your reading experience
as enjoyable as possible, we have chosen not to
right margin justify the typeset text,
although this is industry standard.

Studies have shown that people with reading
difficulties, including those with dyslexia, find
it easier to follow free-flowing text, with better
reading comprehension as a result.

"We are all broken . . . that's how the light gets in."

~ Ernest Hemingway

"The evil that men do lives after them."

~ Wm. Shakespeare (*Julius Caesar*)

Chapter One

Saturday, April 11th
Jacksonville, Florida

They were waiting for him. The two good old boys near the rusty beige pickup—the one sporting a faded bumper sticker of a U.S. map made of guns—had always been lackadaisical about meeting times, showing up whenever they damned well pleased. But today they were waiting for him.

Something's going down.

As Brannon Hardegree pulled his cheap rental car into the parking lot, he swept his eyes over the open area around them. It was early on a Saturday morning, so there were only a few cyclers taking advantage of the Baldwin-Jackson Rail Trail nearby. This lot was empty but for the three of them.

Mason Clarke leaned up against the pickup, his arms crossed and resting on his prominent beer belly. He wore his usual wrinkled shirt, worn jeans, and shitkickers. In his mid-fifties, he had a string of arrests in his past and had been a member of various anti-government groups for over two decades. Right now he was affiliated with one called New America.

It was the other man, Clarke's cousin Craig Bettis, who bothered Brannon most. Bettis was in his mid-thirties, hooked on what he cooked. This morning he was amped up like a high-tension wire, constantly on the move, the drug burning out his body, fix by fix. Bettis had all the classic meth-addict markers: rotting gums, skeletal appearance, delusions. He'd be in his grave by summer. The problem was who else Bettis might take with him on that final ride.

Veritas, a private security agency and Brannon's employer, had been monitoring a series of armed robberies across the South during the last three months. To date, over one million dollars had been stolen, and it looked to have been funneled toward New America, the latest in a growing number of sovereign-citizen militias. New America's leader, a man named Quinton Ellers, had a long history of anti-government sentiment. Sources within the Department of Homeland Security and the FBI office in Washington, D.C. believed that Ellers had something big planned, something as deadly as the Oklahoma City bombing nearly twenty years earlier.

Which was why Veritas was involved because sometimes it was easier to have a private agency do the legwork before you turned the might of the U.S. government loose. In this case, the FBI's D.C. office and the DHS were turning a blind eye to Veritas's operation, which meant Brannon was on his own, at least until he gathered enough intel to interest the feds. In particular, he'd been instructed to remain off the local FBI office's radar, and so far he'd done just that.

For nearly a month he'd been undercover as himself, a former Army Ranger supposedly pissed off at the government and mouthing the expected nauseating rhetoric. Getting these losers to believe he was just as much a racist and anti-Semitic asshole as they were. Did these two finally trust him enough to bring him into the militia? Tell him where all the money from the armed robberies had gone? Was this the day it'd all pay off?

Brannon parked the car, then climbed out, scanning the area again. It was in the low seventies, with a light wind. Typical north Florida day—though right now it felt anything but.

"Hey guys," he said, keeping his tone light. He also kept his arms hanging loosely at his side so he could easily reach the Glock in a paddle holster under his shirt.

"About goddamned time you got here," Bettis said, still jittering around.

"So what's up? Why we meeting here instead of the bar?"

"Got business to attend to," Clarke replied, his brows furrowed.

Brannon walked toward them with deliberate steps. He could feel the tension in the air, smell it. "More important than having a brew and banging some babe?"

"Even more important than that."

Brannon halted about ten feet out from them.

Had he been made?

He channeled his own tension into hyperawareness, the kind that had kept him alive as a Ranger, and beyond. "So what's this about?" he asked.

"We got a job. We need a third," Clarke said.

"Doing what?"

"We're gonna rob an armored truck," Bettis said, grinning. The sight was repulsive.

Maybe I'm further inside this group than I thought.

Then he felt that familiar twitch across the back of his neck, the one wired to his survival instincts. The same instincts that had ensured he came back from Afghanistan alive rather than in a flag-draped coffin.

"Armored truck, huh? How much?" he asked.

"Usually three hundred thou per haul," Clarke replied, watching him carefully. "You in?"

It's a test.

If he declined they'd think he was a federal agent, and that might buy him a bullet. Brannon's mind whirled through his options, such as they were. This may be his only chance to burrow deep into the heart of the militia. If he backed away, and they didn't try to kill him, he might lose weeks of undercover work. But if he went along, he'd be committing a felony. His eyes moved to Clarke's cousin as the man twitched around. Bettis was unpredictable, and nothing prevented him from killing someone during the robbery.

Dammit. He really had no choice.

"Let's see," he began, pasting on a fake grin. "Have a couple cold brews or rack up some serious cash? What do you think my answer would be?"

"You're in?" Clarke asked, surprised.

"Hell yes, I'm in. Why wouldn't I be?"

"Didn't figure a war *hee-ro* like you'd go for this kind of thing."

Brannon never liked being called a hero. Especially out of this bastard's mouth. "I need money just like everyone else. So when and where?" he asked.

Once he got the details, he'd let Veritas know. That way the cops would be in position to take them down. Faced with thirty years in prison for armed robbery, maybe these two would roll over on Ellers, reveal whatever plans he had in the works.

Clarke leveraged himself off the truck. It was only then that Brannon saw the gun stuck in the man's waistband. "We're going now," he said. "We got just enough time to get to the third pick up point."

Now?

"Am I following you to the site?" Brannon asked.

"No."

So much for calling Veritas and giving them a heads-up. They'd done this on purpose.

Clarke noticed his hesitation. "You changing your mind?" the man asked, his hand closer to his weapon now.

"No. Just didn't expect it to go down so quick."

Brannon could take both of these men down now, but then what? So far, they hadn't committed a crime, at least not one in his presence. With no opportunity to warn anyone, he had no choice but to go along with the heist. He knew that with Bettis flying high—mumbling to himself about the roaches running under his skin now—this whole thing could go south in a heartbeat.

Brannon paused. "So who's driving? You or me?" He nodded toward the meth head. "Sure as hell isn't gonna be crazy pants over there."

Clarke frowned. "I'll drive. Once it's done, we'll come back here."

"And then?"

"Then we're all golden."

The hell we are.

As a Ranger, Brannon had a decade's worth of missions under his belt, missions planned and executed with a precision that bordered on obsession. That's what gained you success, and a chance to keep breathing.

Clarke had a plan as well, one fairly well thought out, if not a bit amateur: They'd wait until the armored truck parked in the liquor store parking lot, and when the guard came out with the cash, they'd ambush him, grab the money, and run. Every plan had a flaw, and this one was Bettis.

As they waited at the edge of the parking lot, on foot, the doper quickly began to unravel, his movements increasingly erratic, his head swiveling around like a hyperactive owl. He kept touching his gun under his shirt. Any little noise made him jump.

"Get him on a leash," Brannon warned. "I'm not doing hard time because of some damned meth head."

Clarke glowered at him, then sighed because Brannon was right. "Craig, you with us now?" The man nodded five times more than necessary.

God help me, he's going to blow.

The door to the liquor store opened and the guard exited. The plan had been for the three of them to walk casually across the lot and surround the man. But even before Clarke gave the order for them to move, Bettis took off across the pavement. Shouting obscenities, he grabbed the guard before he could react, and forced him to his knees.

"Shit, I'm going to do him right here. I'm going to kill the fucker," Bettis cried.

As he shouted, a woman exited from her car, talking on her phone. The instant she took in the scene, she screamed. Bettis shifted his gun in her direction. "Shut up, bitch!" he shouted. "Shut up!"

Brannon sprinted across the lot and slapped Bettis's hand

down before he could take the shot. "Get the hell out of here!"

"No, I'm gonna do him," he said, raising the weapon in line with the back of the guard's skull. The man's eyes grew wide as he trembled in fear.

"No! Let's go!" Clarke called out, grabbing the bag full of cash where it had fallen on the pavement. "Go!"

Brannon shoved Bettis away, this time extracting the gun from his grip. The fool tried to fight him, but lost.

"Run!" Clarke bellowed.

Swearing, Bettis finally got a clue and ran across the lot, right behind his cousin.

"Don't kill me, please don't kill me," the guard begged, shaking so hard it was difficult to understand him.

"It's not your day to die, man," Brannon said, then took off at a jog.

He heard a shout as the guard inside the truck broke company rules to come to his buddy's rescue. Bullets impacted the fence near him, and he picked up speed. Once they finally reached the truck, Brannon's temper blew. He shoved Bettis up against the vehicle.

"What the fuck were you doing?" he demanded.

"I was going to kill that spook!" Bettis said. "You stopped me! Why'd you do that?"

"Shut the hell up!" Clarke bellowed. "Let's get out of here."

Brannon muscled the doper inside the cab, and the engine roared to life. As they drove out of town, Bettis continued to fidget, laughing and making shooting noises. Brannon glared out the window while his guts churned.

Jesus, what have I gotten myself into?

Bottom line? He was facing a long prison sentence if his boss couldn't pull a few strings and get the charges dropped. Crispin Wilder would go to bat for him, there was no doubt of that, but it all depended on whether someone at the DHS or FBI was willing to play nice. If Brannon couldn't deliver more than a couple of low-level militia members, he was history. All his years in the military would have been for nothing.

I have to get deeper inside the group. No matter the cost.

As soon as they reached the bike trail, and his car, Brannon hopped out of the truck, his anger down to a slow burn now. If they hadn't been extremely lucky there'd have been bodies all over that parking lot.

"Next time, lose this damned fool," he said, jabbing a finger at Bettis. "I don't work with dope heads."

"Not your call," Clarke argued. "My cousin goes where I go."

"Then you're both headed to prison, or the grave."

Bettis's high had finally wound down. He crawled out of the truck and settled on the gravel. Humming tunelessly to himself, he pulled out the straps of cash from the bag and played with them like they were building blocks, stacking them, then knocking them over.

"God," Brannon muttered. He frowned over at Clarke. "Give me my cut. I want out of here. I got a beer calling my name."

Clarke ignored him, pulled out his phone and punched in a number. His posture straightened the moment the call went through.

"Sir, it's Clarke." A pause. "Yes, sir, he did." The man's eyes tracked to Brannon now. "You sure you want to do that?" The voice on the other end of the phone grew louder. "No, sir. Sorry, sir. I'll tell him."

Sir? Could he be talking to Quinton Ellers?

The call ended and Clarke shook his head in resignation. "Word is you need to stick around until I get further orders."

"Word from who?"

"Commander Ellers."

It appeared that Brannon *had* just taken one big step closer to his goal.

When he didn't reply, Clarke continued, "You said you wanted to help us make this country better, right?" Brannon nodded. "Then you have to learn how to take orders."

"So my time as a Ranger counts for nothing?"

"That's the government's army, not ours. I'll call you when

it's all put together. Until then, stay in town and keep your phone on."

"If you're just messing with me . . . "

"I'm not. You rat us out to the cops, you're going down for a very long time. And we got people on the inside who will shiv you the moment you turn your back."

"Is that what this was all about? Insurance? What if I hadn't gone along with the robbery?"

"Then you would have gone missing, just like that other guy," Bettis said, smiling up at him as he dug grimy nails into his arm, drawing blood.

Brannon tensed. "What other guy?"

"FBI agent," Clarke replied. "He was trying to play us, but we figured him out. He's history now."

"Dead?" Clarke nodded. "What did you do with the body?"

"It's not anywhere it's gonna be found."

No one had mentioned a missing agent during Brannon's mission briefing, which meant that bit of news had been kept so quiet, even Veritas couldn't sniff it out.

"When was this?" he asked.

"A couple days after we met up with you at the bar."

Hell. Would the FBI believe he'd had something to do with the death of one of their own? If they did, he'd have zero chance of walking away from all this.

Clarke squatted down near his cousin, counted out the cash, then tossed it at Brannon's feet. The brown currency straps around the cash indicated that each strap held fifty-dollar bills.

"You need to deliver this when I give you the word."

He stared down at the cash, doing a quick count. If his guestimate was correct, there had to be at least forty or fifty thousand dollars. *Why is he giving me this?*

"Deliver it where?"

"Go buy yourself some camping gear, and keep your head down. I'll call you when I have all the details." He looked at the stacks of money at Brannon's feet. "You take off and we'll find you. We'll hunt you forever. You got that?"

"I'll hang around. I'd like to meet the commander. It's time to take back our country from all these pissy-assed libtards who keep fucking things up," Brannon replied, coughing up the party line and nearly choking on it. "Time to make things right again."

"I told you he's no fed," Bettis insisted, grinning like a fool.

"Time will tell." Clarke spat on the ground, his eyes narrowed. "Time will tell."

Chapter Two

After returning to his two-star hotel room and checking it for bugs of the electronic kind, Brannon called Veritas. The call lasted twenty minutes, and none of it was pleasant. There was no good way to tell your employer that you were now a felon, and that crime had happened on their watch. While the bad news percolated up the command chain to his boss, Brannon headed to the closest big-box store to buy camping gear.

As he shopped in the sporting-goods department, he grumbled under his breath. He had all this at home, and in much higher quality, but that was at the cabin in Kentucky. At least he'd brought his own rucksack and duffle bag on the mission.

Where the hell are they sending me?

As Brannon rolled his cart toward the front of the store, he spied a man following him, and doing a piss-poor job of it. Which meant the guy was either incompetent, or he wanted Brannon to know he was there. Probably a bit of both. After he'd counted the cash, he wasn't surprised: Clarke had given him fifty thousand dollars, currently stashed in the rucksack on his back until he could find a place to hide it in the hotel room. This was yet another test, and one that could easily bite him in the ass.

He'd just loaded all his supplies in the back of his car when his phone pinged. The text was short and to the point: He was to meet up with Morgan Blake, one of his fellow Veritas operatives, at nine *tonight*. He needed to pick the location and devise the "scenario" to protect his cover.

With a sigh, Brannon sent back the requested information, then deleted both texts. Then he dummied up a text to a buddy in Vermont, telling him that he'd be in Florida for a bit longer and that the fishing was great. He sent that to a fake account at Veritas, so if someone confiscated his phone and managed to hack the security code, it would all look legit.

Grumbling under his breath, Brannon headed back toward his hotel room. His employer didn't send someone down from Chicago to check on an undercover operation unless things were really heating up. Whether this was because of the robbery, or something else, he didn't know. He'd find out soon enough.

Though Brannon had been to this particular bar regularly, mostly because it was the best place to meet like-minded separatist types, he still paused just inside the door to conduct a threat assessment. It was habit. As expected, a few of the regulars appeared to be on their third or fourth beers, while the local hustler worked his mark at one of the pool tables. There were new faces, any one of which could be with the militia. Since he was holding their money, he expected to be tracked wherever he went. To his relief, neither Clarke nor the doper was here tonight.

He'd left the cash behind at the hotel because carrying a rucksack into a bar would look suspicious. Fortunately, his seedy room had a serious case of rot just below the so-called air conditioner, the kind that sat just above the floor and managed only a feeble wheeze of air. It'd taken some maneuvering, all of it on his back on the floor, but he'd managed to jam the cash into the hole, encased in a plastic bag. Someone would have to spend a lot of time hunting for it, and he suspected the kind of person who would wasn't that smart.

The smell of spilled beer and body odor hung heavily in the air, along with perfume. Typical watering hole found in the smaller towns outside Jacksonville. Worn tables and chairs, a dartboard, a big-screen television playing some basketball game. There was an American flag on the wall, right next to a Confederate flag. Which actually wasn't the official flag of the Confederacy, but the battle flag of the Army of Northern Virginia. But to some, that bit of history didn't matter.

After winking at a cute server, Brannon made his way to a booth in the back and settled in. His sixth sense told him he was being watched, so he made sure not to let it show. Instead, he pressed an icon on his phone, then tapped in a passcode. A minesweeper game came up, or at least it appeared to be such. He activated the app and the little clock whirled on the screen, then blinked green. No audio bugs, at least not in this corner of the room. That was good news.

Brannon left the game open and set the phone on the table as a server appeared in front of him, her smile genuine. He had that effect on women, and at one time had reveled in it. Not now; something that came easily wasn't usually worth it. He ordered a beer and a plate of nachos, because the ones they served here were actually good. As he waited, he checked out the clientele. One guy in a Royals T-shirt near the bar kept watching him, but other than that, everyone seemed to be doing their own thing.

The beer arrived first and he took a long sip, thinking through his situation. Why trust him with all that cash? Why the camping gear? It made him wonder if the rumors Veritas had heard about Ellers having a base in some remote location were true. If he could locate that camp, this whole mission would be worth it.

A few minutes later his Veritas contact arrived, and as he'd anticipated Morgan Blake was an immediate hit with the testosterone crowd. Dark brown hair swinging freely around her shoulders, she was clad in a tight white T-shirt, painted-on jeans, and cowboy boots. From the male patrons' reactions, it was as if someone had just dropped a busload of Playboy bunnies into the bar. Which was the whole point. Brannon hitting on a hot woman would be expected, and wouldn't ring anyone's alarm bells.

Morgan didn't immediately head his way, but hung out at the bar, where she drank a bottled beer while chatting up the bartender. A former FBI agent, she was suited to this work. Morgan had been with Veritas for a few years now, and if Brannon was going to have someone watching his back, she was on that very short list.

Just last fall she and her partner, Alex Parkin, had taken down a major Russian drug lord in New Orleans. Brannon had been in Calcutta during that time, but from everything he'd heard about the mission it was a miracle the two of them were still alive.

After a quick dance with a beefy biker who kept trying to grab her ass, Morgan drifted through the room, laughing and messing with the males' heads—and the bulges behind their zippers. Brannon had always envied her ability to blend in, be it at a seedy bar or a Fifth Avenue cocktail party.

After ten minutes or so, and after he'd received both his nachos and a second beer, she wandered into Brannon's part of the bar. Then, as if it all hadn't been planned ahead, he raised his beer glass at her and she cocked her head and started walking his way.

He made sure to turn on the charm as she reached the table. "Hi there, babe."

"Hi. You on your own?"

"Not anymore," he said. Lame, but expected.

"Oh no," she said, waggling a finger at him. "You have to answer a question, or I won't waste my time with you."

"So that's why you're not sitting with anyone else?" She nodded. "Okay, what's the question?"

"Which musician has won the most Grammys in one night?" she asked.

They'd set this up in advance, too. If he answered incorrectly he was telling her the situation wasn't secure. At that point she'd wander away and eventually leave the bar. No one would ever know she was his contact.

"Shit, that's not easy. You sure you're worth it?"

She grinned. "Answer correctly and you'll find out."

"Ah . . . Grammys, huh. Was it that Black guy? Jackson?"

"Michael Jackson. You win."

"Damn!" he said, grinning back.

When Morgan slipped onto the bench seat next to him, Brannon didn't need to check the crowd to know there were at least a dozen guys who would have cheerfully castrated him at that moment.

"You're a hunk," she said, running a finger down his cheek. He smiled back, though Morgan was way off limits. He'd thought about hitting on her when he'd first come to work for Veritas, but quickly found out he liked her more as a friend. Most times, dating where you work didn't pan out.

But in her case, it had. She and Alex Parkin were a couple, a seriously into-each-other couple likely headed to the altar. Parkin had worked for the DEA, but he'd also been in federal prison. He could hold his own. Brannon knew that crossing the line with this woman was asking to have his nuts cut off. The only question was whether it'd be Morgan or Alex doing the cutting.

"So . . . " she whispered, nuzzling his ear. "What the hell have you got yourself into?"

In between playing with her hair and acting like he was seducing her, Brannon filled in the missing pieces from his report, mindful to keep his mouth angled toward her so no one could read his lips. He felt her tense when he told her about the dead FBI agent.

"There's been no word of that from any of our contacts," she said.

"They might have been lying to me, but it didn't feel that way."

"We'll check it out. I can't believe they gave you that much money."

"It's a test, like the robbery. Has to be."

She sighed. "The boss isn't happy with the way things are playing out."

"Hell, if there had been any other way," Brannon replied, keeping his voice low.

"He knows that. The D.C. office is acting hinky right now. Something is going on, and they're not sharing intel."

He sighed, then laid his arm over her shoulder as if claiming her. "Let the boss know I'll try to keep in touch, but if I'm out in the middle of nowhere it's going to be hard."

She nodded, then leaned forward and ran her hand up the outside of his thigh, pausing at his pocket. He felt her tuck something into it, and then her hand drifted upward onto his chest. "Plant the tracker in with the cash. We need to know where you are twenty-four seven."

"I will."

Picking up a nacho, Morgan dropped a hot pepper ring onto it. Popping it into her mouth, she licked her full lips, tempting Brannon to rethink his promise to keep his distance.

"You're a tease," he said. No wonder Alex loved her.

She laughed. "You need to get laid, my friend."

"Yeah, I know. But not until this is all over."

Morgan leaned closer now. "There's another problem that might be related to the mission. A significant number of explosives went missing from an Army base in Texas. We think Ellers was behind the theft."

"What'd they steal?" he asked.

"C-4. Enough to do a helluva lot of damage."

"Shit."

"Yeah. Anything else you need from us?" Morgan asked. He shook his head. "Then it's time for Act Two."

Puzzled, he watched as she sent a text message, then tucked her phone into her pocket. She scooped up another nacho, smiling the entire time.

"You're not down here on your own?" Brannon asked, and she shook her head. "But Alex is still in Hungary, right?"

"Nope," she said with a grin.

Out of the corner of his eye, he saw the door open and her lover glaring around the bar. The moment Alex saw her, he stomped toward the booth, pushing people out of the way.

"Incoming," she murmured.

To play to the crowd, Brannon leaned over to collect a kiss

from her. He never got the chance, as a hand grabbed Morgan, yanking her from the booth.

"You tramp! What the hell are you doing?" Alex bellowed. He was in a dirty T-shirt and stained jeans, his hair a mess. Just the opposite of the man Brannon knew.

"Just getting what I can't get at home," Morgan said, pulling free of his arm.

"The hell you can't. You just got to put out, that's the only problem."

"Well, it helps if I've got something worth playing with, you know?"

Brannon whistled under his breath. These two were good. If he didn't know them, know how much they were in love, he'd believe every word.

"Who's this bastard?" Alex demanded, his eyes flashing.

He slowly raised his hands. "Hey, no problem, man. I didn't know she was spoken for."

"Yeah, damned right," Alex snarled. "I see you with her again and I'll kill you."

"She's all yours. I don't need the drama."

As Alex towed Morgan out of the bar, catcalls followed them. The server returned to Brannon's table, watching the door slam.

"Wow. That was something," she said. "Another beer?"

"Nah, I'm done. It's not my night." He handed her enough cash for the meal and a good tip, then headed out.

As he strode across the parking lot, he could hear Alex and Morgan arguing. Then suddenly, they were leaning up against a car, making out.

"Get a room!" he called out, fighting to keep the smile off his face.

He was working with a team of solid professionals who would watch his back, no matter how bad it got. Since he might be headed into the devil's backyard, *that* was a damned good thing.

Chapter Three

Monday, April 13th
South Georgia

Caitlyn Jayne Landry purposely slowed her Jeep as she turned into the long drive that led to the swamp tour's headquarters, watching for alligators that might be sunning themselves on the path. Sure enough, one rose on its stubby legs and waddled across the road. As the seven-foot prehistoric monster slid back into the water, memories of another gator rose.

When she'd been about ten Cait's parents had taken her and her brother on a photography tour in the Everglades. Since her mother was an avid amateur shutterbug, the tour operator had used a trolling motor so they could check out the scenery. Cait had spied a mallard resting on a log, watching the boat as it drew near. As she went to point it out, a gator lurched out of the water, grabbed the duck and vanished back under the surface in the span of a heartbeat.

She'd gaped, stunned at what she'd just seen. When she began to tell the others about it, her dad warned her off. No reason to upset her little brother, or her mom, he'd whispered.

It was the first time she'd seen death up close, and the lesson had struck home: Someone, or something, might be smarter then you, and that could cost you everything. In many ways, her life had changed that day, all due to one hungry alligator.

During her eight years in the Marine Corps she'd been the predator, but that had taken a toll, so much so that her last six months as a civilian had proven a difficult readjustment. She'd spent most of that time camping on her own in various national forests, or in the swamp.

Even visiting her parents in San Diego had proven hard. They pushed her to get back into everyday life, find a job, learn to cope with the horrors she'd seen, lived through. It was like someone telling you to "shake off" an amputation, though she knew they meant well. She'd kept in touch with some of the Marines was her unit, but they had their own problems. Some were homeless, or struggling with drug addiction. Others just wanted to get on with their lives.

As soon as Cait could politely escape the last visit she'd flown back to Orlando and picked up her old Jeep at a friend's place. She'd even managed to catch a few hours of fitful sleep at a Motel Six on the way north, trying to ignore a drunk next door arguing with his wife. When the man had begun to beat her, Cait had intervened, told the asshole if he did not knock it off she would put him down. Considering she was wearing a USMC T-shirt and had a tactical knife strapped to her thigh, it got quiet after that.

Though the swamp tour didn't start until noon—and with it a much-needed opportunity to reconnect with her former commanding officer—she'd risen way before dawn, the nightmares serving as a wake-up call. She slept as little as possible nowadays in a futile attempt to keep them at bay. Sometimes she'd go two or more days without sleep, then crash, only to have the past roll through her mind leaving a trail of blood, bodies, and brains in its wake. Sometimes she wasn't sure if waking up was a blessing or a curse.

After getting breakfast to go, Cait had found a roadside park and eaten at a picnic table, leaving a bit behind for the squirrels. Then she'd taken the scenic route north over the backroads of rural Florida and Georgia, past cotton fields, peach orchards, and run-down shacks.

Her desire for solitude told her she needed this trip into the wilderness, needed the quiet, the lack of people and everyday noises. Mike Montgomery, her former commander and now the owner of a swamp tour operation, would consistently remind her that this was her reality now, that the endless struggle to adapt to "normal" was worth it. She didn't want to argue with him, because he was probably right. Some days the noise in her head just got too loud, and all she wanted to do was make it stop.

It wasn't like Cait hadn't known what she was getting into when she joined the Marines. Her family had a deep military tradition beginning with her great-grandfather. Her grandfather, also a Marine, had been a veteran of the Vietnam War, her mom had served in the Navy, and her father was an Army major. Even her brother had put in his four years in the Army and was now starting college in Phoenix. To her, none of them had shown outward signs of post-traumatic stress. They claimed otherwise, but Cait knew it was a lie to make her feel better. So far, she'd been the only one to crack.

The doctors at the Veterans Administration had recommended various medications for her "issues." She'd tried a few of them, and they only made her a zombie. She flushed them all and tried hard to keep it together, though day after day, hour after hour, she felt the darkness talking to her, giving her thoughts that didn't bode well for a future. With more than twenty-two veterans killing themselves every day, she knew she wasn't alone on this journey, but it still felt like it.

Only after a trip with Mike into the swamp, she'd realized that the wilderness was her drug of choice, her way of keeping herself alive. Once he'd recognized this as well, he'd invited her to join him on the tours anytime she wanted, no questions asked. He'd obtained the proper camping permits, as well as a permit that allowed her to carry a firearm within the national park. He knew what was at stake if she gave up.

She'd found the first tour difficult because of the other campers. Fortunately, Mike had been there as her backup. Once acquainted with the swamp's natural rhythms, from that point on she would split off from the group, going it alone, seeking whatever didn't make her blood pound and her heart race. Seek a tangible means to turn off the nightmares, the memories, the feeling that she'd left too much of herself behind in Afghanistan to ever be whole again.

After swinging into a parking place at the far end of the tour headquarters, Cait turned off the Jeep. While she was roughing it, she stored the keys at the office and Mike's wife Kia would keep an eye on the car. As she pulled out her gear and locked the vehicle, she noticed a group waiting on the building's broad porch, no doubt the others on the tour. She steered away from them; people asked questions, wanted to know what she did for a living, if she was married, did she have kids. The effort to explain was too much, sometimes even made her head ache.

As was her custom, she would bring up the rear of the group until she reached the point where she'd head off on her own deep into the swamp. Mike insisted she check in with him every day via cell phone or satellite phone, and though it grated, she was willing to accept that stipulation. He knew she could handle almost everything, but having a lifeline back to civilization was wise.

If she was lucky this trip would buy her another month or so of sanity. Deep down she knew that one of these days, even nature wouldn't have the power to save her. That would be the day the war claimed yet another victim.

Brannon parked his rental car near the tour office, next to an old red Jeep with Florida license plates. It was dented and had a bit of rust, but the tires looked new which seemed an odd combination.

He'd spent most of his time trying not to worry, especially when he was getting closer to his goal. To chill, he had taken a five-mile run, worked out, then gone kayaking. The exercise had helped, but he'd still remained on edge. Time spent on the militia boards hadn't given him any insights into Ellers's plans, either.

The call finally came in late Sunday night, during which

Clarke had been short and to the point: Brannon was to head
to Georgia the next morning and be at this particular location
in time to take a swamp tour at noon. Everything else had
been taken care of. During that tour, he'd be contacted and the
money would change hands. When Brannon had tried to gain
an assurance he'd be meeting Ellers, he had been told to just
follow orders and it'd all work out.

As he'd driven north from Jacksonville, the armored truck
robbery was still on the news, though so far his name hadn't
been connected with it. His mother would be appalled if she
ever learned her eldest son was a criminal, even in the pursuit
of justice. Still, to Ellers and his cronies, Brannon was the
perfect recruit, an anarchist leader's wet dream: a former Army
Ranger who was a pro with explosives and had experience as
a sniper. Both of those skills could easily be turned against a
government that the "sovereign citizen" types hated.

There were a number of right-wing militant groups,
including those associated with Posse Comitatus, a movement
that believed no law-enforcement official above the rank
of sheriff was legitimate. To show their defiance they often
refused to file income taxes or obey federal laws. Some even
printed their own driver's licenses. Others were affiliated with
the League of the South, a white supremacist group, or the
Christian Identity Movement, which held that Jews ran the
financial institutions and were working with Satan to destroy
civilization.

When these people decided to break the law they were
usually heavily armed and had the capacity to generate
maximum body count. No matter their beef with the
government these guys weren't any different than the Taliban
or Al Qaeda, and he'd had plenty of experience dealing
with those bastards. It was time to use his expertise and do
some much-needed housekeeping stateside. If he'd wanted
armed insurgents roaming the streets he would have stayed in
Fallujah.

As he turned off the car, his cell phone rang. "Hardegree."

"It's Sanjay. I've got mixed news," Veritas's chief data

analyst replied, his Mumbai accent clipped.

Sanjay was one of the go-to folks for information and often served as the point of contact for those currently on a mission. If the intel was on the internet or tucked away in some computer database, he would eventually find it. It was like a cyber game of hide-and-seek to him, and he was incredibly good at it.

"The FBI is going ballistic because of the robbery," Sanjay continued. "Best you complete this mission before they figure out you were part of it, because our boss isn't sure he'll be able to shield you if you're arrested. His contact in the D.C. Bureau office has suddenly grown skittish about our involvement."

"Affirmative," Brannon said. *Dammit.*

"We finished the background check on the tour operator you'll be meeting today. Mike Montgomery is a former Marine with an excellent service record. He's married, three adult kids, has been conducting the tours since he retired two years ago. Financials are solid."

"Any sympathies with anti-government groups?"

"Not that we can find. His assistant, Preston Taylor, isn't as clean. He's spent some time on a few of the sovereign citizen forums. Mostly, he comes across as a wannabe. Lots of talk, no action."

"Let's hope he stays that way."

"Montgomery conducts his registrations by snail mail, not online. It really screws up what intel I can get for you up front."

Brannon grinned at the annoyance in Sanjay's voice because it was a rare thing. "Sounds like the man is a Luddite, or paranoid."

"Probably a bit of both. If you can get me pictures of the campers, I'll run facial-recognition software, try to figure out who is who."

"Consider it done."

"How often do you intend to check in?" Sanjay asked.

"Every ten to twelve hours, provided I have phone service. You don't hear from me after twenty-four, something's wrong."

"Good. We'll monitor the tracking chip."

"At least you'll know where to send the body-retrieval team."

"Let's not joke like that, okay? You may be the Lone Ranger, but we're here to back you up."

Brannon rolled his eyes at the nickname. Everyone who went out on missions had one. Well, except Crispin Wilder, the head of Veritas. No one had the balls to call him anything but "sir" or "boss." It was never smart to jack around with a former international arms dealer.

"How's Iceman doing?" Brannon asked. One of his fellow operatives had been on an undercover mission in South America.

"He's good, headed back to the States. He's your backup if things go bad."

"That works for me." Brannon was originally going to be lead on the South American mission, but the plans hadn't worked out right. Now he knew he was where he needed to be. "Let them know I hope to wrap this up soon."

"I will. Keep safe."

"Always. Thanks, Sanjay."

The moment Brannon stepped out of the car, his back twinged. Stretching his arms over his head, he heard a satisfying pop. It sucked to be an "old man." At least that's what some of his fellow Rangers had called him, ribbing him about being the graybeard on the team. As if thirty-two was old.

Sometimes it feels that way.

It was only after his thirtieth birthday that he began to be aware of the passage of time. Before that he'd been totally focused on the missions and the "downtime" in between. Something had shifted, and it made him pensive.

Once his back cooperated, he gave a slow look around, checking out the scenery. The smell of the swamp immediately filled his nose, but he didn't find it unpleasant. Earthy maybe, but not bad. The vegetation was shrugging off a chilly winter, enthusiastically embracing the warmer temperatures. At least it wasn't full-on bug season yet or he already would have been bitten to death. In the distance, he could see Spanish moss hanging from sprawling oaks and bald cypress trees, hear the lazy calls of waterfowl. Overhead an egret winged by. He'd love to spend time here just enjoying nature, but this mission was too critical. Especially now that his future hung in the balance.

Brannon stowed away his phone and grabbed his rucksack from the passenger seat. Despite the extra couple of pounds the money added, the ruck felt light in comparison to the seventy-five-plus pounds he'd carried on his Ranger missions.

Once the car was locked, he set off for the building. As he passed the rear end of the Jeep, he spied a Marine Corps bumper sticker—the signature eagle, globe, and anchor. Probably Montgomery's car.

The tour office was a nondescript structure, weathered, but the roof was in good shape which meant someone had spent money on the place. He thought it a curious business venture for a retired Marine, but then you had to do something when you reached your "twenty and out." It was better than sitting at home, or comparing war wounds with your buddies down at the VFW.

A knot of people stood on the building's porch, unevenly split between the sexes: two females, four males. One of the females appeared to be in her late teens, with pale-blond hair slashed with a thick streak of blue. Tall and thin, she was accompanied by a young man of the same age. His hair was less outlandish, just everyday brown, a little on the short side.

The other woman was older, prettier, probably in her thirties. Her light-brown hair was pulled up in a messy bun, and she wore shorts and a pink T-shirt. The remaining men were nothing out of the ordinary. Brannon guessed at least one of them had a desk job, if the guy's spreading middle was any indication.

Any one of these people might be his militia contact, the person who would lead him deep inside the organization. With a heavy sigh, he put on his happy tourist face and joined them.

Chapter Four

Cait had avoided the group and headed directly to the dock to check over her canoe in preparation for the trip. Mike kept an eye on it when she was gone, and as usual it had its cover on. She stripped it off and was pleased to see the canoe looked in good shape.

Her phone rang. "Landry," she said.

"It's Kia. We've got a problem."

Cait looked back at the tour office and realized Mike wasn't around. As the tour operator he usually went out of his way to make the campers feel welcome, ease their nerves. "What's up?"

"We got in an accident this morning on the way to the office. We're at the hospital now. Mike needs surgery and—" There was a pause. "Hold on. He wants to talk to you."

"Landry?" a gruff voice called out.

"Colonel." It was impossible not to refer to his rank. "What's going on?"

"It's all fucked up," he said. "Can you believe it? I busted up my leg in some goddamned car accident."

If he was swearing, he was fine; for Mike, cursing was like breathing. Cait began mentally editing out those particular words. Because if she didn't, her own curse rate went up dramatically, something her mother would not tolerate, despite being married to an Army major. Cait's expletives had earned her more than one lecture at the dinner table, even *after* she'd left the Marines.

"Is Kia okay?" she asked.

"Just a few bruises. She got lucky."

"So what happened? Did you hit a deer or something?" she asked.

"No. The brakes failed, and I just had the car serviced last week. The problem is that I have a full tour today."

"I'm sure your assistant can handle it."

"Yeah, but I don't want Preston to handle it. I want you to lead the tour."

"What?" she blurted.

"You heard me."

"I—"

"Sergeant, I need you to keep those folks safe."

He was pulling rank. "You know I'm not in a good place right now."

"What I know is that you're not accepting the fact that you're no different than any other damned soldier who's seen action. That you have bad shit in your head that's doing a number on you. I get that, but you need to SITFU."

Suck it the fuck up.

"Mike . . . " she said. There were voices in the background now.

"Do this for me, Cait. You owe me."

He'd never thrown a guilt card like that before, not in all the years they'd served together. "What's really going on?" The noises increased, then ended. "Hello?" Cait called out.

"They took him back to surgery," Kia said.

"How bad is it?"

"Two fractures in the right leg, both real nasty. They're going to put in some pins."

"Damn." Cait hesitated. "I owe him everything, but I can't handle the tour right now." *I can't handle me, let alone anyone else.*

"I know you're in rough shape, but there's a reason Mike wants you out there. In the last few months, there's been increased activity in certain parts of the swamp. More boats, for one. Mike thought it was because it was spring, more tourists, but now he's not so sure. There've been rumors of people camping out on some of the remote islands."

"Like me?"

"You're not running guns, Cait."

"*What?* He has proof of that?"

"No, but Mike met up with a couple guys in a Jon boat who didn't act right. They didn't have any fishing poles or cameras, and when he tried to talk to them, they blew him off. There was a big wooden box in the bottom of the boat. Mike said it reminded him of what you'd use to ship AR-15's."

"Not dissing him, but that's a stretch. Somebody would have to be crazy to bring unauthorized weapons into a national wildlife area."

"He knows that, but he says something feels wrong and that's why he wants you on the tour. His sixth sense has kicked in. You know what that's like."

Damn. Her former commander's instincts were why Cait was still above ground, or not a prisoner of Al Qaeda. She took a shaky breath. Could she handle it?

Before she could reply, Kia added, "I know what it's like for you. I was there when Mike was going through it. He's better now. You'll get there too someday."

So you all keep telling me.

"We have no one else we can trust," she added. "It has to be you."

"Why not Preston? He knows what he's doing."

"He's not a Marine."

Which meant Mike thought those skills would be needed. Now Cait really had no choice. "Okay, I'll do it. But just this once."

"Thank you," Kia said, not bothering to hide her relief. "I'll call Preston and explain the situation. You met him before?"

"No, I haven't."

"Oh, okay. He only comes along when the tours are full. Where are you now?"

"I'm at the boat dock."

"After I give him the news, I'll send Pres down to talk to you. Don't be surprised if he's way pissed. Please be very careful," Kia added.

Cait ended the call, her hands shaking. She took a series of calming breaths, which failed.

I can't do this. I can't do this. I can't do this.

But she had no choice. She owed Mike her life.

Six days. Just six days.

Then Cait was going off grid for a long time. Maybe she'd never come back.

Brannon had assumed his role with ease. He'd claimed to work in a lawyer's office—that part was easy as his dad was an attorney, so he knew the lingo—and that he was from Florida. Also the truth. It was easier to keep track of your cover story if part of it was based on reality. If someone went digging, they would find information that matched what he'd told them, though his work with Veritas would not be public knowledge.

The others in the group were a mixed lot: an Atlanta real estate secretary named Susan Townsend; a teenaged couple, James Gray and Patti Irwin; Bill Adams, an author; and Keith Rockwell, a professional photographer.

Not one of them struck his "you don't feel real" meter. Which meant they were what they claimed, or someone was as adept at being undercover as he was. None of them had seen the tour operator, though it was nearing noon. That had provoked some concern.

The door to the office opened and a man in his mid-forties exited. Sanjay's research bio pegged this guy as Preston Taylor, the assistant guide. Instead of greeting them, he plowed right through the group and then down the stairs. Looking around, he spied a woman near the dock and set off to intersect her.

"Is that our guide?" Rockwell asked.

"No, I think he's the assistant," the author replied. "I saw his picture on their website."

When Preston intercepted the woman, he gestured animatedly. She appeared about Brannon's age, probably five foot eight or so. She obviously worked out, the subtle curve of her arms showing muscles, and her tan indicated she was not a cube dweller. Her ash-blond hair was caught up in a ponytail and threaded through the back of a baseball cap. He guessed it would reach just past her shoulders if unbound.

She wore khaki green, both T-shirt and pants. The edge of a Blackwork tattoo peeked out from the right sleeve of the shirt. But it was her boots that made him pause; they were military issue, her pants properly tucked and bloused. He'd done the same in the Rangers, mostly to keep out the sand flies. In fact, his were the same today.

The woman's posture was ramrod straight; the way she balanced her weight, telling. He'd bet a month's pay she was either on leave, or ex-military. Was she part of Ellers's team, his contact to guide him to the militia leader? From the woman's expression, he could tell she was growing irritated with Preston, who continued to wave his arms around. Unfortunately, they were far enough away that Brannon couldn't hear them.

Time to change that. He purposefully walked down to join the pair, putting on a pleasant smile. As he drew near, he called out, "Hi. I'm Brannon Hardegree. Are you guys with the tour?"

Two sets of eyes swung toward him. Hers were dark brown with amber and gold flecks. The assistant frowned at the interruption, but the woman pointedly checked him out, from the top of his head to his combat boots. Only fair, since he had done the same to her.

"Yes, we are," she replied, not missing a beat. "I'm Cait. This is Preston."

Brannon nodded at both of them politely.

"The rest of the group is right over there," she said, indicating the others on the porch, as if she hadn't known he'd just come from the office. "We'll be with you in a bit to start the orientation." Which was a polite way of telling him to scram.

"Thanks."

As he walked away, he heard Preston say, "Look, I don't

give a damn how long you've known Mike. This is *my* job, not yours. How do I know you can handle this tour?"

"Kia told you this is how it's going down. I don't like it any more than you, but if that's what Mike wants, that's what's going to happen."

"You have no clue what you're doing," Preston argued.

"Actually, I do. So when you're done nursing your butthurt, come join us and let's get this tour on the water," she replied, heading toward the office.

Brannon smirked. Maybe this mission wasn't going to be so bad after all.

Cait walked away from Preston, counting slowly to ten. The little prick had gotten in her face the moment he'd heard the news, even though Kia had no doubt patiently explained the situation, which meant Preston was going to be a giant pain in the ass if she didn't get him on board quickly. Sadly, she wasn't in the habit of ego stroking, and wasn't particularly good at it.

As she walked toward the tour group, she couldn't help but notice the fine butt on the Hardegree guy. At least that was a plus. He was at least six foot three, probably weighed two-twenty. All muscle, but not buff just for vanity's sake. This was working muscle, the kind that kept you alive in dangerous situations. His face was angular, but not so much that it overwhelmed his good looks, with trimmed dark hair and a hint of a beard. She noted that his brown eyes were highlighted by a touch of rust.

Like her, he wore a T-shirt and cargo pants. She'd already made note of his worn rucksack and how it seemed to be part of him, not just something he'd bought the weekend before. The combat boots, properly bloused, told her he was probably ex-military.

She doubted an active-duty soldier would bother to take a tour like this one. Most guys on leave, unless they were married, headed for the nearest bar and a horny female, or male if he swung that way. Once upon a time, Hardegree would have been the type she'd take for a spin, but not now.

If her guess was right, this man already knew wilderness-survival techniques, could probably teach a grad-level course on the subject. Why saddle himself with a group of clueless newbies? In so many ways he reminded her of the men on her team, Special Forces hunters the country sent to handle the dirty and dangerous jobs. The kind that rarely made the evening news, because they were off the radar or top secret.

She pulled her attention away from Hardegree and checked out the remaining members of the group. A couple of them appeared nervous, others were trying to act like this was no big deal. Once Preston chilled down she needed him to give her the skinny on each one of these people. A successful mission required intelligence, and this one was no different.

When she stopped at the bottom of the stairs she gave her Jeep one last look, the desire to take off colliding with her responsibility to an old friend.

All of the campers were watching her now.

You can do this. At least here, no one was shooting at her.

"Hi. I'm Ser—" She stumbled, nearly revealing her rank. She started over. "I'm Cait Landry and I'm filling in for Mike Montgomery on this tour. Mike had a car accident this morning, and he's laid up in the hospital."

"What?" one of the men said. He was older, with salt-and-pepper hair and tired eyes. "I decided to come on this tour just because of him. He knows everything about the swamp."

"Don't worry, I'll make sure to handle everything just like he would."

Preston joined them now, still sullen, but trying not to look like he'd been sidelined. Time to throw him a bone. "This is Preston. He's Mike's assistant and he'll be helping me on the tour. If you have any questions, ask either of us and we'll get you what you need."

That seemed to mollify Preston, and he nodded solemnly.

"You qualified to take us into the swamp?" the older man asked, frowning now.

"Yes, I am." The Hardegree guy chuckled quietly, which she thought was odd. She ignored him and eyed the skeptic.

"How many varieties of snake are in this swamp, Mr. . . . ?"

"Adams. Bill Adams. And I don't know."

"Thirty-six. The water moccasin, or cottonmouth, is the deadliest. It's a pit viper, like a rattlesnake. You get bitten, things go bad very quickly. But it isn't aggressive until you get in its face." The man stopped looking angry, pulled out a notebook, and began penciling notes. "What do you know about alligators?"

"Not much. Go on."

"Are you a reporter, Mr. Adams?" she asked, confused.

He hesitated, then shook his head. "I'm an author. I'm working on a novel."

Of course you are.

"Then let's make this a learning experience for all of you." She turned to include the others. "You will encounter alligators during the tour. To keep from losing your arm like Captain Hook, your body parts must remain inside the boat. If you come across a gator on dry land, slowly back away. Those things can move a whole lot faster than you'd think, and they can weigh up to nine hundred pounds. I repeat, no leaning over a body of water. Alligators lurk just under the surface and will reach up and make you a meal."

"But wouldn't you be able to see them?" the teenage girl asked.

"No. The swamp waters have a mirror effect, so you can't see below the surface. The gators take advantage of that. They're very well adapted predators. They've had eons to learn how to hunt."

"Is it true they eat you alive?" She sounded fascinated, not afraid.

Cait looked over at Preston now, giving him the stage and hoping she wouldn't regret it.

"Sometimes they do," the man said. "Sometimes they drown you and stick you in their larder for a snack later."

"Yuck," Bill said, but he kept penciling notes.

The cookie needed to ensure the author's good behavior? Feed him information. For Preston, it was the opportunity to show off his knowledge. That she could do. Now all she needed was to find what fueled the others and this trip would be much easier.

"How many of you have been in a canoe before?" she asked. There was a show of hands; only the author was a virgin when it came to that skill.

Better than I expected. When she looked at Preston he nodded his approval.

"Okay, that's good. We'll pair you up with a buddy. The majority of your backpacks and sleeping bags will go with me and . . . " She checked over her potential canoe mates. "Hardegree." Because she had no doubt the man knew his way around a canoe. If she was lucky, he might not talk her ears off. That wouldn't be the case with the author.

"I'll keep an eye on the two younger ones," Preston murmured.

"Thanks." She turned back to the group. "The first day is light—four hours before we make camp. There will be a bio break about two hours in, so use the latrine . . . uh, the restroom before we leave. We'll take it easy today. Tomorrow we'll push harder."

"What if we have to go before we get to the toilet?" the girl asked.

"Then you better be able to hold it. Unless you're a guy, that is." That got a few laughs, which seemed to reduce some of the unease. She turned toward Preston. "How's about you give them a refresher on how to board the canoes?"

"Okay."

Cait lowered her voice. "Before we head out, I need an idea of who these folks are and what they do in real life."

"Can do that, too."

Since he wasn't being a jerk . . . "Look, I know this isn't great for either of us, but we'll get through it."

He didn't reply, but at least he wasn't arguing with her. As she walked off into the office, she wondered why he'd suddenly become helpful.

It sure as hell isn't my charming personality.

Chapter Five

Brannon only half listened to Preston's list of canoeing dos and don'ts. He'd been in and around watercraft since he was a baby. In fact, his mom had gone into labor on a boat.

Susan, the secretary, smiled over at him and he made sure to return it. The other girl, Patti, was glowering at nothing. The distance she'd put between her and the guy named James promised trouble.

"Any of you been in a swamp before?" Preston asked.

Brannon zeroed back in on the conversation and raised his hand. He noted that Susan did as well, but no one else.

"Okay, then, take your gear down to the dock and we'll get you loaded," the assistant ordered. "Stay alert and you'll stay healthy. Zone out and you could get hurt."

There were mumbles in the group and they set off as ordered, except for the younger couple.

"You lied to me," Patti hissed to her companion.

"No, I didn't. I said we'd be camping in the swamp," James replied.

"But for six days? Are you crazy? No way I want to do this!"

"Come on. Don't be a wuss. It'll be fun, you'll see."

Brannon shook his head as he headed toward his car. When someone said "it'll be fun, you'll see," it was always time to walk away.

His buddy Cort had used that line to get them out into the Gulf one summer day. A storm that seemingly came out of nowhere had pushed their kayaks miles away from shore, and it'd taken another twelve hours before the Coast Guard found them. They'd been sunburned, dehydrated, and as scared as two eleven-year-olds could be.

But that half a day spent in watery hell had revealed a toughness Brannon didn't know he had, and that few possessed. He'd kept Cort from drowning, kept him from giving up. That "I refuse to die" mantra had gotten Brannon through Ranger School. Cort had become an inner-city high school teacher, which required a different kind of raw courage and discipline. They remained friends to this day. In fact, his eldest son was named after Brannon. But Cort had never set foot in the Gulf again.

While the others gathered their gear and got to know each other, Brannon walked to his rental car, surreptitiously taking photographs of each vehicle's license plate as he walked by them. He would forward them to Veritas, and then it was just a matter of waiting. Sooner or later, his contact would reveal himself—*or herself*—and it would be time to take this game to the next level.

"Is everyone for real?" Cait asked as she scanned the roster. Preston gave her a confused look, so she rephrased her question. "Does everyone have the skill set they claimed they had, especially when it comes to being in a canoe?"

He gave a half nod. "Keith, the photographer, and James are fine. Susan is pretty good, and the girl? I don't know. I can't get within three feet of her without getting some lip in return."

"Not a willing participant?"

He shook his head. "I think this is her boyfriend's idea. And she smells like weed. Or at least her clothes do."

Cait sighed. "Great. How about the author guy?"

"Bill doesn't have a clue which end of a boat is up. What about Hardegree?" he asked.

"He'll be fine. I just can't figure out why he's on the tour."

"Picking up chicks?" Preston suggested.

"I'd think a bar would be a better hunting ground, but who knows?"

"Any word from Kia?"

"Not yet."

"Let's pray it goes well," the man replied, then walked away toward the group.

"Hardegree?" she called out. He turned toward her and for a moment, she swore she saw him in desert camo, an M4 rifle in hand. Cait blinked her eyes to clear the vision. "Help me load our canoe?"

"Sure."

The packing went faster than Cait had anticipated. He handed down the backpacks and other supplies as she pointed to each one, never second-guessing her placement inside the canoe.

"Why are we carrying so much of the gear?" he asked, sounding only curious, not annoyed.

"The first couple of days we'll have some of the others' gear just in case someone decides they should flip their canoe. Mike warns them about ensuring their stuff is waterproof, but some don't listen. Once I know they've got a handle on things, everyone will have their own gear in their own canoe."

"Makes sense."

Cait checked out the other canoes and found them ready to go. "Load up, we're outta here," she called out. She hesitated. "You've been around boats, right?" Brannon nodded. "You up for steering, so I can focus on the group?"

"Sure." He nodded again, taking his place in the stern. "I was raised in Florida. Spent almost every waking hour on the water."

"That explains it." *But it doesn't explain why you're here, mister.*

It didn't matter. After six days she'd never see this guy again. As long as she could keep her personal demons in check, this trip would just be a quick detour.

✦ ❖ ✦

The first hour or so was filled with the nearly silent rhythm of oars cutting through the water, with the occasional motorized boat passing them, leaving eddies in its wake. As Brannon and Cait's canoe led the others single-file along the broad canal that led into the swamp, she set a slow pace, apparently wanting to break in the newbies as easily as possible.

The water acted as a dark mirror, reflecting the trees and the brilliant blue sky above, dotted with a few airy clouds. The farther they went, hardwoods gradually gave way to cypress trees, their broad bases narrowing to tall trunks as they reached high above the canal. Cypress knobs clustered around the base of those trees, like wooden stalagmites. Birds were in motion, sometimes quickly, sometimes in a leisurely glide over the water. Brannon had already spotted a pair of ibis, an anhinga, and what might have been a sandhill crane.

He savored the silence, and he found himself relaxing more than was prudent. The same could not be said about the woman sharing his canoe. Cait Landry's tension bled through every move. Why had she agreed to take Montgomery's place? Why hadn't the assistant taken the lead?

Knowing the answers would come eventually, he turned his attention to a pair of Florida cooters resting on a log as they paddled by. One of the turtles raised its head to study them. He caught a quick glimpse of an alligator tail sliding into the underbrush.

"Did you see it?" Cait called out.

"Yeah. Smaller one. Probably a couple years old," he replied. Growing up in the Sunshine State had taught him a lot about gators, especially when they ended up in his family's swimming pool.

As the afternoon passed and the day grew warmer, he kept working the oar, switching sides effortlessly when Cait signaled a change. There were quiet conversations and the occasional faint click of a camera shutter. No doubt Keith, who was right behind them, sharing a canoe with Susan. Behind them was the younger couple, then Bill and Preston bringing up the rear.

His attention returned to Cait as they paddled along the

canal. She didn't chatter, but kept focused on the water, constantly assessing the situation around them. Definitely military, and most likely someone who had seen action.

As if she'd known he was thinking about her, she ceased paddling and turned around. "Let's wait here a moment, give the others a chance to rest for a bit. I've been pushing them pretty hard."

"If anything, you've been easy on them," he said, placing his oar inside the boat. Since they had some time, he fetched his refillable water bottle and took a long swig, clearing the dryness in his throat.

"Not all of them are water babies from Florida," she replied.

He chuckled. "Where are you from?"

"Everywhere. Nowhere," she said.

"You were in the military?"

Her brow furrowed. "Why would you think that?"

He pointed at her bloused pants.

Cait glanced down at them as if it had never occurred to her that she did it differently than anyone else. "My mom was Navy, my dad is active-duty Army."

Which doesn't tell me what branch you were in.

Because he doubted she'd blouse her pants just because of her parents. "Married?"

Cait frowned. "Pretty personal with the questions, Hardegree."

"Brannon. Since we're about to spend a week together in the middle of God knows where, I figured I should get to know you better."

"If that's a come-on—"

"It's not. It's just being polite, like my mother taught me." She relaxed a notch. "So, married or not?" he pressed.

"Divorced. You?"

It was time to pony up some info, or she'd close down. "I was engaged once, but she called it off. She didn't like what I did for a living." That gained him a puzzled look, as if she didn't believe him. She appeared about to follow up on that, then closed her mouth as the other canoes slowly drew closer.

"Are we there yet?" James joked, as he and his girlfriend floated up to join them.

Patti groaned. "No kidding."

"Not even close," Cait replied.

The other two canoes circled around them.

"We're about half an hour out from the toilet so rehydrate yourselves, but don't overdo it," Cait warned. "While we're resting, Preston, can you give them a bit of history about the swamp?"

The man perked up. "Sure." Then he launched into a well-rehearsed account of how the canals had been carved into the wilderness, the alligators decimated for their hides, and how the swamp had finally become a national wildlife refuge.

"It's really big, right?" Susan asked.

"Hundreds of thousands of acres," Preston responded, "a lot of which isn't accessible unless you're in a canoe or willing to hike across some of the islands. Me? I stick with the regular routes. You get hurt out there and no one's around, you're in deep trouble."

"Will we have cell phone service once we're 'out there'?" Bill asked. He earned a few stares. "I've got a manuscript on submission at a few of the major publishers, and I'm dying to find out if I'm going to get a contract."

"The cell phone service is spotty," Cait said. "Some places it's fine, others not so much. Like Preston told you at the beginning of the tour, keep your phones on vibrate; that way we can enjoy the quiet out here."

"You know, it's kinda creepy how *quiet* it is," Bill replied, looking around.

"In time you'll crave it," Cait replied. Her eyes met Brannon's, then darted away as if she'd revealed too much.

She pointed back the way they'd come. "See that bird?" Heads swiveled. "That's a great blue heron."

"Wow, it's huge," Patti said.

"They eat small fish, rodents, and reptiles, and are all over North America, not just in this swamp."

As if not pleased by all the scrutiny, the bird took wing and swooped low over the water in a blur of gray-blue, heading down the canal.

"Beautiful," Brannon murmured. That earned him another glance from Cait, who nodded in return.

"Okay, let's head out. We'll stop for the bio break, then continue on to the first night's camp. Don't worry, you won't regret all this exercise."

Patti groaned again. "Riiight."

As they set off, this time the two middle canoes lined up, side by side. James chatted with Susan, which didn't seem to make Patti any happier.

Tuning them out, Brannon found himself watching Cait's back, her muscled arms and her firm butt. If he'd met her anywhere but on a mission, he'd definitely be trying to get her in the sack, despite her aloof behavior.

She stopped paddling, then stripped off her hat and T-shirt, revealing a sleeveless camo tank top beneath. She replaced the ball cap, pulled her ponytail through the back, and began paddling again.

Now, not only was the tattoo completely visible, but Brannon could see a long white scar running down the side of her shoulder to the upper portion of her left arm.

A knife wound.

His eyes moved to the tat again, and he realized what it represented: the distinctive tread on a pair of combat boots. Between the treads, running vertically, were the initials JDS, and a small red heart. He knew what it was in an instant: a memorial for a soldier who had fallen in service to his country. Or *her* country, because death didn't respect one sex over the other.

JDS. The last of the initials didn't match Cait's last name. Maybe she hadn't kept her married name after the divorce, or this was in honor of a family member. Was this an indication that she had an axe to grind with the military or U.S. government?

Cait looked over her shoulder to catch him staring at the

tat. When she recognized what he was doing, she turned back toward the water without offering an explanation. Her way of saying it was none of his business.

Brannon knew when to back off, so he refocused on the journey, paying attention to the snippets of conversation behind him. So far, everyone was acting as he'd expect. But he knew it was only a matter of time before someone made contact; the fifty thousand dollars in his rucksack would prove the ultimate lure.

Chapter Six

Even though Cait had rested the group as often as possible, it'd been a long four hours for those unaccustomed to exercise. She could have easily covered three or more times the distance and still not been tired. The slow pace drove her nuts. She found herself gritting her teeth more often than was healthy as the others talked amongst themselves. It was everyday chatter, the kind she normally didn't have time for. The kind that usually had her bitching at someone to shut the hell up.

The problem wasn't them, it was her. This was what real life was like, and she worried she'd never be able to find her place within it, despite Mike's assurances that she would. To her relief, Brannon had willingly switched to the front of the canoe after the bio break. Steering might take more mental energy, but it took way less physical energy, and her arms were pleased with the rest.

Cait found herself watching the man more than was necessary, trying to figure him out. He was quiet, observant, like a coiled snake. Maybe he was an outdoors junkie and this trip was just another chance to unplug from his day job. Or maybe he had some other reason for heading out into the swamp. Something to do with shipments of guns, perhaps? Or Mike was being overly paranoid and the accident was just bad luck. No matter what, Hardegree was too much like her, which meant he was a helluva threat.

"Are we there yet?" Patti called out, for what had to be the third time.

"Yes!" Cait called back, pointing toward the wooden

platform in the distance.

That announcement spawned hearty cheers from the others. Despite her not wanting to be out here with these people—near anyone for that matter—the group had done well for their first half day out.

"Thank you, God!" someone said. It sounded like Bill. He'd been the most fidgety of the group, but not everyone was cool with sitting for hours at a time, even if they were paddling.

"Race you!" James shouted.

"Go!" Cait shouted, and they dug their paddles into the water, working in tandem, never breaking rhythm. No surprise, she and Brannon reached the platform way ahead of the others. She found herself grinning, and that didn't happen very often.

"You miss it, don't you?" her companion asked. "The team spirit, the competitiveness."

She stilled, caught by what he'd said, and how he'd known that. "Yes, I do."

God help her, she did miss the team. Being on her own sucked, though being around people who didn't understand was worse. Disturbed by the revelation, Cait maneuvered the canoe up to the platform where she could tie it off. The wood structure sat over the water, abutting a small island.

After hefting herself up, she did a quick walk around to ensure the platform was solid, that there were no rotting boards or loitering snakes or alligators. Satisfied it looked safe, she gestured for Brannon to start handing up the various tents, packs, and other supplies. As each load came her way, the muscles on his tanned arms and chest worked with smooth efficiency. Damn, he had a lot going for him.

Their eyes met and he smiled up at her, but Cait made sure not to return it. It was better she kept her distance until this tour was over. If Mike's worries were for real, it'd be unwise to trust anyone, even Hardegree.

The others arrived and their gear was transferred onto the platform in short order. As Preston assigned each of them a place for their tent, Brannon called out a warning.

"I wouldn't do that," he said.

For a second Cait thought he was talking to her, but then she saw his attention was directed toward Patti. The girl had stripped off her socks and shoes, and was about to dangle her feet in the water. She jolted at his voice, looked down, then whipped her feet back.

"I forgot," she said, frowning.

"Trust me, gators never do," Brannon replied. "They love toes with pink polish."

That gained him a coy smile from the teenager.

As Cait had predicted, Hardegree had his tent set up and secured to the platform before anyone else had even begun to dig into their own luggage, her included.

Military. Gotta be.

When they'd been talking about her family, why hadn't he mentioned his own service?

Cait kept the eye roll to herself when she spied the sales tag on Susan's new tent and wasn't surprised when Brannon had to help the woman set up her gear. Cait had been camping since she was eight. *The Major* had insisted on it. He'd sent her and her older brother Jared out to hunt squirrels for supper when she was ten. She still hated squirrel meat to this day, partly because biting down into buckshot was never pleasant.

Once she was sure everyone had their gear set up properly, she asked Preston to do the "here's how we deal with the trash" lecture.

"Alligators steal trash?" Bill asked, his pen and notebook out again.

"No, but raccoons do. They might swarm us tonight. They are ambitious little bastards," Preston said.

"But they're way cute," Susan said.

"They are, but they're a pain," he continued. "Keep your tents zipped shut. You can't be sure if one of them is rabid or not."

Throughout Preston's lecture, Cait watched the young couple. James appeared to be paying attention, but Patti kept eyeing the strip of land behind the platform, like she was going to bolt. Or she needed to have a smoke. Timing it perfectly,

Preston moved on to fire safety.

"It's not like it's going to burn or anything," Bill said. He gestured around them. "I mean . . . water?"

"Actually, besides the trees and bushes, the swamp is composed of peat beds, and those do burn," the assistant said. "There was a major fire a few years back, and it scorched three quarters of the park. And it's not out yet. The fire keeps burning underground because of the peat. Yeah, underground. Really."

"Huh," Susan said, while Bill furiously scribbled notes.

"So if you're going to smoke," Preston continued, "douse the match and the cigarette when you're done. Once a fire gets started here, it's hard to put out."

Cait's phone vibrated. She walked a few steps away and took the call. "Landry."

"It's Kia. Mike's out of the recovery room. The doc says he'll be fine after some PT. One of the fractures wasn't as bad as they thought."

"That's great news."

"Is that Kia?" Preston called out.

Cait nodded. "Mike's out of surgery and doing fine."

The assistant smiled and gave a thumbs-up. "Great news!" He turned back to the group. "Okay, people, let's cook some supper."

"There's more," Kia said, her voice somber now. Cait walked out onto the island for privacy. "The cops checked Mike's car and they found that the brake line had been intentionally tampered with. They've opened an investigation."

Cait slowly turned back toward the group. "You're saying that someone didn't want him on this tour?"

"That's exactly what I'm saying."

Holy shit. "But why?"

"Mike's not sure, but he feels better knowing you're out there. He wants you to send me reports twice daily. He says to include something he'll recognize as a code word. That way he'll know everything is okay."

Mike was never that paranoid. Cautious, excellent in the sixth-sense department, but not paranoid.

Cait barely suppressed a shiver. "Okay. Tell him I'll always make a reference to the St. Louis Cardinals. I know how much he loves them."

"Don't get me started." She paused. "If we or the cops figure out what's going on, I'll let you know."

Hopefully before things go to hell.

"Until then," Kia continued, "best to act like everything's normal. We don't want to tip off whoever's behind this."

"What do you know about the people on the tour?"

"Their applications looked routine, what I can remember of them. Preston handled them for me. The only one that was weird was the Hardegree guy. He took another guy's place. Preston should have had him fill out an application and sign a waiver."

"He did. Has anyone else done a substitution before?"

"A couple times, but not very often," Kia replied.

Cait's attention zeroed in on the man in question now, who had set up a camp stove and was emptying cans of beans into a pot.

"Tell Mike I'm thinking of him. Preston is too."

"I will. You stay safe."

Cait disconnected the call. As she set up her tent, she thought through the conversation. Someone hadn't gone to the hassle of trying to kill or injure Mike and Kia just for fun. Someone had wanted Preston to lead the tour. Now she stood in that someone's way.

Brannon stretched out on the platform, letting his supper settle. It hadn't been anything fancy—hot dogs and baked beans cooked on a portable camping stove—but it beat an Army-issue MRE, a Meal Ready to Eat, any day.

He'd kept an eye on their guide because she'd been eyeing him, and not in a friendly way. Whatever had been said during her phone call had spooked Ms. Landry, rattled her enough that once she ate her supper she'd moved to the far end of the platform, away from everyone else.

Knowing he'd have to tackle that issue later, Brannon chose to sit near the photographer. Keith was taciturn, at best, and spent a lot of time texting back and forth on his phone. Brannon had dated a woman who was a professional photographer, and they'd been together for a few months before splitting up. Last he'd heard, Shelly was somewhere in the Middle East, photographing refugee camps, which sounded like complete hell to him. Because of her, he knew how to get a shutterbug talking.

"So what kind of gear do you use? Nikon? Canon?" he asked, partly out of curiosity, and mostly to vet the guy.

"Whatever works," the man replied, and then pointedly rose and moved away from the conversation.

Whatever works?

Professional shutterbugs were fanatic about what type of cameras and lenses they used. Usually they'd rattle off the brand, the model, then go into all the features, like they were an infomercial. But not this guy. Rockwell had just earned himself a slot on Brannon's people-to-watch list.

Susan took the photographer's place. She smiled over at him, and he knew that kind of smile. Had been the recipient of it time after time, usually at a bar after a few beers.

"How you doing?" he asked, taking a sip from his water bottle. It was warm, but that didn't trouble him. If he ran out, he had an adequate supply of purification tablets to get him through the tour. Truth be told, he'd drank far worse.

"I'm good. Thank you so much for helping me put up my tent. I had no clue how to do it."

Which is why there are directions inside the carry bag. "No problem."

"I'm so tired. My arms are really sore." She looked over at him now, her eyes wide and her lips parted. "I really need a shoulder massage. Do you know anyone who could help me out?"

That was more blatant than he'd expected, especially since they weren't at a bar. Or alone. It felt off in some way, as if she was acting like a fluff bunny for a reason.

"I'm sadly lacking massage skills."

"I bet you could learn," she said.

"Probably not."

Susan frowned at him, but the expression seemed more like she was studying him than upset. "Got it," she said and set off in search of someone else to charm.

This time she zeroed in on Preston, who seemed pleased by the attention, however Brannon noted she didn't make the same massage request of him.

A glance over at their tour guide indicated that Cait had witnessed the exchange. Her eyebrow rose as she returned to sharpening her knife on a whetstone. Her distance from the rest of them clearly said she didn't want to be the center of attention, unlike her assistant, who was holding court a short distance away. Brannon had also noticed her sharp jerk when Preston had accidentally dropped a cooking pot during the washing up.

He remembered being that on edge. Some of it had faded in the last eighteen months, but not all of it, another bit of baggage he'd brought home from the war, like the back injury and the nightmares. Given her reactions, he bet she hadn't been "back in the world," the U.S.A., for that long.

Though he knew she wanted to be alone, Brannon decided to push her, see how she'd react. When he joined her, Cait looked over at him and then back at the knife. It was a black KA-BAR, and he knew it was razor sharp even before she'd begun working on it. She handled the blade like a pro, which told him it wasn't a prop. A Kydex sheath sat near her leg.

"So which branch of service?" he asked quietly.

Cait didn't reply, like it was a state secret or something.

"I'm betting Marine. You guys have a certain way you hold yourself. Like you're better than the rest of the world."

Her eyes caught his again, but this time he thought he saw amusement. She flipped over the knife to reveal the initials "USMC" stamped on the hilt.

"I knew it," he said, smiling. "You're a lot prettier than

most of the jarheads I've met."

He'd been half joking, half serious. He'd learned long ago never to assume a woman couldn't be a warrior. Cait stared at him, looking for something, perhaps clues about who he really was.

"So why keep it a secret?" he asked.

"It leads to questions." She frowned at him now. "You know that as well as I do." Another four heartbeats. "SEAL or Ranger?"

It was his turn to feel uncomfortable. "Ranger."

"Sniper?"

"Better with explosives, but I'm a decent shot."

Cait stared out over the water for a time, as if thinking it through. "You're right, I am nicer looking than most Marines. Some of those guys are butt-ugly."

"Rangers, however, are all smoking hot," he said, waggling an eyebrow.

"And not the least bit egotistical."

"No, that would be the frogmen. SEALs believe the sun rises and sets on their golden little heads."

Cait began to laugh and he joined in. A few of the others stared at them, but Brannon didn't care. The sound of her laughter was rusty, like it'd been a long time since she'd last succumbed.

"I knew you were military," she said, wiping down the knife. "I figured you were regular Army, but then I got thinking you were Special Operations. I've been around too many of them not to recognize one when I see one."

She'd pegged him pretty close, which was uncanny.

"Why do you think that?"

"You're deadly quiet. It's like you go invisible. It's what those guys do best, besides killing, that is."

He suspected that description could easily fit her as well. "How did you get to know special ops so well?" he asked.

"Just do," she replied. He realized she was shutting down again, and he didn't want that. It felt important to keep her talking.

"How long have you been out?"

"A little over six months. You?"

"A year and a half. You been doing the VA shrink thing?"

She nodded as she sheathed the knife. "Yeah. Does it get . . . any better?"

It was his turn to stare into the distance. "Yes. It takes time though. A lot of time. I'm not there yet."

"It's why I like the swamp," she said. "It's quiet out here."

"No sudden noises, right? At least not the man-made kind. Out here, things are trying to kill you, which means you feel right at home. Back in the real world? Not so much."

Their eyes met again. "That's it exactly. Because all the real world does is mess with my head."

She was up and moving away before he could comment.

A Marine, one who hadn't found a way to adjust to civilian life.

At least not yet. There was sadness and anger in her eyes. Hopefully that anger hadn't found a home in one of the anti-government groups, because if she had joined up with them, he'd have to take her on. One thing he knew for sure, Marines never went down without one helluva fight.

Chapter Seven

One by one, the exhausted campers turned in about an hour after sunset. Even Preston called it a night after yet another warning about the raccoons. Cait sat on the platform, listening to the night sounds and watching the stars come out.

In the distance a bull gator bellowed. Another joined in. In contrast, an owl hooted nearby as the heavy dampness of the swamp blanketed the air. She'd already picked out a few reflective eyes in the water as the gators trolled around the platform. That might keep the raccoons at bay. Still, she and Preston had made sure the food was secured in the rafters, along with the trash.

Her nerves were still on edge, like fire ants racing up and down her back. She wanted to be anywhere but here, and the urge to jump into one of the canoes and take off was nearly overwhelming. And if she didn't want to be found, Cait knew how to hide, even from a Ranger. Learning that Hardegree was one of them had helped fuel that desire. Those bastards were deadly—she'd seen them in action. Disabling a car would be child's play to him.

The sound of deep, slow breathing came from the tent next to hers. *His* tent. Hardegree had wished everyone a good night, zipped up the flap, and was asleep in a few minutes. Another sign he'd spent time doing special-ops work: You slept when you had the chance.

75th Ranger Regiment. The elite of the elite. What were the odds? Too unlikely to be coincidence. The ex-soldier wasn't the only one who made her skittish; the photographer was closemouthed, not fiddling with his camera gear nearly enough. Susan's constant prattling had nearly driven her nuts, until Cait realized it was far too targeted for the woman to be an airhead.

Patti was bitchy, slinging biting comments at her boyfriend anytime he came near, and James looked nervous if you caught him just right. Only Bill was oblivious, writing reams of notes on a legal pad. He, of all of them, seemed true to character.

Why would someone want Mike off the tour? Why did they think he was a threat? She had no answers to those questions.

Knowing it'd be another night wrestling with insomnia, Cait made one last trip to the toilet, then unzipped her tent. If she was lucky, she'd fall asleep for a couple hours. She knew better than to let herself sleep for much longer than that, or the nightmares would crowd her mind. They were bad enough when she was alone, but these folks would not understand her flashbacks, her screams.

Crawling in, she settled on her bedroll. After taking a series of deep breaths to relax, she tried to clear her mind. She'd just let her eyes drift shut when she heard the creak of someone walking on the platform. Instead of moving past her, to the toilet, the footsteps left the platform and headed into the woods.

You've got to be kidding me.

Cait crawled back out of her tent, closing it behind her, then strapped the knife sheath to her leg. She gripped a flashlight in one hand and headed into the woods. It was easy to track her quarry. She'd expected it to be one of the guys, out for a rustic pee, but it wasn't. A match flare illuminated Patti's face and then went dark. The distinctive smell of top-grade marijuana came Cait's way.

Tempting as it was to get in the girl's face, she waited as Patti smoked part of the joint, then ground it in the dirt. To Cait's surprise, she unscrewed the cap on a bottle of water and drowned the spot where the weed had landed. At least she'd paid attention to the fire safety briefing.

Patti turned and began to walk in her direction, then came to a sudden halt when she saw Cait. "Holy shit! You scared me."

"Better me than an alligator." Cait had a couple ways to play this, both of which could go bad. Instead, she waited to see how the girl would react.

"So go on, give me the lecture," Patti began. "No wait, I have it memorized. I'm a supreme disappointment to my family, a drug addict, a bitch, and a loser."

Cait shook her head. "Maybe you are all of those. Maybe not. I don't give a damn. You want to smoke pot, fine. I just don't want you getting toked up out here. Too many critters can kill you if you're stoned and not paying attention."

"Why would you care?" the girl shot back.

"Because I don't want to tote your dead ass back to base camp. In this heat, you'll just draw a bunch of flies and I hate it when that happens." Patti stared at her, stunned. "Now let's go to bed. Dawn comes too early around here, and I'm a bitch if I don't get my sleep."

"Sounds like you're a bitch anyway."

Cait winked. "Now you're getting the picture." She gestured back through the woods toward the platform. "After you."

Patti threw her a middle finger as she stomped past.

Cait made sure the teen didn't see her smile. It was like looking in a mirror when she was about that age. Mouthy, disrespectful, pissed at the world. At least until the Marines had gotten hold of her.

"Some folks never change, until they're forced to," she muttered.

Brannon was up at dawn, long before any of the others. Except Cait. From the dark circles under her eyes, he wondered if she had slept at all. She'd already made coffee and was frying bacon on both of the portable camp stoves.

"Good morning," he said, keeping his voice low.

"Morning," she replied. Clearly, she wasn't up to believing

anything was good about it.

"Raccoons wake you?"

She shook her head. "There weren't any. We had a couple gators cruising around last night, and that kept them away."

"Who said those monsters aren't useful except for fancy shoes."

Keith rolled out of his tent, followed shortly by the others. Brannon took the opportunity to walk a short distance away and turn on his phone. The e-mails scrolled in, one by one.

The first reported that the tour operator's car had been tampered with, and that the cops had opened a criminal investigation. The second e-mail relayed that another armored-car robbery had occurred in Jacksonville late yesterday afternoon. This time, one of the robbers had been caught and it was the addict, Craig Bettis. While it was good news he was off the street, it was bad news for Brannon. Clarke wouldn't have ratted him out, probably because he feared Ellis more than he did the FBI. Bettis would crack once he went into withdrawal. It was only a matter of time before he fingered Brannon for the earlier robbery.

The third e-mail said that the team at Veritas was still working on the background dossiers of his fellow campers, based on the photos he'd sent them last night. The Jeep belonged to Caitlyn Landry, the sedan to a Wiley Davis, last known address in Alabama. Had one of the campers borrowed it from a friend or a family member? And if so, which one? The remainder of the cars were rentals, like his. Those would take longer to track down.

Brannon quickly e-mailed back what he'd learned about the Marine, her time in the military. That'd make the process a little quicker, at least in relation to her. He requested further info on her, but also Keith and Susan's bios. Something about both of them twitched his antenna.

He finished his e-mail in time to get a cup of coffee and listen to the secretary chatter about how hard it was to sleep because it was so quiet, and how disappointed she was that no raccoons came to visit them.

Finally, James crawled bleary-eyed out of his tent. He accepted the coffee Preston handed him, took a sip, and then strolled to the toilet. When he swung the door open and found it empty, he looked back at the group, confused. Searching faces, he frowned. "Where's Patti?" he asked.

Cait came to her feet. The girl's tent flap was open. "Patti?" she called out. There was no reply. She walked out into the woods and called again. No reply.

On a hunch, Brannon went to the far side of the platform, where the canoes were tied off. He did a quick count. "We're missing a boat," he announced.

"Ah, hell. Is she crazy?" Cait said, shaking her head.

"She had to have left in the middle of the night," Brannon said.

"Yeah, sometime between three and five, when I was asleep." She grabbed up her rucksack and hastily repacked it. "Preston? Can you take these folks on to the next platform? I'll go find her and make sure she's okay."

Surprisingly, the assistant didn't give her any lip. "No problem."

"I'll go with you," James offered.

"It's best if you stay here."

"No," the young man protested. "She's my . . . girlfriend and—"

"You're staying here," Cait insisted. "This might require some serious tracking skills if she went off the main canal." She looked over at Brannon now. "You game?"

He nodded. "Let me pack my gear."

Cait used every curse word she knew and invented a few more as she and Brannon paddled their canoe back the way they'd come the day before. Leaving in the middle of the night was an insanely stupid move, especially if the girl had still been stoned. If she got lost, headed in the wrong direction, God knew what might happen to her. She could tip over her canoe and end up in the water. They'd never find a trace of her if a gator found her first.

At least by sending Preston and the group to the next destination he could check if the girl had gone that way. Unlikely, though, unless Patti got turned around. Cait's guess was that she was headed back to the tour headquarters, especially after James announced his car keys were missing. Somehow, Patti managed to lift them out of his pack, probably when he'd made a toilet run.

"You keep thinking that hard for too much longer and your head's going to start smoking," Brannon called out from the back of the canoe.

"Just wondering if I screwed up somehow."

"Why would you think that?" he asked, as their oars dug into the water at twice the speed of the day before.

Cait abruptly stopped paddling and he did the same. As she turned, she could see the concern on his face. "I caught her smoking weed last night. I got in her face."

"As one does," Brannon said, setting his oar aside and loosening up his shoulders. They'd been at it hard for the last hour, gliding along, and they hadn't seen anything more than the usual wildlife. No sign of the missing teen.

"Maybe if I hadn't gone off on her, she wouldn't have bailed on us," Cait replied.

"You're guilting yourself for no reason. She's what? Eighteen?"

"Seventeen, according to the paperwork."

"Well, right now she's acting like a spoiled child."

Cait sighed, rubbing her neck. "Something had to make her bolt."

"I don't think it was you. I think it was her boyfriend. Did you notice how they weren't sitting together last night?"

"I chalked it up to her being jealous because he was fawning all over Ms. Flirt," Cait replied.

He grinned. "No, I think it was more than that. James wanted her to share his tent and she refused. The girl doesn't feel comfortable with him."

Cait frowned, thinking that through. "He didn't strike me as creepy. Well, not any odder than most young guys."

"I know, but something's off with him."

"I'll trust your gut on that. If we don't find her, we'll have to call in the search-and-rescue folks."

"We'll find her. She couldn't have gone that far," Brannon said. "I think she just needed some space."

"God, I hope you're right."

Chapter Eight

It was her companion who spied the canoe two hours in, tucked up near the shore, but not tied off. Just resting there. As they drew near, Brannon leaned over and grabbed its front gunwale. To Cait's dismay, the canoe was empty.

"Damn." She raised her head, looking around. "You think she went ashore somewhere?"

"No, I don't." He retrieved a half-empty bottle of cheap whiskey, holding it up. "I suspect she got drunk and then had to take a leak. I bet she stopped at the toilet and failed to tie up the canoe, so it floated here. Probably why it's headed in the wrong direction."

"If we're lucky, that's the case," she replied. "If not, she's lost somewhere in the woods."

And my responsibility. Dammit, Mike.

Brannon carefully transferred over to the other canoe, then paddled alongside hers. As they neared the structure, he smiled and pointed. Patti was asleep on the platform, curled up in a fetal position.

"God, I was just like that at her age. Minus the blue-hair thing," Cait groused.

"You got drunk and stole boats?"

"For me, it was a neighbor's Harley. Luckily, my dad found me before the cops did. And before I wrecked it."

Brannon gave a low whistle. "How old were you?"

"Sixteen, going on terminally stupid."

He laughed. "Been there, done that. For me, it *was* a boat and a bottle of vodka. I still can't touch the stuff, makes me sick just thinking of it." He pounded his oar on the side of the platform. "Time to wake up, sunshine!"

Patti's head shot up, revealing a pea-green face that screamed brain-pounding hangover. "Go . . . away."

"Not happening," Brannon said, rapping the platform again. "We missed you at breakfast. We had lots of *greasy* bacon and scrambled eggs in butter." None of which they'd gotten to eat, but that didn't matter, as Patti's eyes went wide, her throat convulsed, and she scrambled to the side of the platform to retch.

Cait shook her head. "That was cruel."

"Absolutely," he replied, grinning now. "Used to do that to my younger brother when he stayed out all night."

"I'm surprised you're alive to tell the tale. I would have killed you in a heartbeat." She turned back to the girl. "Patti? You hurt?"

The girl raised her head weakly. "No, I—" Without warning, she leaned back over for a new round of vomiting.

"Yeah, *just* like me at that age," Cait said.

It took some time, but eventually Patti was settled in Cait's canoe, once again in a fetal position. Cait sent a quick text to Preston, letting him know the missing camper was safe. As she turned her canoe around, Brannon did the same.

"If I were you, I'd just drop her off at headquarters, since she's going to be a pain in the ass," he said.

"Ditching on the tour is what she wants. She needs to learn that she has a responsibility to others, not just to herself."

"I can hear you," Patti groaned from the bottom of the canoe.

Brannon rolled his eyes, trying to keep the laugh out of his voice. "Your call."

They set off at a strong pace, side by side.

"Was that a lesson you had to learn as well? That you had a responsibility to others?" he asked, watching her closely now. When Cait nodded, he added, "Is that why you joined the Marines?"

"No, I wanted to piss off my dad. He was regular Army, all

the way. We had a gigantic argument, and The Major said he was going to send me off to some Christian college in Texas. I was so mad I signed up that afternoon. I was eighteen, so they were happy to do the honors."

"Did that piss him off?"

Cait shook her head, frowning now. "No. When I told him what I'd done, I figured he would go ballistic. All he did was slap me on the back and say, 'About damned time you grew up, Caitlyn.'"

"Caitlyn, huh?" Though she thought he didn't really look surprised by that.

"Don't go there."

"I'm cool," he said innocently, but she could see the grin. They were pushing their pace again, Brannon's canoe abreast of hers.

Cait moved her oar to the other side while Patti dozed on. "I hated boot camp. It sucked, but I was used to higher-ranking males telling me what to do, and so I did fine. Once I was deployed, I found my home. My dad said he was real proud of me."

"And now?" Brannon asked. It seemed a very personal question.

"He and my mother worry about me because I don't come home very often. Too much noise. Too much fussing. I tend to . . . overreact."

Her companion grunted in sympathy, no doubt knowing exactly what that word might mean.

"PTSD?" She nodded. "Ever considered getting one of those service dogs to help you with that?"

She thought on that for a time. "No, there are other guys who need one more than I do. I'll be okay."

"Most of them say that, Caitlyn."

She shot him a glance, realizing it was true. "Cait."

"I like Caitlyn better."

She took a few more strokes. "I might get a support animal someday, but not while I'm out here in the swamp. The gators think dog is a gourmet meal. I wouldn't risk it."

"Someday you'll have to come out of the wilderness."
Only if I knew how.

Over an hour into the return trip, Patti raised her head, blinking. "Please tell me you're taking me out of this hellhole."

"Sorry," Brannon said. "You're headed back to the group. They miss you."

"No!" she said, sitting up abruptly. "I don't want to. I don't like . . . " She hesitated, then looked from Brannon back to Cait.

"Is it your boyfriend?" Cait asked.

"He's not my boyfriend, okay?" Patti said. "You got any water?"

Cait stopped paddling long enough to extract a full bottle and hand it over. Patti rinsed out her mouth first, spitting over the side, then took three big gulps.

"So what's bugging you about the tour?" Brannon asked. It was a smart question, coming at the situation from another angle rather than zeroing in on James first.

"It's not the tour, it's *him*. James didn't tell me we were going on this thing. He just said we'd take a tent out and camp for a couple days. Then I find out we're going native in the middle of a damned swamp."

Cait opened her mouth to ask a question, then shut it. Her companion seemed to be able to get the girl talking better than she could.

It's the hormones. Or at least it had been when she was Patti's age.

"How long have you been with James?" he asked.

"A couple weeks. He helped me change a flat tire. We started texting back and forth. Then he asked me to go camping with him. It's not like we're dating or anything."

Cait ground her teeth. She could just imagine what The Major would say about *his* teenaged daughter taking off in the middle of nowhere with a guy she hardly knew.

"What makes you not trust him?" she asked.

Patti looked back at her, complexion pale. "He asks a lot of questions, but he doesn't tell me anything about him or his family. He's always in my face if I look at another guy. Wants to know where I am and what I'm doing every minute of the day."

"That's not good."

"No. Or maybe I'm just being weird or something. Who knows? I'm not great at judging people."

"Who is?" Brannon said, ramping up the charm, which caused Patti to smile in return. "Do you know where he's from?"

Patti shook her head. "I asked and he said it didn't matter." She took another swig from the bottle. "I really have to go on the tour?"

"You have anyone who can pick you up if we do take you back?" Cait asked.

Patti sighed.

"Tell me the truth," she warned.

"No, my mom is out of town and my dad is working on some big project. He's hardly ever home."

"Then you should stick with us. We'll keep an eye on James. You let us know if you're spooked about anything, okay?" Brannon said, as he skillfully glided the canoe through the water, powerful stroke after powerful stroke.

Patti gave him an adoring look. "Okay. I'll do it. Ah, do you guys have any food? I'm kinda hungry."

"Yeah, we might just have a protein bar or two," he replied.

She smiled at him again as if he'd just handed her the moon.

Definitely all about the hormones.

By the time they reached the first platform, Patti had come to life after being fed and given some aspirin. While she and Cait packed the remaining supplies into the canoes, Brannon made a trip to the toilet, careful to keep his rucksack with him. He knew it looked odd, but he didn't dare leave it behind, not with the militia's money inside. After taking care of his full bladder, he stepped out and powered up his phone. One of the latest e-mails included the Marine's service record. It made for interesting reading.

Caitlyn Jayne Landry had enlisted at age eighteen, just as she'd said. After eight years in the Marine Corps, she had risen to a rank of sergeant and been awarded numerous commendations and a few medals for her time spent in Afghanistan and Iraq.

She'd been on one of the FETs, the Female Engagement Teams that had partnered with Special Operations units. Their purpose had been to interact with and potentially interrogate village women, since men were not permitted to speak to them due to religious restrictions. It had been a dangerous, but rewarding assignment.

Brannon knew exactly what it was like to enter a small hamlet, looking for the enemy. How sometimes you found them, and how sometimes they were women and children. The FETs had been disbanded in 2012, and Cait had been assigned to another unit. When it had been time to re-up, she'd left the service. He suspected PTSD had kicked in and she'd found it hard to function. Not an uncommon story. Pensive about what he'd learned, he typed a "thanks" in reply to the e-mail and went to join the others.

Cait spied the phone in his hand. "Keeping up with the sports scores?"

He shook his head. "I wish."

"Your girlfriend?" Patti asked, joking. He shrugged and didn't answer, then noticed that Cait was watching him closely.

Once they were back in the canoes, she gave Patti an oar and put her to work.

The girl wasn't impressed. "You're like my mom. She never lets me slack."

"You can slack tonight, once we catch up with the others," Cait said.

Patti muttered something under her breath. "Yeah, *just* like my mom."

Brannon kept the smile off his face. The more time he spent with Cait, the more he liked her. Depending on her loyalties, that might prove to be the worst mistake of his life.

Chapter Nine

It was about an hour out from dusk when they finally made it to the campground on one of the smaller islands. The instant they reached shore, the other campers swarmed down to meet them.

"Patti!" James called out, appearing relieved she'd returned to the group.

"Hey," she replied noncommittally.

"So where'd you go?" Bill asked.

"She decided to check out the wildlife," Brannon said. "Take a moonlight cruise. No harm, no foul."

Good answer.

The look the girl gave him said he'd made a new friend. Hopefully the gentle lecture Brannon had delivered on the return trip would do the trick. In the end, Patti had promised to tough it out and not cause any more trouble. Cait hoped that was the truth.

"So what's for supper?" she called out.

"We got stew," Preston called. "We saved some for you."

"As long as it's not made out of squirrel, I'm starved."

Once the canoes were secured and the packs unloaded, she looked up to find Patti glaring at James, who was giving her an earful of grief. She headed that way, remembering how uncomfortable the girl had been about the kid.

"Who do you think you are, running off like that?" he demanded, gripping her arm hard enough that Cait bet it would leave bruises.

"Back off," Patti said, yanking her arm away. "I don't answer to you." She hurried away even as he made another grab at her.

"Patti," he warned.

"Stop getting in her face and let her work things out in her own time," Cait said.

"This isn't your business," he snarled.

"It is as long as I'm heading up the tour. So chill out, and put the drama in neutral. Got it?"

He swore under his breath and stomped off in the opposite direction.

"Males. They're always trouble," she muttered.

"Present company excluded, right?" Brannon said as he joined her.

Cait gave him a long look. "I suspect you're as bad as the rest of them." Then she hesitated. "Thanks for helping out with the kid. She won't listen to me, but then, I didn't listen to my mom either."

"No problem. Let's get some food."

To Preston's credit, he'd arranged the camp in an orderly fashion, the tents pitched on higher ground in case of rain and the area around the fire pit cleared of debris. In the center of the pit, on an old metal grate, sat the bubbling stainless-steel pot of stew.

Once she'd gotten herself a big bowl, she sat near her gear. Preston joined her.

"Everything looks great," Cait said. "Thanks for taking care of the others."

The assistant nodded. "Girl going to toe the line now?"

"She said she would. You know how it is at that age— sometimes the brain just doesn't work right."

Preston huffed. "Happens at any age." He lowered his voice. "What did you find out about Hardegree? What's his story?"

Why would you care?

"We didn't talk much," she lied. "We were too busy looking for the girl."

"Okay. I just wondered."

"Our photographer ever start being sociable?"

"No. But he couldn't get a word in edgewise with the Townsend woman or the writer yapping all the time. Gonna be a long week."

"That's for sure."

As he walked away, Cait couldn't help but wonder if Preston had messed with Mike's truck. Had he wanted to lead the tour so badly that he'd risked his employer's life? But what would be the point?

If not him, then who?

Her attention tracked back to Brannon where he sat by the other two women, eating his supper. If she kept it up, she'd be seeing enemies everywhere.

After supper, though it was pure busywork, Cait reorganized her rucksack. It was soothing, in a strange sort of way. She'd always done the same right before a mission.

Trust your instincts.

That had been Mike's mantra for as long as she'd known him, and right now her instincts were twitchy. A sidelong glance proved that it was only her: Brannon leaned back against a tree, seemingly mellow. Maybe she was imagining things.

One of the shrinks had cautioned that she was probably hooked on the adrenaline rush. She could easily find that in the swamp, especially when she was camping solo. Get hurt? She was on her own unless she could reach someone by phone. That part, she could deal with because she liked trusting her skills to keep her alive. But she missed her team as well. They'd been like a family, watching each other's backs, joking, sharing life—and death.

Occasionally, there had been some jackass who thought the women had joined up solely to keep his dick happy. That was until whoever was in charge got in the guy's face, told him if he didn't straighten the hell up, his life was going to get very unpleasant, very quickly. Most of the dudes got a clue and fell in line. If not, the women took care of the situation themselves. In one case, a private had learned exactly how brutal Cait could be when cornered.

She reluctantly pulled herself out of her memories, because too often, they led to that dark voice whispering to her. Instead, she tuned in to the others' conversation and found they'd moved from swamp life and history to politics.

"No way you can trust this government," Preston said. "If you think you can, you're not paying attention."

She couldn't resist. "Why don't you trust them?"

"You see what's going on. Our liberties are disappearing, more each day."

In some ways, Preston was right; post-9/11 America had seen an erosion of personal rights, courtesy of Washington—some of which she didn't think served any purpose. The new laws had been too heavy handed in some cases, a knee-jerk response to a horrific attack, one that security analysts had been sounding warnings about for years. The politicians had decided they didn't want to scare the public with what *could* happen. Then reality had bitch-slapped the nation and people had died.

"What about you, Hardegree?" she asked, intentionally trying to push a button to see how he'd react.

"We're losing control," he said evenly. "Makes one wonder where it's all headed."

"But what can you do about it?" Susan asked. "Other than sit around a campfire and complain?"

"There're ways to make it right again," Brannon said. "Just depends on whether you have the balls or not."

Then he closed his eyes and shut all of them out, though she knew he was listening intently. She'd met disgruntled military folks over the years, some who hated the government, others who were gung-ho patriots. Most of them just bitched, but a few of them took it too far. Was he one of those?

God, I hope not.

She turned her attention back to the group. They'd moved on to discussing the military.

"This government, they're crazy," Keith said. He'd spoken

so infrequently that everyone's attention swiveled in his direction. "All this *politically correct* bullshit. Now they're talking about having chicks in the Special Forces. No way that should happen."

"Combat experience helps you advance rank," Cait said, surprised she was even bothering to explain. "Right now, women are at a disadvantage."

"That shouldn't even be an issue. Women have no place in the military," Keith said. "They just don't. Can't handle the stress, can't handle any of it. They fall apart when the first few bullets go flying. They get people killed."

"You've been in combat then?" she asked, suspecting he hadn't. The people who tended to run their mouths hadn't had bullets coming at them.

"No, but I heard it from some of our vets. It's God's honest truth."

"It's only a matter of time before a woman qualifies for Special Operations," Brannon said, his eyes open again. "They're getting close to it now."

"Then the government's bending the rules for them."

"Not if they want to become Rangers."

"No, I'm not buying it," Keith said.

Hardegree rose and poured another cup of coffee. "A buddy of mine got shot in Fallujah. The medic crawled fifty feet through enemy fire to get to him, pulled him back to safety," he said. "My friend is home now and has a brand-new baby. He wouldn't have lived to hold his son if it hadn't been for that soldier."

"See?" Keith said, nodding. "No woman could have done that."

Brannon looked up, pinning him with his eyes. "The medic's name was Corporal Alice Meyers. She took a round in her shoulder, but she still saved my friend's life. So I suggest you rethink your position about women in the military, because it's complete bullshit."

Patti whistled under her breath. "Slap down," she murmured.

Keith rose. "It's not bullshit. It's the truth, but you just don't want to hear it." He stalked off to his tent and crawled inside. The sound of the zipper closing caused sighs of relief to run through the group.

"Nothing quite like the peace and quiet of nature," Preston said.

Cait snorted while Brannon retreated to where he'd been sitting, squatting down to drink his cup of coffee. She gave him a nod of respect and he returned it. Then he reached for his phone to check his messages, as he did frequently.

Must be a girlfriend. For some inexplicable reason, that made her sad.

Later, Cait did her usual rounds before heading to her tent. She'd made sure that Patti's was on the far side of hers, away from James. That hadn't gone down well with him. The girl had looked pointedly relieved and crashed early, no doubt still nursing a hangover.

Cait glanced over as Brannon passed her on the way to his tent, which sat just next to hers.

"'Night," he said.

"'Night."

Cait stripped out of her coat, then unzipped the flap and began to crawl inside. A faint rattle began, followed by a hissing sound. With a yelp, Cait rolled to the side as the snake struck at her. She flung her coat on top of it and it whipped underneath the garment, hissing louder. Slowly, she tugged the garment outside, praying it would keep the creature confined.

"Something wrong?" Brannon said, leaning out of his own tent now.

"Yeah, you could say that." Cait carried the wriggling coat to the edge of the platform and shook it out. The snake dropped into the water.

Brannon leaned over, watching it swim away. "Canebrake rattler?"

"Yup."

"You get bit?"

"Nope." She frowned back at the tent. "I always keep the flap zipped. How did that thing get inside?"

"That's a damn good question."

He held the flashlight while she carefully removed everything from inside the shelter, verifying there was nothing else waiting to harm her. The rattler's bite wouldn't have immediately killed her, but she would have had to be evacuated to a hospital for treatment.

Leaving Preston in charge.

Brannon quietly called out her name, beckoning to her to join him at the back of the tent. She joined him as he shined the flashlight along the base of the shelter. There was a long, smooth slit in the nylon, like a knife would make.

"Hell," she muttered. This had been deliberate. "I guess I'll have to duct tape it."

Brannon stared at her. "Someone just tried to kill you," he said evenly. "You're awfully casual about this."

"No, I'm angry, but I'm not going to waste that anger until I know who did it. Then I'm going to rip that person apart, slowly and with considerable malice."

His lopsided smile said he understood now. "Ooh-rah!!"

"Exactly."

As he crawled into his tent, he said, "Goodnight, Caitlyn."

"Goodnight, Hardegree."

"Brannon."

After fixing the hole, Cait pulled all her gear into the tent and lay down on her sleeping bag. She had an enemy on the tour, one who wanted her incapacitated, or dead. Problem was, it could be almost any of them.

Even the Ranger.

Come morning, though Brannon watched each one closely, none of the group seemed surprised that Cait was unharmed.

James remained surly, which seemed the norm now, especially when Patti insisted on sitting as far away from him as possible. As for Cait, you'd never know she'd come face to fang with a poisonous snake. The lady was a very cool customer.

The morning also brought more e-mails. Brannon made a quick read through them, fired back a few questions, then turned off his phone. With the drizzling rain, his solar charger wasn't going to work so he needed to conserve the battery.

Cait had juggled the configuration in the canoes. He was still her partner, and that pleased him, though he wasn't sure why. Susan and Patti were paired now, which put Bill and James together: Cait's attempt to diffuse the tension between the couple. The younger man hadn't been pleased, but he made the shift with a minimum of bitching. Brannon knew a hothead when he saw one and James fit the bill. He was first on Brannon's suspect list for the snake incident. According to Sanjay, the kid's initial background check had come back clean, other than a DWI conviction a year before.

Keith Rockwell was indeed a photojournalist, more known for gritty inner-city work than nature photography. Nothing on his blog or other online interactions tagged him as being part of the sovereign-citizen movement. He was going through a nasty divorce, which had no doubt fueled his anti-female rant of the night before.

Bill Adams's last book had been about the Mexican drug cartels. Like Rockwell, he had no interactions with anti-government groups. That left Susan Driscoll and Preston Taylor. Sanjay had run into a dead end when it came to the secretary, at least so far, and he was still trying to obtain her rental car record. She'd continued to chatter about this and that, but had grown quieter as the trip had progressed. Was her earlier behavior because of nerves, or was something else at play?

Brannon suspected that Preston was his likely contact, what with his political leanings and his inside access to the tour. But if he was Brannon's contact, why hadn't he taken him aside and told him that?

Cait's cell phone rang and she set her oar aside and answered the call. "Hey. How's it going?" He saw her tense, and then she half turned and looked back at him. "Okay. I got that." She slowly turned away, but something in her demeanor had changed. "How soon?" Cait listened for a time, gave whoever it was a thank-you, then put aside her phone.

"Trouble?"

"Yeah."

She picked up her oar and began moving the canoe forward. He joined in, matching her increased rhythm. Whatever that call had been about, it had unnerved her. He bet it had something to do with him.

Chapter Ten

Cait kept her eyes on the tannin-stained water and the azure sky in front of them. They were deeper into the swamp now, an area lush with slash pines, pond cypresses, and water lilies. Birds were more abundant, and she caught sight of a goldfinch and then a woodpecker in the air above them. Keith's camera shutter clicked repeatedly.

Kia's call had delivered double bad news: The weather forecasters predicted a line of heavy thunderstorms were headed their way out of Alabama. Lightning storms in the middle of nowhere were never good, but if Cait could keep the others on schedule they'd be at the campground before it hit, just barely.

The other news had been even more disturbing: FBI agents had visited Kia and Mike at the hospital. They'd wanted to know if a particular man was on this tour, someone who'd been involved in an armored-car robbery, and who was associated with one of the militias. That man was Brannon Hardegree.

As Cait paddled she tried to reconcile the image of the Army Ranger with the man the FBI sought. Was it possible? Her mind said it was because not all vets stayed on the straight and narrow. Yet for some reason her heart said Hardegree had too much honor to steal, to join up with some armed crazies.

Since when do I trust my heart?

If he *was* a criminal, what was he doing out here? Stashing his loot? His rucksack was big enough to hold the money, and he was never without it. He even carried it with him when he went to the head.

Maybe Hardegree planned to vanish into the swamp. In that case, let the FBI come after him, if they were foolish enough to take on a seasoned warrior in the wilderness. She sure wouldn't want that mission. Her knife was good for close combat, but that wasn't going to happen in a canoe, and her gun was in her rucksack, which was behind her.

Damn.

"Caitlyn?" he said. "What's going on?"

She half turned, hoping her eyes didn't betray her. "We got some heavy weather coming in. As long as we make the island, we're in good shape."

His eyes rose to the sky. "I wondered about that. But that shouldn't have surprised you, because I'm guessing you know the swamp's weather patterns. So what else is going on?"

"Just that."

"Try again," he said, his voice harder now.

Maybe being honest was the best way. "Some reason the FBI is looking for you?"

Hardegree didn't even blink. "Yes, there is a reason they're after me. I'm guessing you know why."

"Yeah, I do," she muttered. "What are you doing out here?"

"I have my reasons. I swear, I'm not a threat to anyone on this tour. Well, not unless someone gets in my face."

She frowned back at him. "I don't care what you've done, but you try to hurt any of these guys, the FBI will only have to worry about body retrieval, you understand?"

His eyes locked on hers, and then he issued a terse nod.

"Then we know where we stand."

It took every bit of her courage to turn her back on him and keep paddling. All he had to do was reach into his rucksack, draw a weapon and put a round into the back of her head. Then he could easily pick off the others. He had the cold-blooded skills to do just that. Sweat broke out on her forehead, and she forced herself to keep her focus on the water and the sky. All she could do was pray that the man behind her would do the same.

Dammit to hell.

Brannon had wondered when his luck would run out, and now it had. Apparently, Bettis had rolled over on him. All they'd had to do was deprive him of his high, and he'd come apart like a cheap toy. He couldn't imagine that the FBI would send a team after him out here. Or would they?

One consolation in the shitty news: Cait's stunned surprise meant she probably wasn't his contact, unless she hadn't received her orders from Ellers yet. That didn't mean she'd hold to her agreement, wouldn't take him down the first time she had a chance. Because that's exactly what he would do in her shoes.

The light rain had cleared off and the sun was out, a brief respite before the big storm. When they stopped for a quick lunch on a small island, Cait delivered the news about the incoming weather. The general response was groans and anxious looks at the blue sky, as if it was suddenly going to rain hailstones and toads.

"We can't go back to the tour headquarters?" Bill asked.

"Too far away. I need you folks to push hard so we can get there ahead of it. We need time to get the tents up and secured. There's likely to be some wind."

"What if it reaches us before then?" Susan asked, her eyes on Brannon as she spoke.

"As soon as we hear thunder, we head for shore," Cait replied.

"If that happens, I'll explain how to keep from being hit by lightning," Preston added.

"Okay, let's get moving, people."

They broke out their rain gear and loaded up. Brannon made sure to take the bow position, his way of saying he was trusting her, at least for the present. Cait gave him a strange look, then climbed in the back of the canoe. He noted her rucksack was at her feet, and he had no doubt there was a loaded firearm inside. This time, he pushed hard, moving at a faster speed. To his surprise, the others were almost keeping up. Apparently, the notion of being caught on open water during a thunderstorm was a serious incentive.

Brannon made sure his solar charger was soaking up a charge, trickling it into the phone, which was currently on. The instant he'd checked his messages during the lunch break, he'd received Sanjay's warning about the FBI getting too close for comfort. If they arrested him before he got inside the militia, all of this was a waste of time—and his future would go up in smoke.

"Why'd you do it?" Cait asked from the back of the boat. Fortunately, they were at least five canoe lengths ahead of the others so none of them could hear her.

"Didn't have a choice," he said without turning around. "Needed to prove I could be trusted."

"That's the weirdest-ass excuse I've ever heard."

He had to agree, but it was the truth.

There was a huff of disgust. "Like a dick-measuring contest, except you're facing prison. What? Ten Years?"

"In Florida it's thirty because I used a firearm."

"Are you an idiot? What the hell were you trying to prove?"

Her vehemence caught him off guard. Why would she care? *Because I'm one of the band of brothers.*

It appeared that Cait's loyalty to those who'd been in the military extended to him. Or was it something more?

He stopped paddling for a moment and turned to look at her. Her face was sweaty from the exercise, and she was burning holes in his back with her eyes. "I had a reason. Once this is over, I'll tell you why."

She gave a reluctant nod. "You really believe all that hardcore militia crap?"

He had no choice but to live the lie, even though he was fairly sure she wasn't his contact. He'd been wrong before.

"Of course. It'll be them against us one of these days, and I'm going to be on the right side for a change," he replied.

"Stupid bastard," she muttered.

Brannon turned back to the job at hand, feeling that ache in his gut again. Now she thought he was some loony anarchist, and that troubled him. This mission had become a total Charlie Foxtrot, and he still hadn't met Ellers.

In the distance, the sky grew darker, seething cloud layers in dark blue and black. A rumble of thunder rolled out to meet them. Brannon instinctively picked up his pace. A quick look over his shoulder proved the others had done the same. Cait's face was set, her mouth in a grim line. No way around it: They were facing two storms, one of Mother Nature's doing, the other entirely manmade.

The wind began to kick up just as they neared the island where they were camping for the night. Working together, Cait and Brannon unloaded their boat, then pulled it far up on the shore. He attached the cover, the gusts making the task difficult.

Preston beached his canoe next to theirs. "I'll help the others unload their gear. Can you check out the campsite, make sure it's okay with the storm coming in?"

"Will do." Cait pulled on her rucksack and picked up her tent.

"I'll go with you," Brannon offered.

They hiked through the wind and rain to the spot, which was about three hundred feet from the shoreline. Mercifully, the lightning wasn't close by.

"Damn, this is one helluva storm," she shouted over the wind.

"Yeah, but it's not a *sand*storm. That's all that counts."

She gave him a thumbs-up for that observation.

The campsite was about thirty by thirty, with a fire pit in the middle and rimmed by shrubs and hardwoods. Branches littered the ground and more joined them with each wind gust. Brannon and Cait shrugged out of their rucksacks, dropping them near the pit along with their tents and sleeping bags. As he helped her clear the ground of debris, he felt an itch roll over his back, that sense that he was in someone's crosshairs. Cait straightened up and turned toward him, frowning as if she'd sensed the same thing. As she did, a red dot appeared and centered on her chest.

"Sniper!" he shouted, diving toward her.

They tumbled to the ground—the shot missing them—then scrambled toward the bushes, seeking cover. With his weapon in his ruck, it was their only choice. Brannon stumbled once, but kept going as more shots impacted the tree trunks around them. In the distance, there was more gunfire, and Patti's screams.

They ducked behind a large bush. "I count one, maybe two," he said.

She nodded. "More down by the water."

"Seems so. You hit?"

"No. You?"

"Nope. Rangers move faster than Marines."

"Your ass," she replied, and that made him smile. They drew their knives in unison. "Let's go hunting."

As they headed back toward the campsite, Cait felt the adrenaline fueling her. Her eyesight grew keener, her muscles primed and ready for a fight. It was a response as old as mankind, and she accepted it for the gift it was. She knew Brannon did as well. She could see it on his face.

The rain grew heavier, which worked in their favor, cloaking their passage as they moved cautiously through the darkness. No more red dots, no more screams. Either the others were dead, or they were under armed guard. What the hell was this all about? Who would attack a swamp tour?

When they drew closer to the fire pit, Brannon signaled that she should circle around. Cait didn't hesitate to follow the order. Once she was in position, they moved in. With every step she expected the punch of a bullet, but none came their way.

Their gear seemed to be gone, all except his tent and sleeping bag.

"Shit," he muttered, shaking his head. "They took my rucksack."

"They get the money?" she asked. He stared at her now. "Come on, I'm not stupid. You've been carrying your ruck around like a lover the entire tour."

He gave a grim nod and they set off for the shoreline, each step deliberate, though the storm reduced the need to be stealthy. She reached the shore before him and squatted down, allowing her eyes to adjust between the lightning strikes. In the distance, thunder boomed as the storm swept toward the east. A Jon boat sat offshore with two occupants, rocking on the waves. One was in a park ranger's uniform, the other in camo. The one in camo raised his AK-47 and sprayed the line of canoes, blowing holes in the fiberglass.

Once the shooting ceased, the ranger called out, "What about Hardegree and the woman?"

"Dead. Get moving. We're done here."

The boat headed away from shore and then disappeared in the rain. Cait swore under her breath. At least there were no bodies on the shoreline, which meant the others were alive. Why take them? And what did this have to do with Hardegree?

As he rose slowly from his hiding place, she walked across the open ground to join him.

"I got the reg number off the boat," Brannon said solemnly. "If we get to a phone, I'll call it in."

"To who? The FBI? I bet they'd love to talk to you right now."

"I have . . . resources," he said.

He was playing games with her and it made her angry. Rather than get into an argument, which most likely wouldn't gain her any information, Cait jammed her knife back into the sheath. Though she knew it was a wasted effort, she checked the canoes. They were history.

"Why destroy these if they thought we were dead?" she asked, rising to her feet.

Brannon didn't answer, staring at the dark water like he could see to the other side of the planet. "One of the tangos was wearing a park ranger's uniform," he said quietly. "How hard is it to get one of those?"

"You can probably buy them online somewhere. Or kill a ranger to get one."

"That's a cheery thought."

Scouting the area, Cait spied her rucksack, tossed near a stump, grateful they hadn't taken it. Some of its contents lay in the mud. Digging inside, she knew what would be missing. "They took my phone and my weapon," she said, repacking her wet clothes.

"Same with me," Brannon announced as he rifled through his ruck where it'd been dumped near the shoreline. "They were in a hurry and didn't get all the money." He held up a plastic bag. "They missed this one."

"How much is that?"

"Ten thousand."

Cait blinked. "How much was there to start with?"

"Fifty."

She whistled under her breath. "Who says armed robbery doesn't pay off?"

Before Brannon could reply, the wind picked up again as another squall line advanced toward them.

"Let's get camped for the night. We'll work on our options in the morning," he said.

She nodded, shouldering her rucksack, knowing there was nothing they could do for the others at the moment. Nevertheless, she expected some answers from the former Ranger, and if she didn't like them he was about to learn just how unforgiving a Marine could be.

Chapter Eleven

Susan held onto Patti's trembling hand as the boat traveled over the open water, her visibility cut by the cold rain. The boats had come out of nowhere, like modern-day Orcs raiding a village in a *Lord of the Rings* movie. Except these were heavily armed men who'd made it clear they'd kill anyone who didn't do what they said.

She and the others had been ordered to load all their personal gear into one of the boats, and then they'd been parceled out into the remaining ones. Susan had kept the girl with her, fearing their kidnappers had more in mind than just abduction.

"Why'd they take us hostage?" Patti whispered, shivering.

"I don't know."

This kidnapping hadn't been on the spur of the moment; it'd been too well executed. Which meant this trip was unlikely to have a happy ending. Especially if they went through her backpack, where they'd find her driver's license was issued to Susan *Driscoll*, not Townsend, because she'd used her mother's maiden name to register for the tour to help maintain her cover story. That, in itself, wasn't a big deal, nor the fact she'd used a rental car. Having them find her FBI badge and ID would be.

Initially, only Special Agent Brad Wiseman, a buddy of hers at the Brunswick Field Office, knew she was out here. She owed him one, so she'd offered to help him discover the whereabouts of Special Agent Vandermeer, who had gone missing while investigating Ellers's group. Since she was due some vacation, Susan had headed into the swamp to determine what had happened to him and if Vandermeer was still alive.

But when she'd received Brad's text about Hardegree, that the man was wanted for armed robbery, she knew she was hosed. Wiseman would have had no choice but to share her location with the Jacksonville office, and with her home office in Atlanta.

That meant her boss would guess what she was up to, and Special Agent in Charge Maxine Rhodes wasn't going to look favorably on Susan's extracurricular activities. Despite the still-missing agent, Rhodes would claim that Susan was trying to find trouble where it didn't exist. Which was a completely different message than what she was receiving from Wiseman. Susan could tell the SAC that the sky was a lovely shade of blue and her boss would disagree. They had that kind of adversarial relationship.

Now the shit had gotten real with seven kidnappers in camo, and one in a park-ranger uniform. Who were these guys? Why take the tour hostage? And more importantly, were they tied to Quinton Ellers and New America?

Susan had managed to count noses and knew that they were two people short. She'd heard gunshots from the campground and saw one of their kidnappers bring Hardegree's rucksack down to the shoreline, the one he *always* had with him. That told her that he and Cait were either wounded or dead. This was all on her shoulders now.

"Don't worry, we'll be okay," she whispered in Patti's ear. *Liar*.

Brannon collected his tent and sleeping bag when they reached the campsite, and they continued on through the woods, each deep within their own thoughts. Fortunately, the latest squall had been brief, and the only moisture falling from the heavens now came from the trees.

The swamp smell was overpowering, that of soaked earth and wet vegetation. They needed to find a defensible location in case their attackers returned; hunker down, get warm, get fed, get some sleep. Come morning, they'd work out a strategy based on what assets they had left. Which were damn few.

"Thank you," Cait said.

He looked over at her, unsure of what she was talking about.

"You saved my life."

He hitched a shoulder, which she probably couldn't see because of his poncho. "You would have done the same."

A nod returned. "You owe me an explanation of who you are, and if you had anything to do with why we just got hit. Because I'm not buying that you're some misguided vet who decided to add armed robbery to his resume."

"I'll explain everything once we're settled for the night."

She huffed and kept walking.

Now that he'd promised to tell her the truth, Cait fell silent. That's what warriors did. You spoke when you needed to, kept your head in the game. He knew he had a pro by his side, and that was the only bright side to this whole goat rope.

When he found a suitable location, she helped him lay out the ground cloth and pitch the tent. Once it was in place and branches strategically placed to help conceal its location, Cait crawled inside.

"I'm going to do another perimeter check," he said.

"You do that," she said. Her tone of voice told him that her patience with him was at an end.

Sighing, Brannon moved out into the woods again, on the alert for danger. After completing a large circle around their site, including another trip to the shoreline, he reluctantly returned to the tent. He owed her an explanation, and he hoped she'd know it was the truth.

Removing his poncho, he folded it up, and crawled inside. Cait clicked on a flashlight, laying it in such a way that it gave them adequate light. Once he had his boots off, he found a bottle of Gatorade in front of him.

"We need to share?" he asked.

She shook her head. "I've got one of my own, and two

bottles of water. That'll be enough to get us out of here."

Apparently, she had a plan. "Where are we going without a canoe?"

"First, I want to hear your story."

It was then that he noticed her knife was out of its sheath, lying on the floor of the tent near her right hand.

"Fair enough." But instead of spilling his guts, he emptied out his rucksack, laying his wet clothes near his boots.

She studied his possessions. "Between us, we have two knives, a first-aid kit, two compasses, my swamp maps, some protein bars, and the fluids. Also, matches and iodine tablets. Better than some missions I've been on."

"Same here."

They fell quiet as he changed out of his wet pants, stripping down as far as his underwear. He didn't bother to gain himself any privacy, as you lost your embarrassment gene in basic training. He knew she was checking him out, noting the old scars on his legs. As he twisted, he winced, his back complaining. It ached more than usual, but sometimes that was the case. He'd landed pretty hard when he'd thrown Cait to the ground.

When he looked up, she had stripped off her shirt. Her bra was black, with a bit of lace, not what he'd expected. He couldn't help but notice her smooth, toned stomach, and he felt his heart rate kick up. Then he saw the scar on her rib cage, another knife wound.

"What happened to the tango who gave you that?" he asked, pointing.

"Dead."

As if it would be any other way.

"Who does the tattoo honor?"

"Why do you care?" That must have been one question too far.

"I'd like to know. I think it's cool."

That seemed to mollify her. "He was a good friend, like a brother to me. Every time I see the tat in the mirror, I remember him."

"I'm sure he appreciates it."

No reply.

As Brannon shimmied into another pair of cargo pants, she pulled on her shirt. When he was done, he moved to the front of the tent and carefully undid the flap. Peering out, all he could see was darkness. It was raining again, heavily. He zipped the tent shut. "Going to be one soggy mess come morning."

"It's already that way."

She offered him a bar and he took it. "Thanks, Sergeant."

Her knife was in her hand before he saw her move. "How the hell do you know my rank? I never told you."

Shit. He'd let his guard down and blown it.

"Okay, here goes. I *am* Brannon Hardegree," he began, his attention on the knife. He had no doubt she could kill him if her timing was right. "I did rob an armored car in Jacksonville, and I had a very good reason for doing so."

"Uh huh. How do you know my rank?" she demanded.

"My resources. We have access to military records."

"Really," she said flatly. "So you're a felon on the run from the FBI, you have people feeding you private, perhaps classified information, and you think I should trust you?"

"Yeah, pretty much." He rubbed his fingers over his stubbled jaw. "I didn't put that snake in your tent. If I wanted to kill you, you'd be dead. You know my skill set."

That brought her up short. "I'll give you that one. You wouldn't have used a rattler; you would have cut my throat."

"Or driven my knife into your neck at just the right place so you were a corpse before you hit the ground." Because she would know he wasn't lying. "Whoever went after you wasn't a pro."

"James. That's my guess."

"I think you're right. You were cock-blocking him and he didn't seem like the type who could handle that."

Cait nodded her agreement as she returned her knife to the leg sheath. Apparently, he'd passed muster—for now. She stripped off the wrapper on a protein bar, and he did the same.

A truce of sorts. They ate in silence, washing it all down with drinks from their bottles.

When her bar was gone, she shot him a glare. "Spill it. All of it."

"Okay. I work for a private security agency called Veritas. There have been a string of robberies in Florida and Georgia, and we believe that money is being funneled into a militia, one that might be located somewhere in this area.

"I'm working undercover, hanging in the chat rooms and in the bars, mouthing all their anti-government bullshit. When I finally figure out what's going on, we'll send that info to the FBI and Homeland Security so they can shut down the militia's operation."

"Go on."

"The group is run by a man named Quinton Ellers. He's got aspirations to become the next Timothy McVeigh."

"Jesus," she muttered. "But how'd you end up becoming a robber?"

"It was the price of admission so the group would trust me. If I hadn't gone along with it, I would have had to incapacitate or kill my two contacts. Or they'd have killed me. They had already taken out an FBI agent who hadn't passed their test."

She frowned. "Why are you in the swamp?"

"I was told that someone would contact me on this particular tour, and then I would hand over the cash. That I might have a chance to meet up with Ellers."

"Were the guys who attacked us part of Ellers's group, or someone else?"

That was a good question. "I'm guessing they're his people. Not many knew I was out here with that kind of cash."

"When you say this Ellers guy wants to be the next McVeigh, is he a bad enough customer to pull it off, or does he just have a big mouth?"

"Everything indicates that he's crazy enough to try something big. It's possible he's behind the theft of some C-4. We do know he's been stockpiling weapons. We just don't know his target, or targets, yet."

"It fits," Cait replied. At his puzzled look, she added, "Mike said he saw a couple guys in the swamp who made him uneasy, mostly because they seemed out of place. He said there was a large wooden box in the bottom of the boat. He figured it held guns. Or maybe it was that C-4 you mentioned."

"But how can Ellers hide in a national wildlife area? There are rangers all over the place," Brannon said, frustrated. "It doesn't make sense."

"Unless a few of them are on his side. All it would take is one to turn a blind eye. Besides, parts of the refuge are pretty remote, which means if he is out here, he's figured out a way to bring in men and supplies without being obvious," she said.

"Which might explain why one of those guys was wearing a ranger's uniform."

"Yup. Tell me more about this private security agency you work for."

He took a long swig of his Gatorade, finishing off the bottle. "Veritas is multi-national. We take on missions that governmental agencies won't tackle, perhaps because of potential political fallout, or because the risks are too high. Or because the bad guys have bribed the local authorities."

"What types of missions?"

"Just about anything. Human trafficking, illegal drug manufacturing, arms sales, terrorism, you name it."

"The FBI is okay with you folks?"

"It all depends on the day. The D.C. office is decent with us, others not so much. Sometimes they don't like that we can get the job done. I know that sounds arrogant, but it's the truth. We're damned good at what we do."

She cocked her head in thought. "Do you like working for these guys?"

"Yes, they're good people," he said, smiling now. "They watch my back, and there are no bullshit mind games about not treading on someone else's toes. My boss is there for us, one hundred percent."

"So you were supposed to connect with someone on the tour and hand over the money. Why didn't that happen?"

"I have no idea. Originally, I thought you might be the contact, but that's obviously wrong. Preston's still high on the list. He's been sympathetic to some of the militia's propaganda."

"Hmm . . . what about James? I know he's young, but something about that kid bugs me."

"It's possible. He's a prick, but he's a smart one. He had to have had some ulterior motive for bringing Patti on this tour."

"You mean besides having someone to screw for the week?" she asked.

He grinned. "Do I detect overt hostility to the male sex?"

"Only assholes, which James is."

"I'll give you that one."

She yawned, then rubbed the back of her neck. "I need some sleep. My brain's getting foggy."

"Unfortunately, the sleeping bag is damp," he said. "And there's only one." He gave her a look. "No, I'm not going to be a gentleman and let you use it. We can share."

He knew she wouldn't pull the fragile-female card, not this woman.

"Okay. We share. Remember what you learned in kindergarten?"

"To drink all my juice, then take a nap?" he asked, puzzled.

"To keep your hands to yourself. Because in this case, you violate that rule and you won't have hands come morning."

"Roger that." Cait looked away now. For a half second he wondered if he'd acquiesced too easily. "Now that I've told you my story, what's your plan to get us out of here?"

"I'm going to take us to my cabin. We can restock weapons and food and contact the authorities there."

"Your cabin?"

"Yup. I usually follow the tour partway, then go off on my own. Well, except this time."

He thought that through. "I'm liking this plan, Sergeant."

Her mouth twitched upward. "Let me guess—you were a lieutenant, right?"

"Yes, ma'am, I was."

"Figures."

When he rolled out the sleeping bag, she hesitated. "I have nightmares. Sometimes I react . . . violently."

He knew what it had taken for her to admit that. "Same with me. Let's find a way to ensure that neither of us kills the other."

"What do you recommend?"

"We put our knives in a neutral location. That way it's down to hand-to-hand combat if one of us isn't connected to reality." A nice way to say that either of them might be having a full-blown flashback.

Cait weighed his offer, probably working through all the negatives.

"Do you honestly believe I would knowingly try to kill you?" he asked, disappointed.

"You're still on probation. It's more that I'm not used to someone who understands what's going on in my head."

He nodded. "Let's put the knives inside our boots. That'll require an extra step to get to them. I find I'm better if the weapons are some distance away. I have a stronger chance of waking up before I reach them."

"Same with me," she said.

Pleased they had worked out a compromise, he stored their blades as he'd suggested, then draped his wet clothes over the footwear. He turned off the flashlight as Cait stretched out in the sleeping bag, scooting to its edge. He lay next to her, adjusting to the lumpy ground and the drone of rain on the tent roof. He smelled flowers, perhaps her shampoo, but he wasn't sure. It was pleasant, and for a moment, he just enjoyed that fact.

Over the last year or so, he'd had a few one-nighters, but even those didn't seem to work as well as they once did. He was still gun-shy after his fiancée had left him behind. What with the job at Veritas, he'd been too busy for anything more than the occasional hit-it-and-quit-it.

Watching this woman, the soft rise and fall of her shoulder with each breath, made him realize he envied what other men had. He wanted a wife, maybe a few kids. Wanted to share his days with someone who loved him as much as her loved her.

He shook his head at his daydreams. First, he had to finish the mission.

Chapter Twelve

The sun burned down on them like it always did. The other Marines were horsing around, relaxing. One of them had just told a crude joke, and there was laughter. Jeremy, her best friend, said something that made them laugh even harder.

In slow motion, one of the Afghan soldiers turned toward them, his weapon up. She heard his coarse yell, and then the sharp bark of bullets as they sped toward their targets. Even before she could move, one of them struck Jeremy in the forehead. He blinked once, then crumpled to the scorching sand.

Cait screamed and fired back at the rogue soldier, emptying her gun into him just as the others did, at least those still standing. Then she was holding Jeremy, crying, begging him to live. He heard none of her words, already gone, already another statistic in a war full of them.

Now the familiar darkness rose, pulling at her, chiding her. Demanding to know why she was still alive when he was dead. Why did she think she was so special? If she'd been quicker, she could have saved him. It was her fault he was gone.

Cait cried out, flailing in the sleeping bag. Warm hands touched her, and she tried to wrench away. The hands became arms and they cradled her, strong and secure, rocking her like a baby.

"Come back, Marine. It's over. Let it go."

She fought the arms, but they didn't release her. Not hurting her, just keeping her secured.

"It's over," the voice repeated, soft and low. "Come back to me, Caitlyn. You can do it."

She fought again, but only halfheartedly.

"Can you hear the rain?" Brannon whispered. "Hear how it falls on the tent? It's washing us clean, one drop at a time. All the blood, all the guilt. Do you hear it?"

She felt the sobs inside of her, but couldn't set them free. If she could just cry, maybe it would stop hurting, stop suffocating her.

"Caitlyn? You back with me?"

She slowly nodded, knowing now who held her. Somehow, it felt right that it'd be him. Her mind cleared, the remnants of the nightmare leaking away like Jeremy's blood into the sand. With it, the darkness receded, at least for now.

"You're safe," Brannon whispered. "No one will hurt you. I won't let them."

She so wanted to believe that.

He shifted his arms and for a moment, she thought he was pulling away from her. Instead, he moved close, so now her head lay on his chest. She heard his measured breaths, his slow heartbeat. Felt his calm reassurance fill her empty places.

"You want to talk about it?" he asked.

"No," she said. It was the only response she knew.

"Then go back to sleep," he said quietly. "I'll be here. I won't leave you."

"Jeremy did. He died and left me alone."

"Your friend had no choice."

"You might not either."

"You know there are no guarantees," he replied.

"No, there never are."

So Cait listened to the rain, tried to let it do what Brannon claimed. Could it really clear away the guilt, the loss, the emptiness? The feeling that it should have been her that day, not her best friend?

"The nightmare," she began—because she had to tell him what had happened—"it was the day Jeremy died. One of the Afghan soldiers attacked us. Gave no warning, just shot us down."

The military had a term for it: green-on-blue killing, when one of the insiders turned on their allies.

"You feel betrayed," Brannon said softly.

"Oh, hell yeah," she snarled. "We gave our lives to save those people, and they killed . . . " *My best friend.* Her voice broke. "Yes. Jeremy and three other Marines. One had just learned he was going to be a father."

"Oh God," Brannon said. "Were you wounded?"

"No."

"I'd argue that." He touched her chest, just above her heart. "Maybe not physically, but the wound is still there. It always will be, but in time, it'll ache less."

"You're an expert on that?" she demanded, frowning over at him.

"Not an expert. Just my experience. When I first came back, I had nightmares as many as four times a night. I went out to my cabin in the woods and stayed there, as far away from people as possible, so I wouldn't hurt anyone during my flashbacks. I thought of killing myself just to make it all stop."

He's like me. "And now?" she asked, her voice shaking.

"I get nightmares maybe once a night; sometimes it'll be a week between them. I no longer want to die."

"You haven't had one on the tour. I would have heard you."

"When I'm on a mission, they don't seem to bother me. It's when I'm . . . idle."

"It doesn't seem to matter to me."

The yawn caught her before she could stop it. The nightmare had sapped the energy from her body.

"Do you get these more than once a night?" he asked.

"Sometimes. That's why I try not to sleep for more than two or three hours at a stretch."

Without asking permission, he laid his hand over her stomach, drawing her even closer. "You're not alone in this. Never forget that."

She looked over at him, hearing the shared sadness. "Neither are you. Alone, I mean."

He didn't reply, as if he didn't trust himself to find the right words. Cait closed her eyes, wrapped in the arms of a man who still might be the enemy. Betrayal had taught her that trust was a fragile commodity, one easily shattered. Or, this man might be the one soul who understood what it was like to die every second of every day.

Their kidnappers had stopped at a small hammock, one of the swamp's mini islands. This one was just a waypoint in the storm, with no fire pit or no toilet. Still, at close to eight in the pitch-black night, Susan and the others had been herded on shore and told to take a bio break in the woods. She and Patti were moved away from the guys so they could do their thing in private.

"Get it done," their guard said, gesturing with his rifle. He was probably in his thirties, with a scruffy beard and a hard frown. His clothes were dirty, like he'd been digging in the mud, and his eyes never left her companion.

"No way, I'm not peeing with some guy watching," Patti replied.

Sighing, Susan tugged a few clean tissues out of her jeans pocket and handed them to her. "He can't see anything, not with your poncho on."

The girl swore, but managed to do the deed. Susan did the same, while their guard watched over them like they were going to bolt into the woods.

"See? That wasn't hard," the man said, smirking.

Jerk.

Once they were done, she and Patti were herded back to join the others. The rain continued to pelt down, but at least the wind had finally eased off.

"Cait and Brannon aren't here," Patti whispered.

"No, they're not," Susan replied.

"Are they . . ."

"I don't know."

Agitated voices came from the shoreline.

"I don't care if he wants us back tonight or not," a man said. "We can't see shit in this weather. We stay put until we can. Commander Ellers will just have to chill."

Ellers?

"He gave you an order, Rafferty. You need to follow it." That was James's voice.

"He's with—?" Patti began, wide eyed, but Susan waved her quiet.

"I'm not risking my life just to bring a bunch of tourists back to the compound," Rafferty continued. "We go when the weather's better."

"Then you call him and tell him that. I'm sure as hell not," James warned.

"Yeah. I'll explain it to him."

Susan dipped her head down to keep the rain running down the poncho and not into her eyes. James was involved with Quinton Ellers, and they had been kidnapped on his orders. Why wasn't Hardegree with them? Had there been a falling out among thieves?

Though she was chuffed that she'd been right, that feeling quickly drained away. Besides the threat to the others, it was anyone's guess what Ellers would do once he realized he was holding an FBI agent hostage.

Chapter Thirteen

Thursday, April 16th
Chicago, Illinois

Crispin Wilder, the head of Veritas, looked up as Morgan Blake entered his office. Through the window to his left, the sun rose over Lake Michigan, casting lines of color across the rippling water. A lone sailboat skimmed across the horizon.

The office reflected the man: a state-of-the-art computer, antique wooden desk with four cell phones arrayed on top of it. On the brick wall behind him hung a medieval broadsword encased in a worn scabbard. It wasn't a prop. She knew of at least one enemy who'd died with it buried in his chest.

Though in his mid-forties, he looked older now, with the dark circles under his eyes. His hair was pulled back in its usual ponytail, but his navy shirt was uncharacteristically rumpled. It'd been a long night ensuring that the authorities in Argentina ignored Veritas's current mission within their borders.

Crispin had been on the phone for hours, calling in favors, promising a few down the line, and making sure sufficient money landed in the right palms. In the end, their two operatives were out of the country alive, and in possession of the data needed to take down a human-trafficking ring.

"You look like crap," Morgan said, sinking into a leather chair in front of his desk. She couldn't stifle the yawn, and it triggered one of his.

Once the yawn ended, Crispin gave a weary sigh. "I always

thought that when I was rich, I'd be on a yacht, sipping fine whiskey, dabbling in online high-stakes poker games. Instead, I keep horrendous hours and find myself longing for a soft bed and a soft woman."

That was uncharacteristic of her boss; he was rarely so candid.

"Sorry to add to your worries, but I think we've got trouble in the swamp."

"Such as?" he asked, straightening up immediately.

"Brannon missed his check-in. That might be because of the storm that rolled through there last night. Maybe he can't communicate with us."

"And your gut says?" Crispin asked.

"It's more what the tracker on the money is saying: He's off course. The group should have overnighted at an established campsite, but they didn't. Instead, they kept moving and finally stopped at about eight o'clock or so. Now they're going farther southwest into the swamp, closer to the Florida border. That's not on their itinerary."

"So that begs the question: Is Brannon off course, or just the cash?"

"No way to know unless we talk to him. I've got a call into the owner of the tour operation to find out what he thinks. Maybe the group had to be rerouted because of the storm, or because of the fire they've got down there now."

Crispin rubbed his chin with a thumb. "In between all the Argentinean negotiations, I received a call from my source at the D.C. FBI office. Susan Townsend, the real estate secretary we couldn't find background on? She's actually Susan Driscoll, and she's an agent in their Atlanta office."

Morgan blinked in surprise. "What's an agent doing undercover on the same tour as Brannon?"

"My source indicated that Ms. Driscoll is there as a favor to a colleague who works out of the Brunswick Field Office. They have an agent missing, one that was undercover trying to gain access into New America."

"Like Brannon, then. You think Driscoll knows he's wanted

for armed robbery?"

"My contact says she does."

"I'd hoped he'd have a bit more time. Has she been given the order to arrest him?"

"Not yet."

"That's something at least. Sanjay says the militia chat rooms have gone quiet. A lot less bombastic, is the way he put it. Almost like radio silence for those guys."

"Like right before something big goes down?"

Morgan gave a shrug. "Ellers is up to something and I'm concerned that Brannon is in the middle of it. He has no idea who to trust. We could lose him if this goes bad."

"I agree," Crispin said, frowning now. "Is Neil back in-house yet?"

"No, but he will be soon."

"When he is, get him as close to the swamp as possible and give him helicopter access. Can you arrange that?"

"I'll handle it."

"If he's delayed in any way, let me know and we'll send someone else down there. One way or another, we must offer Brannon every bit of backup he might need."

Morgan smiled. "That's why we all want to work for you, boss."

"You just keep telling yourselves that," he replied.

Less than thirty minutes later, Morgan stuck her head back into her boss's office. "All the car tags Brannon sent us have been traced, and only one isn't tied directly to the group. That vehicle is registered to a Wiley Davis. He's well known in the white-supremacist circles, as well as a longtime associate of Ellers's. It's our guess that James Gray was driving it. His mom is Ellers's sister."

"Then he's most likely Brannon's contact."

"That's our guess. The tour operator's wife has discovered that two of the campers, Rockwell and Adams, received free vouchers for that *particular* tour. They were paid for by Davis. Those vouchers were handled through her husband's assistant, Preston Taylor, who has also expressed interest in those kinds of separatist causes."

Crispin tented his fingers. "That's curious. Why Rockwell and Adams? Do they have any military background?"

"None at all. Oh, I've arranged for a copter to be on standby for Neil in Valdosta. He'll remain there until we tell him otherwise."

"Good. Let's get Brannon home safe," Crispin said, worry reflected in his eyes.

"You got it."

One of his phones rang. He peered at the caller ID, then answered in fluent Portuguese. "*Boa tarde, Carlos, conseguiu encontrar o assassino chamado Styx?*"

Morgan quietly closed the door behind her.

Brannon woke to the realization that a warm woman slept next to him, and his body responded accordingly. He was so close he could count the faint freckles on Cait's nose and cheeks. Her blond eyelashes were long; her hair lay unbound over her shoulder. He wanted to touch it, see if it was as soft as it looked, but he held himself in check. A woman and a warrior. Any ancient culture would be pleased to call her their goddess.

Now that she'd shared a tiny portion of the hell she'd endured, his heart hurt for her. He knew what it was like to watch friends die, how helpless you felt, how that guilt often turned inside, seeking yet another victim.

It was a rampant cancer, searching for weakness until it finally consumed you. How you went about the final deed was as individual as the pain—some took a bullet, others died by booze or pills. Some let the cops do it for them.

Not her. She's too special.

Brannon carefully rose, restored his knife to his belt, and began lacing on his boots. His movement woke her and she sat up, her eyes blinking open. She looked kissable, vulnerable even. He wondered if that's what she looked like after a night of passionate sex. If it were him making love to her, the tension at the corners of her eyes would be gone. He'd make sure of that.

"Man, was I tired," she mumbled.

Knowing if he remained near her any longer, he might try to kiss her, Brannon crawled out of the tent. "I'll do a perimeter check."

The morning air was still heavily laden with the scent of swamp on overdrive. He did a slow three-sixty, not sensing any danger. As he headed away from the tent, his boots sank into the sodden ground, which meant their trek today was going to be slow and that bothered him.

They had to get to the others, make sure they were all right. Last night, he'd been careless, not on guard. Fighting an ambush in the middle of a raging storm wasn't easy; nevertheless, he had been the most qualified to keep those people safe, and he'd blown it. Right now their enemies held the better hand.

It's time to turn that around.

"It's pretty damned bad when you find yourself wishing for an MRE," Brannon grumbled. They'd taken down the tent, and now he and Cait were sitting on the ground cloth in the feeble sunshine. The tent itself was drying out as best as it could in the hundred-percent humidity.

"Come on," she replied. "A bottle of water and a bar? It's nourishing. It's—"

"Pretty damned pathetic," Brannon said. "I figured that once I was back in the world, I'd be eating regular meals. Looks like I was wrong."

"Same here."

They grinned at each other like two kids. Some barrier between them had fallen, and it felt good. Brannon wanted to keep it that way.

"How are you doing this morning?" he asked.

"Better. You helped. You said all the right things."

"Don't know about that. I just know that it sucks to go it alone."

"Yeah, I noticed."

She removed a map from her rucksack. It was waterproofed, and for a moment Brannon wished he was. He wasn't one for complaining, but right now too many of his clothes were damp. Including his socks. That, of all things, had always bugged him.

Cait opened up the map and laid it on the ground cloth, then pointed a finger at a certain section. "West of here, there's a series of hammocks and then open prairie. On the other side of that prairie is the island where my cabin is located. Well, it's not my cabin, but the one I use."

He studied the map and saw the destination she indicated. "How do we get there? We building a raft?"

"If I can find it, there's an abandoned canoe along this shoreline," she said, pointing to the west side of their island. "I saw it the last time I was paddling around."

"You do that, just paddle around?"

"Sometimes."

"What if that canoe isn't watertight?"

Cait smirked. "Then we build a raft. Should be a piece of cake for a hotshot Ranger like you."

His grin returned. "Sure thing."

A calm resolve filled him. He knew this drill, had trained for it. So had she. Between them, they'd get off this island and find help for the others.

It didn't surprise Susan that morning brought sunlight, but no food or water, and yet another heavily guarded bio break in the woods. Once again, they were herded back into a group and told to stay put. By now, the terror had receded and been replaced by anger.

"What the hell is going on here?" Keith demanded.

James shot him a sidelong glance, but didn't answer as he sipped on a bottle of water. Apparently, hydration was only for the captors.

"Come on, we need to know what's going on," Bill insisted. "Why are you working with these people?"

"You're being taken to New America," the young man replied. "You each have a purpose there." Then his eyes skipped over Susan. "Well, some of you. Others . . ." he continued, his attention moving to Patti now. "Definitely have a purpose." She shrank back.

"What's New America?" Keith asked, eyebrows knitted in confusion.

"Home," James said. "That's all you're going to find out, so just stop asking about it."

"What about Cait? What happened to her?" Preston asked.

Grinning, the young man pointed his finger at his temple and mimed a single gunshot.

"You killed her?" Bill murmured, eyes wide.

"The bitch refused to die when I put that snake in her tent."

"Oh my God," Patti whispered.

"And Brannon?" Susan asked, suspecting the answer.

James smirked and turned his back on them.

"We need food and water," Keith said, standing now. "Can you at least do that?"

It was the other man, the one named Rafferty, who answered. "We've got some extra water, but no food. We didn't figure we'd be out overnight. Once we get to the compound, you'll be taken care of."

There was more grumbling, but no one felt the need to push the issue. A few minutes later, they were herded to the boats and paired off again. It was only at the last moment that James intervened.

"You're coming with me," he said, pointing at Patti.

"No way, you asshole," she snarled.

He reached out and made to grab her arm, but Susan

stepped between them.

"Get out of my way," James ordered.

"Leave them alone," Rafferty said. "You can sort it out later. Let's get out of here."

The younger man gave Rafferty a glower, but headed toward his own boat.

"What a dick," one of their captors muttered.

"Who is he?" Susan asked.

"Commander Ellers's nephew," he replied. "Which means we can't beat his ass like we'd like." Then he looked around, as if worried someone might have overheard him.

As Susan mulled over that bit of news, their boat headed out into open water, joining up with the others in a line. She leaned closer to Patti. "How did you get to know James? Where did you meet him?"

"In Atlanta. He changed my flat tire." The girl frowned. "After that, he was just everywhere I was, or so it seemed. I thought it was kinda cool."

"And now?"

Patti rubbed her nose. "Now I'm wondering why I didn't realize he was a creeper."

"Don't worry, you'll get better at creeper detection as you get older."

"Really?"

"I'd like to think so."

"You're not as much of an airhead as before," Patti observed.

"Let's just keep that between ourselves, okay?" she replied in a lowered voice. It'd been hard to keep up the ruse as long as she had, mimicking her college roommate's flirty behavior.

The teen gave her a long look. "You're up to something, aren't you?"

Susan gave a wink. "Maybe."

Or maybe not. Because it was a good bet that James's uncle had his own plans for her and her fellow campers. Until she knew what those plans were, all she could do was wait them out and hope someone noticed that the group had vanished.

Chapter Fourteen

After claiming a pair of undamaged paddles down by the shoreline, Cait and Brannon tromped along in mud and near silence. An hour had passed and the going had been slow, as she'd feared.

"Are we there yet?" Brannon said, mimicking Patti.

"That was good. You got her whine dead on."

"My ex-fiancée had a younger sister. She was remarkably whiny." He paused. "Come to think of it, the ex was as well."

Cait laughed. "Ex, huh? Didn't make the cut?"

"No."

From that one word, she could tell it was best not to ask for details. "So how did you make the move from the Army to Veritas?"

"One of my platoon buddies didn't make it back, and I promised I'd keep an eye on his wife and kid. Well, the boy gets himself arrested, charged with a Class C misdemeanor because he was being an asshole in school. It should have resulted in a fine and suspension. Instead, he ends up in a private juvenile facility, sentenced to three months."

"What?"

"Yeah, I couldn't believe it. Jake's mom was freaking out, so I started asking questions. Seems the judge was taking bribes from a company that managed the prison. They wanted to make sure they had a steady supply of inmates. When I made a big stink, it got ugly."

"How ugly?"

Brannon walked around a rotting log before replying.

"I was warned off and when I refused to back down, I was arrested and beaten. Next thing I know, there's this lawyer from Veritas bailing me out. They'd been building a case against the judge for some time, and when I came into the picture, they decided I'd make a good ally. Together we shut it down. The judge and local sheriff are doing time, the company who owned the prison went bankrupt, and my buddy's kid is on the straight and narrow." He grinned. "Because if he doesn't stay that way, Jake knows I will seriously kick his ass."

She heard the strength in that commitment. "You're a good friend."

"Just honoring my promises. After it was all over, Veritas's boss offered me a job, and I've been with them ever since. I've never regretted that decision."

"What about the robbery? How's that going to play with them?"

Brannon issued a long sigh. "It's already causing problems. If I get the goods on Ellers, my boss will have a better chance of talking the FBI into dropping the charges."

"God, I hope so."

"Yeah. I hope Veritas called my folks. I can just imagine what will happen if they hear my name on the evening news."

Cait paused and checked her compass against the map, and then they set off again. The humidity was still off the charts, a heavy fog in some of the low-lying areas.

He smiled over at her. "This cabin of yours, does it have hot running water?"

"Only if you heat the water and pour it over your head. It does have a roof that doesn't leak, well not too much, and some supplies."

"Satellite phone?"

"Affirmative," she said. "I've been kicking myself for leaving it there the last time. That was stupid."

"Your cell phone should have been enough. You didn't plan on being ambushed."

"Yeah, and it bites me that we were," Cait replied, frowning. "I really didn't see that coming."

"You're not the only one. So what other features does this fabulous cabin have?"

"Food, a bed, guns, and ammo. It's pretty fancy."

He grunted. "My idea of fancy is a suite at one of the classy hotels, with a king bed, walk-in shower, twenty-four-hour room service, and a high-definition big-screen TV."

"And a hot babe?" she said.

"All depends on the lady," he replied, watching her closely now. "You game?"

Cait didn't reply, because she didn't know what to say. There was no way she should be looking at this guy as anything more than an ally, but she was. That was unnerving.

"I didn't catch your answer," he said, humor in his voice.

"The canoe should be right up here," she replied, trying to change the subject.

"That was a well-executed diversion, Sergeant."

"Glad you think so, Lieutenant."

To her annoyance, it took Cait longer to locate the boat than she'd expected. She put her hands on her hips, studying the area around them.

"If you can't find the canoe, you'll have to answer my question," he teased.

"I'm trying to locate my landmarks."

After five more minutes, he raised an eyebrow. "You sure there really was a canoe on this island."

"If I say I'll find it, I will. Now be quiet."

Brannon raised his hands in surrender, but more importantly, he stopped needling her. A few minutes later, she found the canoe.

"Well look at that," she said, smiling.

"I'm sorry for doubting you. I should know better."

She eyed him. "Did I just hear a Ranger apologize?"

"Yeah, but don't let it get out. It'll ruin our rep."

Cait smirked, and after stowing away the map and her compass, she fetched a thick branch.

"Going to beat me into submission?" he joked.

"Maybe. You into that kind of thing, are you?" she shot

back, feeling feisty.

Brannon blinked. "Maybe. Depends on who's doing what to whom."

She laughed, wondering what it was about this guy that made her say things she never would to any other man. Made her wonder just what he'd be like in her bed.

Cait forced her mind away from those thoughts—and God, had they been steamy. She poked around the canoe until she was sure that nothing called it home, then flipped it over and studied the damage. The fiberglass had a grapefruit-sized hole along one side.

"Perfect." She shifted off her pack. "Can you keep an eye out for company?"

Brannon gave a nod and drifted away. She watched him for a time, how he moved silently through the brush, how confident he appeared. Maybe he was right, and the demons in her mind would eventually call it quits and give her space.

Yeah. Sure.

The patching process was rather straightforward. First, she cleaned around the hole on both sides of the canoe, then laid down a crosshatch of duct tape on the inside. Cutting a piece of tarp a bit bigger than the hole, she placed that on top of the tape, then sealed it with another layer of duct tape. She'd just repeated the process on the outside of the canoe when Brannon returned.

"Anything?" she asked.

He shook his head. "That looks good. I'm smelling smoke, though. Seems to be coming from the northeast."

She rose, frowning. "Could be a fire started by the thunderstorm. That happens out here."

"How do you fight a fire in a swamp?" he asked, as they carried the canoe toward the water.

"About the only way is to dump a ton of water on it. If the peat starts burning, it's hell to put out. It's freaky because you're not only fighting a surface fire, but also another ten or more feet underneath you."

"Which means just walking on the wrong piece of ground

can get you fried?" Brannon asked.

"Good chance of it. I have a cousin who fights those huge forest fires out in Oregon. I think he's insane," she said.

"Like what you used to do was totally normal?"

Cait looked over at him, matching his grin. "Like that, yeah."

Once they reached the water, she shimmied out of her rucksack and left it on the shore. Climbing into the canoe, she waited. To her relief, there were no leaks. After handing in both her gear and his, Brannon climbed into the front.

"Are we seaworthy, Sergeant?" he asked, looking back at her.

"Roger, L.T. We are for the time being. If that hole had been in the bottom, not so much."

They set off. The wind had grown stronger, and now Cait could smell the smoke too. In some ways that was a good thing, as it would mean the park rangers would be checking in on the tour, wanting to evacuate them. When they couldn't reach either Preston or her, someone would take notice.

As if unaware that their world might be in danger, birds actively hunted for food while gators sunned themselves on the banks. Mist still covered the water in places, swirling as they moved through it, uncovering clumps of golden club, some in bloom.

"Feels like some horror movie," he said. "The quiet before it all goes to hell."

"I can't watch those things. They scare me."

"Really?" he said, surprised.

"I keep shouting at the stupid girls. You know, the ones who say, 'I'll just run out to the car for my lipstick' after ten people have been slaughtered."

Brannon chuckled. "I thought I was the only one who did that. Shout at the TV, that is."

"Nope. And I warn you right up front, I have no football genes. It's a stupid game. Now, if you take the padding off those guys and turn them loose, then we got something. Rugby all the way."

He'd stopped paddling and she noticed he was favoring his left side.

"Something wrong?"

"Muscle cramp. My back gives me problems sometimes. I just landed wrong last night when we dove for cover."

"You mean when you kept me from becoming a corpse."

"That too," he said. He touched his back and winced. "It almost feels like there's something in there."

"You rest. I'll take it for a while."

She expected him to argue, but instead he did as she asked.

"How'd you get injured in the first place?"

Brannon turned around toward her, stretching—and wincing as he did so. "Humvee rolled. Luckily, none of the other guys were hurt."

"Ever tried massage therapy? The deep-tissue kind?"

"Yeah. It hurts like a bitch, but it helps. How about you? I've heard you jarheads are fragile little flowers."

"Huh," she huffed. "You do know that ARMY stands for Ain't Ready to be a Marine Yet, right?"

He broke into laughter and she joined in.

"We're going to take Ellers down," Brannon said. "We're going to teach that SOB some respect."

"And we're going to enjoy every damned minute of it," she replied.

It was mid-morning when the convoy of boats reached its destination. It wasn't much different from any of the other parts of the swamp, though the island was more heavily wooded and the shoreline trampled down from use. Once they reached the shore, the captives were ordered out of the boats and bunched into a group, guards surrounding them. James stood near Rafferty, but his eyes were on Patti.

You touch her, and I will tear you apart.

"Any idea of what this is really about?" Bill asked, looking around.

Susan had no choice but to lie. "They must have confused us with someone else. I'm sure they'll let us go soon. It's all a big mistake. You'll see."

Keith shot her a frown like she was an idiot. She just smiled at him, reinforcing the notion.

"Airhead mode engaged?" Patti whispered.

Susan gave a subtle nod in return.

"This way," Rafferty ordered, gesturing.

"What about our gear?" Keith asked, worriedly eyeing his camera bag.

"Leave it. We'll bring it to you. It'll be safe."

Keith muttered under his breath, but joined the others in lining up like good little hostages. Ahead of them, the track into the woods was about eight feet wide, and been heavily used. As they hiked, Susan caught glimpses of men walking parallel to them on either side. There would be no opportunity for escape, at least not yet.

"Why are they doing this?" Bill asked, still pushing for an answer.

Preston didn't answer, his eyes down again.

You know more than you're letting on.

"So, any of you rich?" Keith asked. "Because there has to be some reason they kidnapped us. It sure as hell isn't because of me. My ex-wife took every damned dime."

"Not me," Bill replied. "Everybody thinks authors are rich, but we're not. Well, except the biggies."

"Do you really think they killed Cait and Brannon?" Patti asked, her voice barely audible. Her hand clutched Susan's so tightly it hurt.

When Preston looked over at the girl, his frown softened. "It's not looking good. There was no reason for it."

"Yeah, there was," Keith replied. "Both she and the Hardegree guy were ex-military. They were a threat to these bastards."

"Him, yeah. But why did you think she was?" Bill asked.

"The way she tucked her pants. It was just like Hardegree's. My brother-in-law used to do that when he was in the military,"

Keith replied.

"You know these people, don't you, Preston," Susan said. She hadn't framed it as a question.

"Yes," he muttered. "I suspected they were out here, but I didn't figure Ellers would go this far."

"What the hell does he want?" Keith demanded.

Before Preston could answer, they cleared the woods to where a fifteen-foot-tall fence rose in front of them, topped by concertina wire. Double gates demarcated the entrance to the compound.

Susan shielded her eyes and looked up at twin guard towers that sat at the corners of the complex. They were manned and their weapons of choice were M-4 rifles. The group's chances of escaping alive had just plummeted to zero.

Chapter Fifteen

They'd fallen into a rhythm over the past hour, moving through the water at a decent speed. It wasn't fast, not with the floating debris from the storm, but progress was being made. Blessedly, the patch had held. The only issue was that, every now and then, Brannon would halt for a few strokes, trying to release the burning cramp in his back.

"Another hour or so," Cait called out. "Once onshore, another fifteen minutes to the cabin. We're getting close."

Her idea of "close" wasn't the same as his, not with his back spasming every few minutes. Before he could reply the sound of a boat motor cut the stillness of the swamp.

Cait turned, paddle in hand, listening. "We got company. Could be nothing, or . . . "

"I agree."

Looking back, she pointed at the shore. "See near the big cypress with the Spanish moss? We can slot the canoe in there. Maybe if we hunker down they won't see us."

As the other boat drew closer, they redoubled their efforts, moving toward where Cait had indicated. Once they were up close to the shore, they pulled the canoe in behind the fallen log. Beetles skittered in all directions, and a pair of turtles sitting on top of the log stared at them.

"God, I hate bugs," Cait murmured, flicking one into the water.

Brannon smiled to himself as they crouched down and waited. "If these folks are with Ellers, we could take them out. It'd get us a better boat."

"Tempting, but if some of his people go missing, he'll know something's up. He'll start hunting us before we're ready."

He nodded his agreement. "This is your part of the mission, Sergeant. I'm good with whatever you decide."

Their eyes met. "You're okay, for a Ranger that is."

He stifled a laugh as the motor grew louder. They flattened down and waited. Cait's hand curved around her knife. He already had his out. As they drew near, he could see there were two men in the boat, both of them in ranger uniforms.

"Caitlyn?" Brannon said quietly, not liking the twitch across the back of his neck.

She was frowning now. "Damn, I don't know."

"What's your gut tell you?"

"To hold position. But I could be wrong."

"My gut agrees with yours. Let's hold."

The boat motor cut out.

"See anything?" one of the men asked.

"No. I don't know why the hell we're way up here."

"Because we were told to check the outer perimeter."

"Yeah, well, this is damned far away from the compound. Between you and me, Ellers is too paranoid for his own good."

Brannon smiled to himself. Their instincts had proven correct.

The first man snorted. "What's with those people they brought in this morning? Who the hell are they?"

"God knows. You see anything?" the second man asked.

"What about over near that log?"

"There's nothing there. Those turtles would have split right off. Let's get home. I'm tired of this shit."

"I'm there with you."

The motor cranked up and the boat did a sharp turn, then set off the way it came. Once it was out of sight, both Brannon and Cait sat up. Only now did the turtles crawl off the logs into the water.

"Now we know for sure that it was Ellers who kidnapped the others. Not that I could think of anyone else who would."

"Why take the risk? He has to know someone will miss them eventually. He could have just had his contact get with me and collect the damned money." Brannon ran a hand through his hair, frustrated. "What possible use could he have with a tour guide, a writer, a photographer, a secretary, and a couple teenagers? It makes no sense."

Cait shrugged as she picked up her paddle. "Let's get to the cabin. Maybe things will make more sense there."

If anything, it would only be more complicated. Him and her, alone in a cabin in the wilderness? He could think of a lot of things they could be doing besides preparing for their mission tomorrow. Somehow, he suspected Cait was not on the same wavelength.

"Susan?" Patti asked, her eyes wide in terror as she stared up at the wire-and-post enclosure in front of them.

"If they wanted us dead, they would have killed us hours ago," she murmured, keeping her voice low.

The twin gates swung open on creaking hinges, and they were herded inside. If it weren't for the wire and the armed guards, the compound would look as if it'd been transported from the late 1880s.

The main house was a two-story wooden affair, with a broad porch and a worn roof covered in camo netting. It was encircled with white sand, an old swamper's trick—made it easier to spot if a snake or an alligator came too close to the house for comfort.

Around the edges of the compound, but still enclosed within the barbed wire, were various run-down outbuildings. There appeared to be a forge and a machine shed, both housed in what had to be original structures.

There were newer buildings as well: a dining hall—some kind of low bunker with netting over the windows. A dozen or so tiny cabins sat inside the wire as well, each just big enough for one or two families. A smaller building was located well away from the others, with a padlock on the door. Probably a jail or the armory. All of the structures had one thing in common: camo netting on their roofs to hide them from aerial surveillance.

As they were marched forward under the watchful eyes of their guards toward the main house, the compound's occupants stopped whatever they were doing and stared, as if a circus had suddenly appeared in their midst. Susan's quick count totaled twenty-six individuals. They were of both sexes, some younger, some older. The kids were barefoot and their clothes had been patched a few times.

The women wore dresses that reached their ankles, plain affairs that looked to have been hand made. None were in bright fabrics, but muted tones that blended in with the swamp around them. Their hair was pinned up, often coiled in braids. Some of them had a careworn look, as if each day was filled with too much work from sunrise to sundown.

Susan knew that some religious sects did not allow women to cut their hair, wear jewelry or makeup, or show their elbows. Her research into Ellers hadn't indicated a religious component, but perhaps that hadn't made it into the reports somehow. In contrast, the men were in jeans or camo, and every one of them had a weapon—a rifle, a handgun, or a knife.

"Take their security seriously, don't they?" Keith said.

"Yeah, they do," Preston replied.

"You been here before?" Susan asked. The assistant shook his head.

She found herself staring at the oversized American flag hanging from the front of the main house. Right below was a banner that proclaimed, "Death to Traitors!"

"Who the hell are these people?" Bill asked in a low voice.

"Folks you don't want to cross," Preston replied, still frowning.

"Line up!" Rafferty ordered.

While they shuffled into place, a camo-clad guard on the house's porch knocked on the door, then returned to his position, at rigid attention.

A minute passed, then another. Susan watched the expressions of the guards around them. Most grew progressively uneasy, as if expecting something to happen. James, on the other hand, appeared bored, as if he really didn't care. Like he was smarter than everyone. Some of that was to be expected with a teenager, but his complete lack of remorse over the deaths of Hardegree and Landry told her this boy had deeper problems. Every now and then, his eyes would flick toward Patti, and the way he focused on her made Susan's nerves twitch.

Finally, Quinton Ellers stepped outside the building. After her friend in the Brunswick office had told her about the missing agent, Susan had researched Ellers, reading anything she could find in the FBI's files. Seeing him in person brought those dry reports to life.

He was about six feet tall, heavyset, but didn't seem to have an ounce of fat on him. He wore camo as well, and his sparse brown hair was sprinkled with gray, trimmed in a regulation high-and-tight style.

The son of an oil-rig worker in Louisiana, Ellers had joined the Army in his mid-twenties. It'd been that or go to jail for assaulting a cop. Unlike for some, the military and Ellers had not proved to be a good fit. After his time in the Army, he'd worked in a factory. He'd gone underground right after the 9/11 terrorist attacks and begun "raising" his militia. He claimed it was in response to the Patriot Act, but he'd been sympathetic to the cause far longer than that.

Over the years, he'd had numerous brushes with the law, ranging from assault to shooting two of his neighbors' dogs, claiming their barking drove him crazy. The fact that he'd executed them in front of a five-year-old kid said that he was a stone-cold son of a bitch. If Susan's guess was correct, James wasn't much different.

The militia leader remained on the porch, hands on his hips, raking his unfeeling gaze down the line of captives. Finally, he stomped down the wooden stairs, then stopped, eyeing his nephew first, then each one of them, as if taking their measure.

"What is going on here?" Keith asked, taking a step forward. "Who the hell are you?"

A second later, the photographer had the muzzle of a Glock 18 pressed up against his forehead, courtesy of their "host."

"I ask the questions, you give the answers," Ellers said. "You got that?" Keith carefully nodded, sweat blooming on his forehead now. "Then step back in line and shut the fuck up."

The photographer did as the man commanded. The remaining captives had gone stone silent now, knowing their lives hung on this man's whims. Patti looked as if she couldn't decide between running or vomiting. Susan slipped her hand into the girl's to keep her in place.

Ellers calmly holstered his weapon. He took the stance again, like he had on the porch, feet spread, hands on hips. It reminded Susan of someone from an old news video.

"Welcome to New America," the man began, his voice full of gravel. "This is my world. The only people who are allowed to live here are true patriots. Anyone else gets a bullet in their skull. Is that clear?"

Preston gasped. "*You're* Quinton Ellers?" A sharp nod returned. "I saw your posts on the Freedom Network message boards." Which apparently hadn't included a photo, or the tour assistant wouldn't have been so stunned.

Ellers ignored him. "Explain to me why I shouldn't just shoot you all and go back to my breakfast," he demanded.

"You can't do that," Patti protested.

Oh yes, he can.

Ellers glowered. "Where's Hardegree?"

"Dead," James said.

"How the hell did that happen?"

"He was trying to take off on us."

Rafferty stared at him in confusion. "And go where? He was on an island and we had control of the boats."

"I made the call," James said. "He wasn't trustworthy."

The commander's steely gaze rested on his nephew. "Hardegree had explosives skills I could have used. Next time, you don't make decisions on your own, you hear?"

James's smirk faded.

"Where's the money?" Ellers asked tightly.

The teen hefted the backpack at his feet and then dumped it out. Stacks of bills hit the dirt. They were of various denominations, denoted by the color of the straps.

"All of it there?"

"Most of it. He must have skimmed some off the top before he came on the tour. Probably figured to take his cut right up front."

Ellers frowned. "I thought he was being watched."

"He was. He was smarter than you thought."

The commander's frown deepened. "You got over eager. It's not the first time."

James's smirk returned, as if the death of two people was just a joke for his own private amusement.

"I was told there were eight on the trip. Where's the other one?" Ellers asked.

"Dead. She was with Hardegree." James gestured toward Patti. "That girl? She's mine. That's why I brought her along. You said I should pick someone, so I did."

"I meant a woman *within* the camp," his uncle replied.

"Well, I made my choice and she's it," he repeated.

"I'm not your possession, asshole," Patti shot back.

Susan squeezed her hand in warning. "Don't push him," she murmured.

Her action caught Ellers's notice.

"Who's this?" he asked, pointing at her.

"She's a nobody. A secretary," James said.

"Ah . . . " Susan began, trying to sound breathy and unsure. She raised a hand, like she was a kid in a classroom. They expected an airhead and that's what they'd get. "Hi! I think you've made a mistake. We're just people on vacation, not anyone special. You should just let us go home."

Ellers's eyes radiated contempt, the muscles in his jaw twitching.

"Be quiet, for God's sake!" Bill hissed. "Don't make him mad."

The commander swung away from her, dismissing her just as he had Preston. He appeared to have a narrow focus, and that was a weakness she could exploit.

"Did you check their gear?" he demanded. Rafferty nodded. "Anything I need to know about?"

Susan's heartbeat ramped up. There was no way he hadn't found her badge and gun.

"Nothing out of the ordinary," Rafferty replied.

What had just happened? Why hide her identity from his superior?

"Take the rest of them to the lockup," the commander ordered. "Adams and Rockwell, you're coming with me."

"Why?" Keith asked.

"You two have value. The rest of them don't."

"The girl—" James began.

"Doesn't go with you," Ellers said. "I told you to pick a woman who's in the camp, not an outsider. Besides, I need your head in the game, not thinking with your dick."

The undisguised hatred on James's face promised payback. Was that a rift Susan could exploit?

At the nudge of a gun in her back, she, Preston, and Patti were herded around the side of the building and deeper into the compound. Guards roamed outside the wire, each armed with an AR-15, or in some cases an AK-47. She counted them as best as she could without drawing attention, making note of their locations, knowing that some might be ex-military. In her mind, that made them even more dangerous.

The first stop was at the latrine. The building was sectioned off, like you'd see in a county park: women on one side, men on the other. Once the bio break was complete, they were led to a shed made of cedar. It looked new, which meant that Ellers had been adding to this compound recently. With its location near the Georgia/Florida border, maybe he had a back way in that hid the bulk of his activities.

Why hadn't the park rangers noticed all this? Were some of them taking payoffs to ignore the crazies in their own backyard?

Another guard stood in front of the shed, armed with a pistol and a knife, both of which would come in handy if they tried to make a break for it. Susan and the others waited as he opened the door. Once they were inside, the door slammed shut and the bolt was thrown.

Two barred windows were the only source of light, as there appeared to be no electricity in the cabin. At least there was a potbellied woodstove along the back wall. Pellets of some kind were stored next to it in a bucket. No wood, probably because that could possibly be used as a weapon. The strong scent of cedar permeated the place.

Patti looked around, sniffed, and then sighed. "It smells like a hamster cage—you know, like the shavings." Her eyes met Susan's. "Who are these crazy guys?"

Before Susan could reply, Preston slumped on one of the six bunk beds. Each of them had a rudimentary mattress and a quilt for a cover, but no pillow.

"Quinton Ellers is . . . a legend," the guide replied. "He's stood against a government that doesn't answer to its people. He's gotten folks talking about how wrong things are."

Susan drifted to the wooden table in the center of the room. It had a few chairs and she sat in the one closest to the stove. "So kidnapping us is a blow for freedom?" she asked.

"I don't know about that. I've been reading those message boards for a couple years. Some of those guys are totally on the level. Others?" Preston shook his head. "They're just nuts."

"You believe all that stuff?" she asked.

Preston frowned. "Some of it I do. The government is digging into our personal lives, hacking our computers and cell phones. I don't like that. But I am not good with killing innocent people just because you don't like how things are going down in Washington. Like that McVeigh guy. That was murder, pure and simple."

Susan nodded. Preston might be an ally after all.

"My parents are going to freak when they find out I'm missing," Patti said, shaking her head in dismay. "I never should have trusted James." She looked over at them, fear flaring in her eyes. "You can't let him take me away."

"We won't," Susan said. "Right, Preston?"

"Right. That boy needs to learn that he doesn't rule the world."

As Patti turned away, Susan could see the tears forming. If they were lucky, this was one promise they could keep.

Chapter Sixteen

As the day grew warmer, Cait and Brannon traded war stories. Not the bad ones that still brought nightmares in the dark of night, but the ones that made them laugh. Helped them remember the good times with good friends. Cait was just about to start another one when she paused and pointed to the shoreline ahead.

"This is it."

Brannon couldn't tell anything different about this one stretch of ground from another, but it would be the right place. Cait knew this swamp like she'd lived here for years. With some effort, his sore back not helping the situation, they beached the canoe, then portaged it farther onto the island. From what he could tell, this one was similar to the one they'd left, only a slightly different mix of trees and shrubs. It seemed less marshy, and he appreciated that.

Once she'd propped it up against a tree, Cait frowned at him. "Rest that back of yours while I hide our tracks, just in case the tangos decide to come this far north."

Brannon nodded, pulling the near-empty bottle of water from his pack and downing the remainder. Stuffing the bottle back inside, he slowly sank to the damp ground. One particular part of his back was throbbing now, which led him to believe that something other than sore muscles was involved. The Army docs had warned him that it would give him trouble now and then, and they hadn't been lying.

He reached around and put his hand under his T-shirt, touching the area that hurt. And grimaced in response. His hand came away slightly bloody. He looked up to find Cait watching him. "My back's bleeding."

"Huh. I couldn't tell because your T-shirt's black. You want me to check it out here, or wait until we get to the cabin?"

"It'll wait."

She offered him a hand to help him up and they walked side by side through the trees.

"Right before we arrived you were about to tell me a story about a bet you took on your first R-and-R," he said.

"Oh yeah," she said, grinning. "It was a hazing. We were in Thailand. The squad made a bet with me that I couldn't get one of the guys out of a brothel without help. I figure, how hard can that be? Wait until the guy has done the deed, then haul his butt out of there. So I go door to door to find him, seeing things that I really didn't need to see, and I finally find him.

"Except Frankie isn't in any shape to get it on. No, he'd passed out, dead drunk. The other guys knew that'd be the case, but if I didn't bring him down, I'd lose the bet."

"How much was the bet?"

"Fifty bucks. It wasn't so much the money as the principle of the thing. They figured since I was a 'girl,' I'd freak out about being in a whorehouse."

"They didn't know you very well."

"No, but they learned." She laughed. "I fireman-carried that Marine's heavy ass down two flights of stairs and dumped him in a mud puddle in the street. The other guys just stared at me. They paid their debt and I gave most of it to the girl at the brothel."

"What was your nickname?"

Her grin grew larger. "Wonder Woman."

"Well deserved."

"What about you?"

"They just shortened my name to Bran. One guy tried to piss me off by calling me Bran Flakes. I decked his ass and that was the end of that."

"Bran. It sounds strong," she said. "It fits you."

The brush opened up onto a clearing, and in the center

stood an old log cabin, which had probably been built in the late nineteenth century. A stacked-stone chimney sat at one end, and a long porch graced the front. The windows were covered with shutters. Made of cedar, it would probably be standing for another hundred years, at least.

"How did you find this place?" Brannon asked.

"Mike is friends with one of the old trappers. Walt said he used to live here as a boy, came out to visit it every now and then. I hiked in to see if it was still standing. I had to run some critters out, do some repairs and fix a few holes in the roof, but it's pretty sturdy."

She climbed the stairs, Brannon right behind her. It was then that he noticed the complex knot that secured the door to a bent nail driven into the side of the house.

"Old-fashioned alarm system, huh?"

"Yup. Unless the thief can duplicate a buntline hitch with my own special addition, I know they've been inside. And even if they could . . . " She undid the knot and something fell to the porch. She picked it up, displaying it on her palm. It was a small, rusted fishhook.

"Clever," he said, nodding his approval.

The door creaked open to reveal a dark interior. Brannon remained out of the way as Cait batted away a spider web, then opened the shutters, letting in the light. She angled out a chair, and he sank into it with weary relief. He could still hike another twenty miles today if needed, but thank God that wasn't the case. Running a hand over his forehead, he felt a sheen of sweat. That wasn't good news.

Cait moved the bed aside, which currently had no mattress, just rope serving as the springs. Beneath the bed was a large metal box. She opened the padlock and began pulling out its contents. First a thin mattress, then a large sleeping bag, all wrapped in plastic. She set those aside.

The goods began to pile up on the table: a large first-aid kit, a twelve-pack of water, a bottle of iodine tablets, toilet paper, body wipes, soap, shampoo, all the simple necessities one would require when your house is located miles away from civilization. Finally, a camp stove and kerosene lantern appeared, along with a box of matches.

"You trucked all this in here?"

"Mike helped me. He has a big boat with an outboard motor, so it cut it down to one run."

"What don't you have in there?"

"The weapons and the food. They're stashed elsewhere. Sorry, but some of it is MRE's."

He groaned. "No pizza delivery?"

"Gators would probably like pizza just as much as the rest of us. Unfortunately, they'd like the delivery guy more."

Cait climbed up on the bed frame and clipped a mosquito net above it. After making the bed, which looked pretty comfortable after the night sleeping on the hard ground, she toted all the supplies to a long, narrow table set against the wall, leaving the main table free.

He was intrigued by how she'd stowed all this gear in such a small space. "So where is the food hidden?" he asked, looking around.

Cait opened a rickety cupboard, removing a couple pots, two metal plates and cups, plastic glasses, and silverware. Then, using her knife, she pried off the back of the cupboard to reveal another stash. This time, there were canned goods, medicine, cartridges, a rifle.

And those damned MREs.

"I hate to sound ungrateful, but I swore I'd never eat one of those things again, if I could help it."

She scooped them up and set them on the table. "Feel free to take the rifle and shoot yourself a squirrel. Me? I'll eat these before I touch another tree rat."

"Had to eat a lot of them?"

She nodded. "My dad thought it was a great way to teach my brother and me how to be self-sufficient."

"Tough dad. Mine wasn't like that. He believed food should come from the grocery store, and that having the local Chinese place on speed dial was a blessing."

She smiled. "I like your father already."

"He's a good guy. He raised us right. And my mother rocks, except when she's trying to hook me up with some friend's daughter."

"Luckily, I don't get that so much now. Mom knows I'm not a particularly fun date."

"Not sure about that. You've been a blast so far."

She huffed and ignored his comment, setting a satellite phone on the table in front of him, followed by a bottle of generic pain tablets and a gallon of water. After refilling his own bottle, he downed the pills while waiting for the sat phone to power up.

The moment the call went through, he said, "It's Brannon."

"Thank God," Sanjay said, heaving an immense sigh of relief. "We were sweating here, my friend. You okay?"

"Yeah, but we got a big problem. So I don't have to repeat all of this, can you get me on a conference call with the boss?"

"Sure. Give me a minute to set it up."

He was put on hold and heard blissful silence. If someone was calling this particular phone number, they didn't need to listen to some tinny version of Madonna's "Like a Virgin."

When a noticeable click came through the phone, Brannon pushed the speaker button.

"We're ready," Sanjay reported. "Crispin and Morgan are here."

"Hi guys," Brannon said.

"Damned glad to hear from you," his boss replied. "We had concerns."

"Sorry it took so long. I have Caitlyn Landry listening in on the call."

"Ms. Landry," Crispin said. "Good to speak with you."

"Thank you," she replied cautiously.

Brannon gave his report, laying out exactly what had happened, where they were, and the situation they faced.

"Well, hell," Morgan muttered.

"Sanjay, where is the cash now?" He turned to Cait. "We have a tracker stuck to one of the bundles of money."

"Smart," she said.

"It's still in the swamp, stationary since mid-morning," he reported. "Where are you located?"

Cait retrieved her map and supplied the necessary coordinates.

"Then you're about nine miles northeast of the tracker," Sanjay replied.

"You think that's where Ellers's compound is?" she asked.

"That's our guess," Morgan replied.

"I spoke with Mr. Montgomery about an hour ago," Crispin began, "and he believes that, if Ellers is anywhere, he's exactly where the tracker is at this point."

"How is Mike?" Cait asked.

"Doing well. We'll let him know you're alive and unharmed."

"Thanks."

Crispin went on to explain how Rockwell and Adams had come to be on that particular tour.

"Huh," Brannon said, shifting in his chair. "No matter what, Ellers isn't going to surrender without a fight."

"We have the same concerns, though the feds did learn valuable lessons at Waco and Ruby Ridge. They'll be more cautious this time around," Crispin replied. "Would you be able to reach that location and determine if this is indeed Ellers's compound? And if it is, serve as a forward scouting team?"

Brannon looked over at Cait. She gave him a thumbs-up.

"We're 'go' for that. We'll need coordinates and anything else you can provide."

"We'll get you all we have," Morgan said. "Give us an hour or so and I'll pull it together for you."

"How long would it take you to get down there?" Crispin asked.

Cait answered. "Probably about three hours, if we push it. Usually it would be faster, but there's a lot of debris in the water after the storm. Since it'll be best to do the run at night, and we don't have a full moon, we'll be feeling our way along."

"What do you have in the way of weapons?" his boss

asked.

"Two knives and a rifle," Cait answered. "If we encounter any tangos, we'll acquire more from them."

"There's one issue that is going to hamper both us and the FBI," Morgan said. "As of a couple hours ago, the swamp's airspace was closed, except for park rangers and fire personnel. The fire is nowhere near you, but to keep the news helicopters out of the way, they've shut down the entire area."

"Okay. We'll just have to do it the hard way," Cait said. "'Embrace the suck', as they say."

"There you go," Brannon replied, smiling now.

"There's another player in the game that you're unaware of," Crispin said.

Brannon raised an eyebrow as his boss explained exactly who Susan was. "I wondered what was going on with her," he said. "Does she know there's an arrest warrant for me?"

"Yes," Morgan replied. "At least you have someone inside that can help you."

"Provided she's still alive. If Ellers finds out she's FBI, she's dead."

"Indeed. We'll send you what info we have, and I'll call the FBI, let them know the situation," Crispin said. "You'll have backup in your area in a few hours; Neil will be positioned in Valdosta by nightfall, and he'll have access to a helicopter. We'll obtain permission to access your airspace, if needed."

"Roger. Always good to have Iceman on a mission," Brannon replied. "I'll check messages in a couple hours, but the phone will be off until then to conserve power."

"Understood. See you when this is over."

When the call ended, Brannon turned off the phone and set it aside.

"What happens if they can't get that permit for the copter?" Cait asked.

"Won't matter. The boss will ensure that we have backup. He'll worry about the legal flak later."

"He sounds like a good commander."

"He is. Veritas only hires good people. Unfortunately, there are a lot of bad people in this world, and often it doesn't even out."

"Then let's make sure it does, at least this time."

Chapter Seventeen

As he entered his office, the two hostages behind him, Quinton Ellers felt the need to hurt someone. His nephew in particular.

Lying little bastard.

That was the problem with James—he couldn't be trusted. He wouldn't even be at New America if it weren't for his unique skills. So what had really happened between the kid and Hardegree? How had James managed to kill an Army Ranger? No, he'd have sent others to do his dirty work, and it would have been an ambush. There was more to that tale than his nephew was admitting, and Ellers would have to weed out the lies to get to the truth. But first, there were other matters that needed attention.

He sat on the old folding chair behind his desk—not that two planks spread across a pair of sawhorses was a real desk. It didn't matter. He wasn't here for the long term.

Two campers stood in front of him now. The writer was nervous, opening and closing his fists at his sides. Ellers had read the man's last two books and knew he'd be adequate for the task. The photographer wasn't as scared, or just better at hiding it. Rockwell's eyes were sharp, focused. His biography had put him in war zones, so this reaction was to be expected.

Time to fuck with their minds. "You know why you're here?"

"No," Rockwell replied. Adams just shook his head.

"I'm about to make history, gentlemen, and I need someone to document that moment. That would be you."

Rockwell blinked. "What kind of history?"

"The kind that will be spoken of in awe for decades to come. The tree of liberty needs to be watered, and I'm the one to do it. It's the only way the tyrants in Washington will know we mean business." He let that sink in. "You know anything about Timothy McVeigh?"

Adams frowned. "Yeah, he bombed that building in Oklahoma, killed all those people."

"He struck a blow for liberty."

"I'm sure the kids he killed would disagree," Rockwell said.

Yeah, this one's got balls. "Not McVeigh's fault. The feds never should have put a day care in that building. They had to know they were a target. That blood is on their hands."

Rockwell gaped at him. "You really believe that?"

"Of course I do."

"And you'd do the same, blow up a bunch of babies just to make your point?"

"Yes, I would." He kept the smile to himself. "I was there that day. Not near the federal building, but in Oklahoma City. I was visiting a buddy of mine. I wish I'd been closer to see the explosion."

The photographer clenched his jaw, but managed to hold his silence. The bastard was learning.

"Did you have something to do with the tour owner's accident?" Adams asked.

The writer was smarter than he looked. "Sure did. I didn't want a battle-hardened Marine anywhere near my operation. And if you think the FBI are going to rescue you, you're wrong. The last agent who tried to infiltrate this organization is buried out in the swamp. It took him a *long* time to die. I enjoyed every damned minute of it."

Adams swallowed hard. "So what do you want with us?"

"Every great general has someone who writes his memoirs, makes sure the truth is known after the battle is over. *You* will do that for me. He," Ellers said, gesturing at Rockwell, "will provide the photos."

"And if we tell you to fuck off?" the photographer asked.

"Then I take you two out by the flagpole, make you kneel, and put a round in the back of each of your skulls. I can always find someone new. It's that simple."

It wasn't, but they didn't need to know that. He was on countdown-to-zero hour, and the overnight delay delivering the tour group to the compound had nearly compromised his plans.

The two hostages traded looks and Ellers knew what Adams would say before the words left his mouth.

"Looks like we're writing your memoir, Commander."

Yes, you are.

He retrieved the two hundred-plus manuscript pages and the laptop, handing them to Adams. Three spare laptop batteries went on top of the pile, because there was no electricity in the lockup.

"Clean this up," he said. "It needs to be ready by 0700 two days from now."

"Two days!" the author blurted. "That's impossible."

Ellers only had to touch his weapon to get the man to sputter an apology.

"Sure, sure. Two days. Okay."

"What am I to do?" Rockwell asked, his tone indicating that he was barely reining in his anger.

"When I'm ready, you'll walk around with me so you can photograph the camp. If I tell you not to take a photo of something, then don't do it. You do, you're dead."

Rockwell gave a curt nod, his jaw locked again.

"Will our names be on this book of yours?" Adams asked.

"Of course," he lied. It'd be damned hard for them to argue the issue after they were dead. "Any other questions?"

When there were none, he waved them off. As the guard ushered them outside, Ellers called out, "Tell Rafferty I need to talk to him."

When the man arrived, Ellers could read the worry on his face. That was smart. He had reason to be worried.

"What happened with Hardegree?" Ellers demanded.

Rafferty shook his head. "From what I could tell, he and the tour guide went up to the campsite." He stalled out, growing more agitated.

Ellers smiled to himself. His reputation as a hard bastard worked wonders with his people. They feared him, and that was what it took to be a leader.

"And?"

He looked down at the floor now. Anywhere but at him. "James sent a couple of our men inland. I just figured they were going to round up Hardegree and the woman. Instead, I hear gunshots and the guys come hot-footing it back with their gear, telling me they're dead."

"Did you check the Hardegree's rucksack like you did the others?"

"No. James had it. Wouldn't let me touch it."

The little prick thought he could outfox his old uncle. The kid didn't have a fucking clue. "That'll be all."

Once the door closed, he rose and made his way to the window, looking out on the parade ground. Maybe it was good the Ranger was dead. Hardegree had been too perfect. One of Ellers's contacts in the Army had said as much, claimed the man didn't seem to be the kind to cross over to the other side.

Still, Hardegree had gone on the robbery, hadn't even hesitated that much, according to Clarke. Now that he was gone, Wiley would have to handle the explosives, and he wasn't a pro. But you did what you had to get the job done.

Ellers still remembered the rumble under his feet, the sound of the car alarms, the shattering of the window glass, and the piercing screams that day in Oklahoma City. At the time, he hadn't understood what it meant or what it stood for. Now he did. McVeigh had done his best; so would he. And by the time he was done, Tim's strike would look like child's play.

"It all comes down to body count," Ellers muttered. "That's the only thing those assholes respect."

About half an hour had passed since they'd arrived at Ellers's compound. During that time, Susan had inspected their "jail"

and determined there was no way out except through the bolted door. There were also no hidden microphones or cameras, which meant their conversations would be private. Down the line, that might become important if they plotted an escape.

She curled up on one of the bunks and stared at the ceiling rafters, her hands laced behind her head. Patti slept on one of the other bunks, worn out, while Preston sat near the woodstove. He looked lost, like he'd found the most perfect diamond in the world, only to realize it was a fake.

"I have no damned idea what this is all about," he murmured.

"So what do you know about this guy?"

"Only what I read on the Freedom Network. It's an online community. We share stories about how the government is trampling on our freedoms. Some of those stories are pretty scary."

"So you think Ellers is a good guy?"

He sighed. "Well, I did. Now that I'm inside this little world of his, I'm not so sure."

"Any idea why he took us hostage?"

"No." His eyes moved to Patti, sleeping peacefully through their conversation—the girl must have needed it. "I don't think any of us are important enough to warrant a ransom. And that kid, James? I figured he was just a horny pain in the ass. Certainly not Ellers's nephew."

There were voices outside the building, and then someone threw the bolt. The door swung open and Bill entered, followed by Keith. Both looked exhausted. Following them were two armed men and a young boy. The boy staggered under the weight of the tour group's packs, which he dropped by the door.

"You going to feed us?" Preston asked.

"Not until we get the order," one of the men replied tersely. Then their captors were gone, the bolt sealing them off from the rest of the world. Patti yawned and headed over to the pile of gear, rummaging through to find hers.

"The bastard is nuts!" Bill sputtered, dropping a stack of

papers on the table, followed by a battered laptop and batteries.

Keith retrieved his camera bag and slumped into a chair. "He wants Bill and me to 'tell his story.' Says he wants it all down for posterity, so they'll know just what a patriot he really is."

"How would he know you're on this tour?" Susan asked.

"Keith and I both received free vouchers, but only for this week's trip. When I got it, seemed odd, but I figured what the hell, why not?" Bill replied.

"Same here," the photographer said.

Patti gasped. "We were kidnapped because of you two?"

Keith actually looked embarrassed. "Yeah, I'm guessing that's the reason."

Maybe not the only one.

"Shit, guys," Preston said. "I sent out those vouchers. I just figured they were gifts or something. People do that every now and then. I had no idea the commander was behind all this."

"Any idea what he's up to?" Susan asked.

Keith shook his head. "Just that he's going to 'water the tree of liberty.' He was talking about that bastard McVeigh. How it was the feds' fault all those kids got killed. How he'd do the same. The man is a freaking psychopath."

Preston whistled under his breath. "He didn't come across as batshit crazy on the message boards, just really intense."

"I bet he's been planning this kidnapping for some time," Bill added. "He told us he made sure that Montgomery wasn't on this tour. He even confessed to killing an FBI agent. He boasted about it."

Susan lowered her gaze to the floor so they couldn't see her reaction. "Does Ellers have a timetable for this blow for freedom?" she asked.

"It felt that way, but he wouldn't tell us what it was," Keith said.

The author nodded his agreement. "These," he said, gesturing at the pile of papers and the computer, "are his notes. He has written a rough draft, and now he wants me to edit it into some sort of order. And he wants it done in two days. Like

I said, the man is nuts."

Two days? Was Ellers just being pushy, or was that deadline tied to his plans in some way?

"You guys, he needs. What keeps him from killing the rest of us?" Patti asked, her voice shaking. She was back on her bunk now, her hands knotted around the strap of her backpack.

"Nothing," Bill admitted. "Though I think your boyfriend will want to keep you around."

"He's not my boyfriend," the girl replied. "He's too weird."

"Then why did you come out to the swamp with him?"

Patti hitched a shoulder. "I was bored."

Teenagers.

Susan's attention swung back to Bill and the pile of papers. "How's about we help you sort all that out. It might tell us exactly what Ellers is up to."

Bill was nodding even before she finished talking. "Works for me. All I want to do is get the hell out of here and not get dead like Brannon and the tour guide."

"Just like the rest of us, then."

Chapter Eighteen

At Cait's request, Brannon stripped off his shirt, feeling the fabric pull against dried blood.

"Yeah, you got a wound back here. You land on something?" she asked.

"Must have. How bad is it?"

"Don't know yet." She pushed on the area and he grimaced. "It's getting infected. Turn around and straddle the chair for me."

Brannon did as instructed while she retrieved the first-aid kit. As Cait pulled supplies out of the kit, placing them on the table, he couldn't help but check out her honey-wheat hair, still mussed from the trip. Even with not a lick of makeup, she looked beautiful to him. A real woman, through and through.

What would she be like in bed? Probably as take-charge as she was a soldier. He could imagine her astride him, moving at her own pace, making him suffer until she made him come. He groaned at the images in his mind, his groin tightening.

She touched his back near the wound. "That hurt?"

The discomfort was much lower, but he didn't dare admit that. "A little." When her hands began to probe the area, his hard-on faded. Nothing like pain to overload that part of his anatomy.

"You had a tetanus shot recently?" she asked.

"About six months ago. A mission went wrong and I took a knife in the thigh."

"Youch."

"Yeah. Iceman and I got even. We took down the drug lord

responsible for wiping out an entire village in Mexico."

Looking over his shoulder now, he saw her respect.

"Damned fine job. Thank you for what you do." Then she grew solemn. "Me? I'm just . . . coasting."

"No, you're recharging, like a battery. You've been through hell, and it takes time to deal with all that. I have no doubt that once you're back at full capacity, you will kick ass at whatever you do."

She quirked an eyebrow. "You sound so sure of that."

"You will kick ass at whatever you do," he repeated. "I'd bet money on that."

Cait returned a soft smile. "Thanks. I just have a lot of stuff to work through."

"I'm doing the same. Meanwhile, I get to hang out with a pretty warrior woman in a remote cabin. That doesn't suck." His eyes strayed back to the pre-packaged food on the table. "Well, except for the MREs."

She laughed as she picked up a set of tweezers. "You really hate them, don't you?"

"Yes, ma'am, I do."

"Back when we were paddling here, you were going to tell me about what happened in Tangiers. Now would be a good time to tell that tale. It might keep your mind off what I'm about to do."

"Which is?"

"I'm going to dig around in this wound to make sure you don't have anything embedded in it. It's not going to feel good."

"Oh shit. All right. My story is about a monkey with a very wicked temper. It started when a working girl hit on me. I turned her down."

He gritted his teeth as she dug in the wound. "Next thing . . . I know, the monkey comes out of nowhere, trying to bite the shit out of me. It chased me down the street, and I found myself taking refuge . . . in a brothel."

"Nice excuse," she said, chuckling.

"Actually, I hadn't intended to go there. Since I couldn't

leave the place, not with that evil beast waiting for me, I stayed." He looked over his shoulder again. "I stayed all weekend."

Her reaction proved worth the discomfort as Cait paused in her digging, her eyes widening. "*All* weekend?"

He grinned. "Yup. Since I stayed that long, I got a special rate. I finally quit when I ran out of condoms."

"Damn," she replied, then mock-fanned herself.

He laughed. "I found out later that the girl had trained the monkey to herd potential johns to the whorehouse. I thought that was so smart that I wasn't upset at all."

"I bet you weren't. Not after a whole three days of *personal attention*."

"I was young and stupid. What can I say? Doing that kind of thing lost its appeal when I got older." He paused, then blurted, "What about you? How did you scratch the itch?"

She dug some more before answering, making beads of sweat pop out on his forehead. It also made him wonder if he'd gone too far with that question.

"I didn't scratch that itch," she replied. "I couldn't sleep with anyone in my squad because the other guys would think I was easy, so I went without. Lots of cold showers."

"What about when you were on leave?"

"There were a few hookups when I was back in the States," she admitted. "Nothing long term. My career came first."

"I understand. How long were you married?"

"Three years. The husband didn't seem to comprehend that marriage vows meant he was supposed to keep it in his pants when I wasn't around. I caught him and an ensign going at it in our bed, so I kicked their asses out and filed for divorce that same afternoon."

Brannon huffed in disgust. "You should have introduced him to my fiancée. They would have gotten along just fine."

"She cheated on you?"

"Yes. Repeatedly. Dammit!" Brannon said in response to a particularly deep probe with the tweezers.

"Found it." Cait held up a long sliver of wood. "That seems

to be all there is. I have some antibiotics. If you're not allergic, I'd suggest you start taking them."

"I will. Thanks."

Her eyes held his for a time, then went back to the wound. "I'm sorry about your fiancée."

"I'm sorry about your husband."

"So all around, we're just sorry."

Brannon reached over and lightly touched her cheek. "Not so much anymore," he said.

A faint blush spread across her cheeks.

He hoped that simple gesture would convey how much he appreciated her. Respected her. Wanted to get to know her better. *Way better.*

"Let's get you bandaged and then make us some food."

Outside the cabin, the sound of a light rain began. Then it grew heavier. She looked toward the window and smiled. "Change of plans. I'm getting a shower first."

"You have one rigged up?"

"No, I do it the old-fashioned way—I strip and stand in the rain. When it's this heavy, it's just like standing under a real shower."

His mind conjured up what Cait would look like nude, raindrops running down her tanned skin. Down her breasts, down her thighs.

"Brannon?"

He thought of the water beading on her nipples.

"Bran?" she repeated.

"Huh?"

"I'll put on your bandage unless you want to bathe too."

We could share the rainstorm together and then . . .

"Leave it off for now. I need a shower," he said, though he knew it'd be solo.

The pressure south of his belt buckle edged up a notch. The missions had been coming so close together, he hadn't had time to deal with that issue, and being alone with this alluring woman wasn't helping.

Cait gathered her shampoo, a bar of soap, and a microfiber

cloth. "This heavy a rain is great for washing clothes. Just in case you need to."

He heard the clump of her boots hitting the porch, and then she was out in the downpour. He imagined her getting all wet, then using the soap to wash her clothes, even as she was wearing them. Then stripping down to her smooth skin.

Brannon groaned at the images in his head. To keep himself occupied, he inventoried the food and found two cans of ravioli. After rinsing out a saucepan, he fired up the camp stove and began heating the food.

At least one meal would be decent. As he moved to set the table, he caught a glimpse of Cait through the window, even though he hadn't meant to do so. She was naked, looking up, catching raindrops on her tongue like a child, her face filled with joy. Her breasts were small but firm, and her butt curved in the most blood-firing way.

Damn, you're smoking hot.

Brannon made himself look away in case she saw him. He hadn't meant to violate her privacy; it had just happened, and now he'd always have the image of her in his mind. With a groan, he adjusted his trousers and made a mental note to get laid once he got back to civilization.

Cait toweled off on the porch, then dressed in clean clothes. Winding her hair in a towel, she began drying it. She could have sworn she'd felt Brannon's eyes on her, but she couldn't be sure. If he had been watching her, she suspected it'd been by accident. But then, most guys could not resist the temptation to check out a naked female.

She entered the cabin to find her companion stirring something on the stove. "You can cook. I'm impressed."

"I hardly call opening a can a major culinary feat."

"It would have been for my ex. He claimed to be clueless when it came to feeding himself."

Brannon stopped stirring. "How'd you get hooked up with

him?"

"I was young and stupid," she said, echoing Brannon's own words. "He was funny, good in the sack, and I thought that was all I'd need. I was wrong." Cait sank onto the bed, then carefully dried her feet. Fresh socks came next. It felt great to be clean again.

"At the time," Brannon said, "I didn't understand what my fiancée saw in me. I was messed up big time."

"Have you looked at yourself in a mirror, Bran? You're handsome. You're ripped. Any woman with eyes would go for you."

"Even you?" he asked.

Cait blinked, realizing she'd set herself up for that question. "Ah . . . "

"No need to answer right now. The food's ready," he said, giving her an out.

Time to set the boundaries. "I'd be dead not to notice you," she said, "but I'm not interested in making things more difficult right now. I'm too screwed up."

"Maybe not as much as you think," he said, laying paper plates of ravioli on the table. "So, will it be white or red wine for the madam this evening?"

She rolled her eyes because they had no wine. "I'll go with water, thank you."

They ate in silence, the ravioli, cheese and crackers, and canned peaches disappearing at a quick rate.

"God, was I hungry," he said, leaning back.

"Funny how some meals stick in your mind. This one will, for sure."

"I'll take that as a compliment," he said, smiling. "I remember the first pizza I ate after I left the service. It was deep dish, Chicago style. And there was beer. Lots of it."

"I went to the closest hot-dog place and loaded up. Onions, chili, you name it."

"A woman after my own heart," he said. She smiled. "You know, I wasn't entirely honest. My fiancée wanted me for a couple reasons."

"Besides the fact that you're handsome and ripped?"

"Besides that. Her dad owns a string of sporting goods stores. It wasn't until after we broke up that I realized he'd intended to use me as his 'mascot.' Army Ranger, all-American dude, God and Country. He wanted was a 'hero' to brag about, put me in his store's ads."

"What an asshole. I'm sorry," she said, meaning it. "That had to hurt."

"It did," he said, standing now. "I need to wash up while it's still raining."

Then he was out the door to take his own shower, as if somehow the past still had the power to wound him. In Brannon's wake, she felt disappointment. Not in herself, but in the stupid woman who'd treated him like that. Then she frowned. Her ex hadn't deserved her, either.

As she cleaned up the plates, burning them in the fireplace, she made sure not to sneak a look out the window. Her imagination was good enough to guess what he looked like standing in the rain. The strong muscles on his arms, his six pack, his strong thighs, and what rested between them.

Why wasn't she out there, seducing this virile man? Was it because she was afraid?

Yes.

Brannon Hardegree was the real thing, and the more she opened up to him, the more power he'd have to hurt her. Especially when he found out exactly how many pieces of her soul were missing.

Chapter Nineteen

Cait waited until she figured he was dressed. Moving into the doorway, she caught a flash of his firm butt as he tugged on a pair of clean trousers. Did he usually go commando?

He turned and grinned. "Eyeballing me?"

"Only by accident, honest. Sorry."

"Same thing happened when you were showering. You're a beautiful lady."

She snorted, which wasn't at all ladylike. "Right."

"No, I'm serious," he said, slowly moving the towel over his broad chest. She followed every movement. "You're for real."

Their eyes connected. "Bran . . . we . . . "

"There's no one around for miles. We're both adults, and I want you, Caitlyn," he said softly.

Cait opened her mouth, then closed it again, unsure of what to say. Because she wanted him just as badly.

I can't.

He moved closer, not reading the answer in her eyes. "No strings attached, just you and me. I've wanted you since the moment I saw you loading the gear into the canoe. I know whatever happens here tonight will be incredible." He hesitated. "Even if my back hurts like hell."

Brannon hadn't gotten all the water dried off and it still beaded in his chest hair. She longed to touch each bead.

He took her hand in his, caressing it. "If you don't want us to be together, just say so, and I'll back off."

Cait looked up into those deep eyes, saw the heated desire.

She shook her head. "I'm sorry, I can't do this. I want to, but . . . "

He gently touched her cheek and placed a chaste kiss on her forehead. "Understood, Caitlyn. If you change your mind, just let me know."

That, she hadn't expected. Resisting the magnetic pull he seemed to generate, she fell back on her training. "We should plan our mission."

Brannon didn't move, just gazed at her like she was the only woman in his world. It was sincere, not just designed to get her in the sack.

"I like it when you call me Caitlyn," she admitted as tears pricked at her eyes. "Jeremy used to call me that before he—" She turned tail and vanished inside, like the coward she was.

There'd been fear in her eyes. Not the stark dread of combat, but the deeper, more personal panic of allowing someone too close. With a sigh, Brannon followed her inside, rubbing the towel down his chest and arms, not only to dry off, but also to warm up. His shower had proven colder than he'd anticipated.

After she'd applied a bandage to his wound, he pulled on a clean T-shirt. Cait hunted for a pen, then dismantled a brown grocery bag to create a makeshift sheet of paper. Flattening it with her palm near the map, she looked up at him from the table.

He saw the plea in her eyes: *Please let it go. Please don't push me, or I'll take a step I might regret.* So Brannon played the gentleman and took a seat opposite her at the table, knowing that he'd rather be in that bed making love to her. Showing her that life could be good again, that he was the one who could guide her back from the darkness.

"Like I told your people, it'll take at least three hours to get to the island where the tracker is located." She pointed at the map. "I recommend we land here and hike in. Less likely to run into any of Ellers's patrols that way."

"What is the terrain like?"

"I've never been that far south, but I suspect it's much like this island."

"If the compound is there, Veritas will pass on what we know to the FBI. We'll have to sit tight until they arrive. None of us want another Ruby Ridge."

The siege at Ruby Ridge in Idaho had cost three lives and broken open a hornet's nest of anti-government sentiment, fueling the growth of militia groups like New America. Almost every one of the federal alphabet agencies had screwed the pooch on that one, which meant they'd be extra skittish about taking on Ellers and his people.

"On the plus side, we're both highly trained," Cait said. "You were Special Operations and I worked with them, so I know how you think. We're both stealthy. But we're going up against an armed camp, and I'm guessing there're women and kids in there as well, besides the hostages."

"So no explosives," he said. "Too high a chance of taking out friendlies. Of course, no guarantee the women or kids won't come after us themselves."

"Yeah, we learned that one in the sandbox, didn't we?" she said.

He grunted. "What time do you want to leave?"

"We should be on the water by 0400. That way we'll be under the cover of darkness until we hit the island."

"Sounds like we've got ourselves a mission," he said. "So you know, I'm pleased you're along on this one."

Cait nodded. "I feel the same about you." Then she rose and left him behind to stand on the porch, staring out into the downpour.

As time passed, the rain grew lighter, a soft patter on the roof. It was calming, and the frog chorus added to the natural symphony. They cleaned what weapons they had in companionable silence. Cait found Brannon watching her, his expression thoughtful. Hopeful. As if he hadn't yet realized she wasn't for him.

Sunset came early and after a meal of MREs—she'd opted for the beef stew and he'd chosen the chicken with noodles—Cait dug out the whiskey.

Brannon's eyes brightened. "I'm loving these accommodations of yours, Sergeant."

"Thought you would." She poured them each two fingers. "To victory," she said, touching her plastic glass to his.

"To good friends and a long life," he said.

"Those too."

She took a good slug of the liquor and felt the burn. When she set the glass down, she found Brannon nodding his approval.

"You drink like a Ranger."

"No, I drink like a Marine. And a woman."

He blew a stream of air through his lips. "You smoke cigars too?" She nodded. "God, where have you been all my life?"

That sounded like a come-on, so she ignored it. "How many hostage rescues have you done?"

He followed her change of topic without a hitch. "I've lost count. Well over a dozen."

"I've been on three." His expression indicated he was surprised at that admission. "Of course, you didn't hear that. Those missions were all off the record. I was only on them because I speak fluent Pashtun and some of the hostages were women."

"Understood. If this mission implodes, secure the hostages and I'll take care of Ellers. Unless I'm out of commission, in which case he's all yours."

By "out of commission," he meant dead. Cait barely suppressed the shudder.

Brannon ripped off a piece of the paper sack, and after writing a phone number on it, he pushed it to her. "Worst-case scenario, Veritas will get you out, one way or another."

"I'm not going anywhere unless you're with me. I don't leave anyone behind."

He didn't answer for a time, taking a long sip of his whiskey. "Neither do I. Especially someone who is smart, brave, and has the heart of a lioness."

Cait felt herself warm, and it wasn't just because of the liquor. "Thank you. That means a lot."

He nodded solemnly. "When this is over, you might consider applying to Veritas for a job. We need people with your integrity and skills."

"No," she said, shaking her head. "I'm tired of watching people die, tired of killing. I want to build something. You know, help make things better, not tear it all down." Then she realized what she'd said, how disrespectful it'd sounded. "Sorry. I'm not dissing what you do. I'm not. I just don't have it in me anymore."

Brannon caressed her hand, running a finger over the knuckles one by one. It was both reassuring and sensuous. "You want to make things better in your own way."

"Dad keeps pushing me to become a military contractor. That's the last damned thing I want to do. If I never see the Middle East again, I'll be happy."

"So what does Caitlyn want to do?" he nudged.

She knew the answer, because she'd put a lot of thought into it when the darker emotions weren't filling her brain. "I'm good at teaching, and I love animals. I was thinking I could learn how to train service dogs. You know, the kind that are paired with vets who are suffering from PTSD."

A warm smile bloomed on his face. "I think that's a great idea. You'd be good at that. You're patient, and you know exactly what those folks are going through. It'll give you an edge in helping make their lives better."

Cait looked away for a second, then back. "There has to be a reason for all we went through, right?"

"There is. I've found mine; you'll find yours. Besides, training service dogs is a lot less dangerous than what I do. That way I won't worry so much about you."

That confused her. "Why would you worry about me? We just met."

"I know this will sound corny, but it feels like I've known you for years. What about you?"

She pulled her hand away. "I don't know what I'm feeling. You mess with my head, Bran, and that scares me." It was a tiny step forward, that confession. One she hadn't wanted to make.

"I'm right there with you," he admitted. "You intrigue me, Caitlyn. I want to find out why."

"I . . . we should get some sleep."

There was an uncomfortable silence, and then he sighed. "I'll take the floor," he said.

Cait shook her head. "Things have been known to creep in at night. Things that are poisonous. If you promise to behave yourself, you can share the bed with me."

"Behaving myself is the last damned thing I want to do."

"I know." *Because I'm right there with you.* "But I also know I can trust you."

"True. Our weapons have to be on the table, out of reach. We're both under a lot of stress, and sometimes that causes trouble. At least for me."

She couldn't argue with that. She looked at her watch. "It's a little after twenty hundred hours now. I'll set my watch for 0300."

"Sounds good."

Once Brannon was in bed, Cait secured the cabin for the night. She knew he was watching her every move, from closing the front shutters to locking the door and jamming one of the chairs under the doorknob.

"Thinking we might have visitors?" he asked.

"No, but just in case we do, we want time to react."

"Then we're on the same page."

"On some things," she replied, not wanting him to think she was falling for his charm. Or his rugged face, or the rest of him lying under a thin blanket with that "come here, baby, and I'll make your night explode" gaze. A gaze that seemed to strip her naked with little effort. Then she spied his trousers hanging on the chair. "Are you commando?"

He shook his head. "I've got boxers on. I put them on during that last bio break."

Now she felt like some sissy schoolgirl.

"What about you? Do you sleep in the nude?" he asked, those bedroom eyes still tracking her.

"Usually, but not tonight. Don't want to upset your delicate sensitivities."

He laughed, causing the bed to shake. "Oh honey, you're already there. Let's get some sleep. We got a heavy day tomorrow."

She set their boots on the table so nothing would creep into them overnight, blew out the candles, and crawled in beside him, causing the mattress to dip. It had always felt like a big enough bed, until now. Not with a large and muscular man lying right next to her, their hips touching.

It's just for one night.

She turned on her side, pointedly giving him her back. He sighed, as if he'd expected that, then settled in. To her annoyance, she was still awake half an hour later. Apparently, she wasn't the only one.

"You awake?" he whispered.

"Yeah."

"What day is it? I've lost track."

She worked it out. "We left on the thirteenth, so it's the sixteenth. Why?"

"Not sure. Just something I need to think through."

She turned her back to him again. If she didn't, they wouldn't be getting any sleep tonight.

Brannon listened as Cait's breathing finally evened out and she fell asleep. She smelled of fresh air and orange shampoo. So did he, but luckily, none of his squad was around to give him hell about the orange bit. No matter how hard he tried to think through what they faced tomorrow, his attention kept wandering back to the woman lying next to him.

Maybe when this is all over . . .

He was kidding himself. Once Ellers was neutralized, she'd vanish like a mirage in the desert. If not back here in the swamp, then somewhere else. Cait craved solitude, or at least thought she did. Until she craved him more, he would always come out the loser. He'd seen the look of resignation in her eyes, and he knew it well. He'd seen it in others and at one time, in himself. He knew how close she was to giving up. He wanted to be the reason she didn't.

Chapter Twenty

Brannon came awake instantly at the noise. It wasn't the sound of someone outside the cabin, but of his companion murmuring in her sleep. The murmuring grew more intense, more filled with terror.

"No!" she cried out. "God, no!"

He took her in his arms. "Ssh. It's okay. It's just a nightmare. It's okay."

"Jeremy . . . " she whimpered, her eyes coming open now. He saw the instant she was fully awake, the realization that her best friend was still dead and there was nothing she could do to change that.

"You're safe. I won't let anything happen to you."

She stopped struggling and then began to cry. It was soft, like she didn't want to admit she was human.

He hugged her close. "Go on. It's what you need. We all need to cry sometimes."

"Even you?" she whispered.

"Even me. Some nights, I wake up and my face is wet from tears. It doesn't make you weak. It means you're strong enough to grieve for those you lost."

The tears continued, but at least she'd stopped shaking now.

"One minute he was laughing, the next he was . . . dead. It was like the angels just picked him up and took him straight to heaven."

"Maybe they did. He's still watching over you. You have to know that."

He felt a faint nod against his chest. "He loved Irish

whiskey. And hot dogs. It's why I eat them, to remember him by."

"You loved him."

"Yes. He was like a brother. He left behind a girlfriend and a little boy. He looks just like Jeremy, at least in the pictures."

"Have you seen them yet?"

"No. I couldn't make myself . . . " She sniffled. "God, I'm a damned wuss. He died, and I don't even have the guts to go see his lover and his kid. What kind of friend am I?"

"One who loved him very deeply," Brannon said. "One who will never forget him." He swept away a few strands of her hair. "You better now?"

Cait nodded, then pulled out of his arms and crawled out of the bed. It took her a bit to hunt up some tissues. She blew her nose, then rinsed her face in the wash basin. He didn't need to see her eyes to know they were red from crying. He knew that sense of loss, the feeling that you'd failed somehow.

When she turned, he said, "I've been there. I still go there sometimes, depending on how bad things get. But I always know that it'll be better in the morning, that it's worth waking."

Cait walked to the bed, then stopped. Her eyes met his, and he saw her wavering on the point of a decision. In that moment, he felt something change within her.

"You said one night, no strings attached, right?" she asked, her voice quieter than usual.

"No strings, just a chance to forget all the sadness and pain. A chance to truly feel alive again."

"I want to forget it all, if only for a short time. I want that with you."

Brannon knew how much trust it took for her to say that. He sat up, ignoring the ache in his back, and extended his arms. "Then come here, and I'll make it good again. I promise you that."

He swore he could almost hear her thoughts: *One good night's scratch and the itch will be gone.* He suspected that was a lie, that the moment their bodies united, it wouldn't be enough. Or at least, that's what he hoped would happen.

Why her, out of all the women he'd met? He didn't know. As his mother had once explained, 'The heart wants what it wants.' Right now, he wanted Cait's body and more, which meant every touch, every kiss, every second of this night had to be perfect. It was his only chance to prove himself to her.

She slowly stripped off her T-shirt, revealing a plain, navy-blue sports bra. No lace this time. He found it as arousing as anything he'd ever seen.

Brannon ran a finger along the upper seam. "What do you like when a man makes love to you?"

"You mean, what kind of sex?"

You're still distancing yourself. He changed tactics. "What turns you on?"

"A man like you. Strong, virile . . . kind."

He hooked his finger in the bra at the point between her breasts and lightly tugged her forward. Cupping her face with both hands, he ran his tongue across her lips. She moaned in response.

"I want a man who is as strong as me, who takes as much as he gives when I'm with him," she whispered. "Are you that man?"

He laid her on the bed, his lips on hers. His hands curled around her hips, pulling her tight against his erection. She pressed herself into him, making his head spin. With her help, he pulled off the bra. Trailing kisses down her neck, he lightly bit just above her left breast, then took the tight nipple in his mouth, rolling his tongue over it.

Cait arched into him, her eyes closed. His hands skimmed down to her waist, then deftly removed her shorts. He cupped her, feeling the heat spread through his fingers. Dipping one inside her briefs, he sought the center of her pleasure and began to stroke it lightly. This time she nearly came off the bed with a gasp of surprise.

"Like that?"

"Hmm . . . yeah."

He continued his attentions, stroking her, then suckling a breast. She cried out again. This time, Cait dug her fingers into his neck, pulling him closer. "Now, Bran."

"A little bit more, honey."

"No," she said. "Now!"

"You are bossy." There was no way he was going to rush this.

As Brannon reached down to pull off her panties, his back went into a spasm. "Oh, hell."

"You hurting?"

"Yeah," he said through gritted teeth.

"Lay down," she said.

He did as she ordered, moving slowly so as not to make it ache any worse.

"Not one of those Hollywood heroes, huh?" Cait said, smiling down at him. "Can't take four rounds in the chest and still bang the babe?"

"No. Sorry," he said, the pain gradually easing.

She yanked her panties down and they fell to the floor. Then she began kissing him, from lips to neck to chest, touching him with her hands.

Maybe this is for the best. It put her in control, and right now, that would be important to her. When she wrapped her fingers around his shaft, making him grow hard again, he sucked in a sharp breath.

"Caitlyn . . . " he warned. "It's been a while. You might not want to . . . "

The fingers were gone and he heard the rip of a foil package. Then he sucked in another breath when she sheathed him. As she slowly slid down onto his length, he gritted his teeth, feeling her tightness. Cait lowered herself again, and he skimmed his hands down her belly and rubbed her core. She arched in pleasure, tightening even more around him.

"Oh, honey," he moaned.

Cait began to move with more urgency now, using him, taking him along with her to that peak they sought. He placed his hands on her hips, moving his own up with each thrust. His back protested, but the pleasure was stronger.

"Oh, God, Bran!"

Her screams echoed off the cabin walls as she took everything offered. In return, she gave him everything, her muscles rippling around him, making sweat break out on his forehead. Her fingers dug into his shoulders as she gripped him, plunging him even deeper inside.

When she came again, it was like fireworks in the heat of summer, high and bright, beautiful to behold. Brannon's climax followed quickly as he exploded in waves of pleasure. When the spasms ended, she sank down onto him, panting. The scent of their lovemaking hung in the air, mixed with that of shampoo and whiskey.

"My God," he muttered, barely able to catch his breath. "That was . . . "

Cait gazed down at him, her eyes languid, the face of a woman well pleasured. He'd brought her joy. "Yeah, that was . . . "

"I've never slept with a Marine before," he said, purposely keeping his tone light. "Clearly, that was an oversight."

Cait smiled down at him, her breasts glistening and her lips swollen from his kisses.

She gently touched his face. "Thank you."

He placed his hand over hers, but didn't reply. He knew her gratitude was for more than just the sex.

Cait woke in the middle of the night, disoriented. Then she remembered where she was, who was lying next to her, and what they'd done. Usually, she would have just gathered her clothes and slipped away, avoiding that awkward after-sex conversation.

But she couldn't do that in this circumstance, and it wasn't just because they were in the swamp. She'd felt something when they were together, something unusual. Maybe it was because she was very fond of Brannon. Who wouldn't be? He was a good man doing a tough job. A man she deeply respected. Sure, the sex had been mind blowing—that, she *had* expected. Brannon would always ensure that the woman he was with had a very good time. Still . . .

Cait slipped out of bed, pulled on her shorts, and retrieved the mini flashlight. After checking the insides of her boots, she pulled them on, not bothering to lace them. Sticking a pack of tissues in her pocket, she removed the chair from under the doorknob. Brannon didn't stir, which meant he was soundly asleep. That pleased her; she'd given him enough of his own good time that he was down for the count.

She made sure to open the door as quietly as possible, then made a quick trip into the woods. When she returned, she stood on the porch for a time, watching the stars. In a few hours, they'd set off to find Ellers. That would either go really well, or they would be injured or die. It was the nature of the business. The creak of a floorboard told her Brannon had noticed her absence, and she wasn't surprised when he joined her on the porch, wearing only his shorts and his boots. It looked funny, but so did she.

"Trouble sleeping?" he asked.

She shook her head. "Are you kidding? I just needed a bio break."

"Me too." As he walked around her, he pecked a kiss on her cheek. "I'll be right back."

Cait returned to the cabin to give him some privacy. The bed was rumpled, just as you'd expect after a round of energetic sex. Her mind was already chattering about what they could do after they settled the bill with Ellers. Like how it'd be great to spend a weekend with Brannon at a nice hotel, just like he'd mentioned. Room service would keep them fed, and the rest of the time, they could explore each other's bodies. Hours and hours of . . .

What the hell am I doing?

Before she had a chance to address that question, the door closed and she heard the chair being wedged back in place. Then he wrapped his arms around her, pulling her back against him.

"Do you want me?" he whispered.

She slowly turned in his arms, looking up into those brown eyes that seemed bottomless. She should step back, give them some distance, and yet . . .

"Yes, I want you."

"Slower this time," he said, running a finger across her lower lip. "Slower and more intense."

"Is that even possible?" she breathed.

"Let's find out."

Brannon heard her moving around the cabin, smelled fresh coffee, and still his eyes didn't want to open. Once they did, their night would be over and he wasn't ready for it to end. Hell, he was just getting started.

If they'd been anywhere else, he'd have pulled her back into the bed and made love to her again and again until they fell back to sleep. But there was a madman to stop and hostages to be rescued. There were times he didn't like his job very much—this was one of them.

He reluctantly sat up on the bed. Cait was at the table with a cup of coffee in hand, staring down at the map, an electric lantern lighting up one side of her face. He took in her rumpled clothes, her hair in a tight, regulation Marine bun, her tanned legs wound around the chair legs. She was special, someone worth caring for. In that moment, he realized he could fall in love with this woman. Maybe was already on the way.

With a long sigh, he rose off the bed and pulled on his boxers. As he opened the front door for another nature call, he heard her chuckle.

"Nice butt," she said.

He gave her a mock frown over his shoulder and went to take care of business. Once he was done, he studied the night sky. It was clear, the rain having ended, but there was little, if any, moonlight.

April seventeenth. Something about that nudged at his mind, other than that it was two days before his birthday. At the moment, he couldn't pull the memory free.

He found Cait still at the table and a cup of fresh coffee waiting for him.

"Any new thoughts on the mission?" he asked as he pulled on his clothes. She shook her head at his question.

Once he'd laced his boots, he sat across from her and pulled the cup closer. He took a sip of coffee, finding it remarkably good for being brewed on a camp stove. When Cait rose to stir something else on the stove, he powered up the satellite phone and was pleased to find there were no new messages. That meant they were still on track. A short time later, he had a protein bar and a metal cup full of instant oatmeal to go with his coffee.

"Not only are you great in bed, but you can cook," he said. "Definitely my kind of woman."

"You keep telling yourself that," she said drily. Preparing the oatmeal had seemed to allow her time to regroup her thoughts. "Thank you for last night," she said. "It was . . . really good."

"Same for me."

Cait stared at him for a few moments, as if trying to discern whether his words were just polite after-sex chatter, or how he really felt. Apparently, she couldn't decide, so she rose to wash their cups, then methodically began to repack the supplies in their various storage cubbies, getting ready for departure. As she worked, he took another dose of the antibiotics.

"How's the bandage look?" he asked, pulling up his T-shirt so she could inspect it.

"Clean," she replied. "Does it feel better?"

"Yeah, it does. Anything I can do to help?"

"Not really. If you get out of my way, I can pack faster."

He took the hint, and after tucking in his shirt, he left the cabin, gear in hand. In her own way she was telling him that she needed space to work through all they'd shared.

By now, most women would be clamoring to set up the next date, especially of the horizontal variety. Cait wasn't like that; she moved at her own speed. He could respect that, as long as she understood that it wasn't only her decision. Not with what they'd shared tonight.

She didn't know it, but there was more than one mission in play; dealing with Ellers was the obvious one. There was another one: getting Cait to realize that her life hadn't ended that day in Afghanistan. That her friend would want her to live on, to find happiness, to have the kind of life he'd been fighting for. Of the two missions, Brannon suspected that hers would be the hardest.

Chapter Twenty-One

They were on the water right on time, with sunrise three hours in the future. Cait found that her mind kept skipping back to what had happened between her and the Ranger. The second time they'd had sex had changed everything, revealing that underneath all her military-grade emotional armor, she was still a woman who needed a man, if nowhere else than in her bed.

Irrational as it was, that revelation made her feel weak. And made her angry. Trying to keep her surly temper in check hadn't worked, and she'd growled at Brannon a couple of times for no good reason. He didn't respond in kind, which pissed her off more.

"Hey, Caitlyn? What's wrong?"

What could she say? That she had found more happiness in his arms than she had in years, maybe forever? That she was just as silly as Patti, all crazy for some dude with six-pack abs and the lovemaking skills of a romance-novel hero?

"It's not my fault that we hit it off in bed," he added.

Oh, hell. "No comment."

"You came, what, five times? We hit it off big time, sweetheart, at least by any sane person's measure."

Six orgasms. She wasn't going to correct him. "It's just that—"

"You didn't want to feel that close to anyone ever again. I got that," he said, keeping up his measured paddling as if this conversation wasn't punching holes in her armor. "Something happened between us, and I'm not going to let you act like it didn't."

Damn you. "Just paddle."

"I am. You're the one who's *back* paddling, at least when it comes to us."

She ground her teeth. "Okay, damn you, it was good. Great. Actually . . . the best sex I've ever had, but that doesn't mean you have a place in my life." *Because there isn't much life left in me.*

He stopped paddling and turned toward her now. "That darkness in your head doesn't like good things. It'll lie to you, tell you you're not worthy of any of it. Warn you that getting close to someone else will destroy you. I've been there, Caitlyn. I know what it's like."

"You could destroy me," she admitted.

He sobered. "The risk goes both ways, honey. Remember that when you push me away, because it's going to hurt me just as much as it does you."

He turned his back on her and resumed paddling, his warning ricocheting around her brain like a bullet in a metal pail. Her anger fizzled and now she just felt tired. Old. Nearly an empty husk. Deep down, she knew the man in front of her could make it better, help her feel alive again. For a time last night she'd felt that way, and those emotions had been as strong and rich as they once were.

Biting her lip, she took the risk. "Okay, we've got something going. Maybe . . . " *God, why is this so difficult?* "Once this is done, we could . . . spend a weekend together. See if all this is just a flash in the pan or something else."

Brannon's posture relaxed. "I'd like that. A lot." He looked over his shoulder now, his eyes laced with desire, making her breath catch.

"Mission first, then . . . whatever happens."

"Roger that," he said, pushing the canoe forward with renewed conviction.

She made sure to memorize every movement of his arms, his muscles, how he looked on the water. Because she knew as sure as the sun rose every morning that what he thought they had would never survive.

As per Cait's prediction, they made the island right before dawn. To Brannon's relief, they didn't run into any patrols. After camouflaging the canoe under a pile of brush, they pulled on their rucksacks and headed inland. Cait carried her rifle, the strap slung over her shoulder, her knife in its sheath, attached to her right thigh. He had his attached to his belt.

Once they got their bearings, Brannon used the sat phone to call in a report. "We're on the island."

"Good," Morgan replied, followed by a long yawn. He heard the unmistakable sound of a coffeemaker gurgling in the background. He bet it'd been going all night. "When Crispin told them about the hostages, the FBI suddenly became more helpful.

"They put the thumb screws to a couple of their informants and confirmed you are in the right place. Ellers has his compound on that island. They're trying to decide how to handle the situation."

"Which means?" Brannon asked. Since Morgan used to be with the Bureau, she understood how they worked better than most.

"There'll be a bunch of meetings, a lot of weighing of risk factors, you name it. Once everyone signs off on a plan, they'll be in the air headed your way. They don't really have any other choice."

"How long will that process take?"

"No clue. Sorry."

So was he. "Any idea of how many people are inside the compound?"

"Forty or so. About a third of those are women and children."

"Okay. I'll contact you after we've completed our recon," Brannon replied.

"Stay safe, my friend," she replied, and she ended the call.

He turned off the phone and then relayed the information to his companion.

"So we're on the right track then," Cait said.

He nodded, sweeping his eyes along the area in front of them. "Ellers is enough of a paranoid bastard that he'll have patrols outside the compound. It's what I would do."

"If you were a paranoid bastard, that is."

He smiled over at her. "Who says I'm not?"

She chuckled. "Want me to take point?"

"No. Let's fan out. I'm wondering if he's set some surprises out here."

"IEDs?"

"Possible. Or maybe not. Best not to find out the hard way."

"Roger that."

As they moved cautiously through the swamp, Cait about twenty or so feet away to his left, Brannon could feel the warrior taking full control—the constant reevaluation of his surroundings for any potential threats, the heightened senses.

Like a human computer, his training gave him an edge, one that might keep both of them alive. The adrenaline buzz was full throttle now, and he lived for that. Missed it. A quick glance over at Cait told him she was feeling the same way. They'd become nearly silent, carefully placing their feet in a way that caused them to pass unnoticed.

Birds were waking up in the trees around them. A raccoon pushed his way through some brush after a night's foraging. Above them, clouds built as more weather moved in. As they donned their rain ponchos, he smiled, knowing the crappy weather worked in their favor.

Guards would hunker down, trying to stay dry, and that inattention increased Cait's and his odds of survival by a slight margin. Raindrops began to patter down, heavy at first, then growing lighter. A Georgia spring in all its wet beauty.

Brannon slowed, then halted. Glancing over at Cait, he gave the "stop" hand signal and she immediately complied.

"What have you got?" she asked.

"Not sure. The ground looks wrong." Kneeling down, he studied the muddy depression that sat about five feet ahead of him. He carefully edged forward and pushed back some of the brush. Then stared down into a remnant of the Vietnam War.

"What the hell?"

It was a tiger trap, a hole about six feet deep, filled with stagnant water. Sharpened stakes rose from that muddy water, promising serious injury or death to anyone who bumbled into it. They'd been used by the Viet Cong, an ingenious and low-tech weapon.

"Believe it or not, we got a tiger trap," he said.

"You're kidding me."

He shook his head. "There has to be some sort of marking up where the guards can see it, or they'd fall into one of their own pits."

Rising, he took a slow look around and then finally spied a thin paint stripe on the closest tree. "Got it. Red slash on the tree about seven feet up."

"Roger that," came his companion's calm response.

Brannon carefully skirted around the trap, and they continued to work toward where the tracker had indicated the compound might lie. Through the rain came a sound he hadn't heard in a long time: a bugle blowing "Reveille," the military's version of a wake-up call.

Cait stared over at him. He gave her a thumbs-up, and she returned it. They'd found Ellers and he was leading them right to him.

"Reveille" pulled all the hostages out of their bed.

"These guys are nuts," Patti muttered. "What time is it?"

"Too damned early," Bill replied, rubbing his eyes.

Susan had barely swung her feet off the side of her bunk when the door to their jail opened.

"Everybody out!" the guard barked. "Move it!"

She laced on her shoes as the others struggled into theirs. Once they were ready, they were marched toward the front of the compound. It was barely dawn, the air heavy with oppressive humidity from the recent rain. Occasional droplets still fell on their heads.

For Susan, there'd been little sleep. While the others had crawled into their bunks one by one, she'd read Ellers's ravings by the light of an electric lantern. When she had finally given up at about two, the dreams were so damned vivid, she could have sworn she wasn't sleeping at all.

Then came "Reveille," one of the many reasons she'd never wanted to join the military. That thought brought her back to Landry and Hardegree. Were they really dead? Someone might have gotten the drop on one of them, but both? Especially Hardegree—not that the guide didn't look like she could take care of herself. If Cait had survived, she'd be letting the world know exactly what had happened to the rest of them. Unless Hardegree had killed her and then got topped himself.

Prodded by rifles, she and the others were lined up in front of Ellers's house. They weren't the only ones present; other militia members slowly formed up in groups on either side of them. Mothers did their best to quiet the young kids as they whined or cried, having been pulled out of bed far too early for their liking. Susan gave a quick look around but didn't spy a bugler. The morning wake-up call must have been a recording.

Rafferty stood by a tall blond woman and a pair of young boys, his family no doubt. His eyes met Susan's, then quickly looked away. So far, he'd kept her secret, but for how much longer?

While she waited, eyes gritty and the urge to yawn nearly overwhelming, she sorted through what she'd learned from Ellers's writing. The manuscript had been a jumbled mess, almost a steady stream of diatribe, something that had driven Bill nuts. But ignoring all the bullshit, Susan had begun to see the man behind the rhetoric and Ellers was as scary as she'd feared.

Anyone in authority, especially a female, was never to be trusted. Unless, of course, that person with the authority was Ellers. He had a quartet of "ists" going for him: misogynist, racist, egotist, and anarchist. He was convinced that he was the only one who could save America from the Blacks, the Jews, the government, and the "feminazis."

Susan knew where she'd fall on his hate list: She was Jewish, had two X chromosomes, and was a federal agent. Three for four. He wouldn't even hesitate to put a bullet in her brain.

The commander had an arrest record, which included domestic violence, which in his manuscript he'd claimed was his wives' fault. Wives, as in plural. In short, he was a loud-mouthed, hateful, and abusive SOB. Who held them hostage, which said he wasn't as stupid as she'd hoped.

The door of the house swung open and their lord and master strutted out to study them. His hands were on his waist as he turned to survey his minions. The way he held himself twitched Susan's memory again. This time, the answer came to her.

Mussolini. He acts just like him. Which made total sense, as Ellers had devoted one whole chapter of his memoirs to his admiration for the Italian dictator.

"How do we start and end every day?" he bellowed.

"By remembering we are the ones who will restore liberty to this once-great nation," came the rote response from the members of the compound. Most sounded a lot less enthused than their boss probably expected.

"How will you do that?"

"By shedding our blood and that of our children and that of the traitors."

Susan blinked. *Their blood, even their children's, but not Ellers's.*

Of those she could see, the expression on his followers' faces ranged from true zeal to sad resignation. Rafferty's and his wife's were the latter, as if they were trapped and had no way to get out.

Maybe I can change that.

"When will you give yourselves to this noble cause?" Ellers continued.

"When you command us to do so," the others chanted.

"And what will be the result?"

"A free nation, clothed in liberty and justice."

It was pure indoctrination. Repeat the same phrases, most likely day after day at the crack of dawn, and the message would sink in: an unintentional affirmation that these people were nothing more than cannon fodder for this man's delusional fantasy. The Pledge of Allegiance came next. As they reached the end Susan frowned, realizing it'd been changed. She replayed what she'd just heard.

'. . . one nation under God, indivisible, with liberty and justice for all. . . who believe."

"For all who believe?" she whispered. What did that mean?

Then Ellers tromped down the steps to take his place in front of them. "Are you working on my book?" he asked, his eyes on Bill.

"I am."

"Be done tomorrow, will it?"

Lie, Bill. He hates challenges to his authority. Not delivering the manuscript on his insane time schedule would be just that.

"Yes," the writer replied, sweat forming on his forehead, despite the chilly temperature.

Ellers looked over at the photographer now. "What about you? What pictures do you need?"

Keith swallowed hard. "I'll need some of you, whatever parts of the compound you're willing to reveal."

"All of it! No reason to hold back."

"But yesterday you said—"

"All of it! This will be our final battleground. We will all be martyrs here. No one will be left standing."

Rafferty's face paled as his hand sought his wife's. Clearly, not everyone wanted to be on this crazy train.

"Once you get the photos," Ellers said, "we'll go through them, one by one. I'll tell you which ones to keep and which ones to delete."

Keith's mouth twitched, but he wisely held his silence.

The commander's attention moved to her. "You got any skills, woman?"

Like putting you behind bars, asshole?

"I can cook," she replied. If she spent time with some of the women, she might be able to learn more, figure out how to get her people out of here alive.

"Maudie!"

"Yes, Commander," an older woman replied, stepping forward. She wore a plain dress like the others, but Susan swore she saw a spark of defiance in the woman's eyes.

"Take these two females and put them to work," he said, jerking a thumb toward Susan and Patti.

"What about me?" Preston asked, his nerves causing him to fidget.

Susan gave Bill a quick look, and the message was passed.

"He could help me organize your notes," Bill cut in. "You've got a lot of details in there, and I need to make sure they're right in the final draft."

"Do it then," Ellers said dismissively. "Let me know if he isn't pulling his weight, and we'll take care of that problem." He looked over the assemblage. "Where's Sweetman?"

"Here, sir," a man said, stepping forward. He seemed surprised that he'd been singled out.

Ellers waved him forward until the man was standing directly in front of him. "You got anything to confess?"

"What—ah, no, sir," the man replied, but his eyes darted around, looking panicked.

Ellers gestured to one of the guards, who came forward, a backpack in hand. "That yours?" Sweetman nodded.

"Dump it out." The guard turned the pack upside down, and banded stacks of cash hit the ground, probably from the armed-car robbery. Apparently, James hadn't turned in all the loot.

Ellers glowered. "I was told that Hardegree was bringing me fifty thousand dollars. Then I was told he skimmed some off the top so only twenty thousand made it to the camp. Now I find another twenty in your backpack. Why is that?"

"Oh, Jesus," Sweetman said, backing up. He pointed at James, his hand quaking. "He told me to do it. Said I should kill that Hardegree guy and the woman."

Ellers turned toward his nephew, an eyebrow raised. "James?"

"Not true," the young man replied, but Susan heard the tremble in his voice.

"What? Wait! No, he's lying," Sweetman cried out. "He said I should kill them and hide the money, and then he'd make sure I got out of here safe, because you're crazy and—"

"Silence!" Ellers bellowed.

Sweetman took another step back, only to bump into the solid bodies of the guards behind him, who pushed him back toward their leader. Sweetman shook in fear. "James, come on, man. Tell him!"

"How do we handle traitors in New America?" the commander demanded, his eyes blazing.

"Death!" someone called from the ranks.

"No! No, I swear he told me to—"

When Ellers placed the barrel of his gun against the man's forehead, Susan buried Patti's face in her chest. The single shot ensured that Sweetman was dead before he hit the ground.

"Oh my God," the girl whimpered, shaking in fright.

"Anyone else think I'm crazy?" Ellers demanded, stomping up and down the ranks of his followers. "You?" A man shook his head vigorously. "What about you?" The woman he'd asked cowered in response.

He swung back toward the line of hostages. "Any one of you?"

Susan made sure to lower her eyes so he couldn't see the "Hell, yes" that was in them. Apparently pleased he'd made his point, Ellers walked to his nephew.

"You try that bullshit with me again, and I'll kill you. Doesn't matter if you're family or not. I demand absolute loyalty, you understand?" The young man gave a jerky nod. "Then get back to work on that project. I expect it to be done on time, even if you are my sister's useless bastard."

Holstering his weapon, Ellers climbed the steps to the porch. "Rafferty? Bring that money inside." He slammed the door of the house behind him, missing the look of pure hate that James sent his way.

"Come on," Maudie said, tugging on Susan's arm. "Best to be out of sight until he calms down. Invisible is best. You live longer that way."

"Unless you trust his nephew," Susan said.

The woman eyed her. "That's gospel, for sure."

Chapter Twenty-Two

Brannon drifted on, keeping silent, searching for any additional markings that might indicate explosives or traps. Cait was still to his left, moving as silently as he was. She'd covered her blond hair with a dark handkerchief so it wasn't as noticeable. Once night set in, he bet she'd vanish entirely into the landscape, just like he would.

She abruptly came to a halt, and her hand came up in a "stop" signal. He held his position, checking for any tangos. There weren't any.

"What's wrong?"

"IED. You need to move away," she said, her eyes riveted on her feet.

Ah, fuck. "Pressure plate?"

"It's near my left toe, and there's a trip wire right behind that leg. I didn't see it until it was too late."

He moved toward her cautiously.

"Bran, back off!"

He ignored her, studying the situation. "You don't do anything half assed, do you?"

She shook her head, fear in her eyes. But there was more there too: the cold acceptance of fate.

"Once this detonates, they'll be out here in force. You need to go on with the mission."

He judged the distance from the closest tree to where she stood. Perhaps there was a way to get her free.

"Bran," she said, "are you listening to me?"

"I'm hearing you, but right now, I'm not buying what

you're telling me."

"Why? This isn't a survivable situation, *Lieutenant*. We both know that."

Only now did he look up at her. "Because you want it to be that way?"

His blunt question rendered her speechless for a moment.

"Maybe. At least the nightmares will end," she admitted. "Ironic that some tin-pot dictator might have done me a favor."

Brannon's gut churned at the thought. "Trust me, someday the nightmares will give way to good dreams. Dreams of the future. Ones that come true."

She glared at him. "What are you, my damned fairy godmother or something?"

He couldn't stop the grin. "Something like that."

"Please, Bran, go! I don't want you hurt."

He shook his head. "You see, that's the problem. If I walk away and you die, I *will* be hurt. I'll always remember your beautiful eyes, your full lips, how you cried out my name when we made love. You're as much a part of me as my own heart, Caitlyn. If you die, I will always grieve deep inside."

She blinked at him in shock.

"Now shut the hell up, Sergeant, and let me figure this out."

Cait snapped her mouth closed and it formed into a tight white line.

He pulled off his rucksack and set it aside, then scaled the nearest tree, a big white oak. Bits of bark fell as he climbed, broken free by his fingers. Brannon peered down at her, then nodded to himself. Once he was back on the ground, he reached out his hand. "Remove your ruck and give it to me. Be careful not to shift your weight."

"What are you going to do?" she demanded.

"Rescue a damsel in distress."

"You have got to be kidding me."

"Nope." He saw the plea in her eyes. "Trust me, please."

She heaved a sigh and gingerly removed her pack. When he took it from her, he was careful not to inadvertently alter her balance. "Stay put."

"Like I'm going somewhere?" she snapped. "Other than that big recruitment center in the sky?"

Brannon would have laughed at that, but he was focusing on what was about to happen. If it went wrong, they'd both end up maimed or dead. He carried both of their rucksacks and the remainder of their gear about thirty feet away from the IED, then returned to where his companion stood immobile. Cautiously clearing the area around her of debris, he began to pile it up on Cait's right side: fallen logs, brush, anything that might act as a shield from the blast. It was a piss-poor substitute for body armor, but it was all they had.

"Once I'm in place, I'll do a count of three, and then I want you to jump toward me, grab my hand, and I'll swing us both to the other side of this tree. We're going to the ground hard and fast."

"This isn't going to work."

"It has a chance. The IED has sunk into the ground at least a foot, so if we're lucky the force of the blast will be directed up, not out."

"Huh. You really think this is an option, Ranger?"

He swung himself back up into the tree. "Let's find out, Marine."

She looked up at him, and he saw a faint glimmer of hope.

"You were right, last night was special. Thank you," Cait said softly.

God, she's so strong, even now. "Then let's make sure there're more of those kinds of nights." He extended his arm. "On three. One . . . two . . . three!"

As Cait sprang toward him, he clasped her arms in a circus hold and swung them around the broad tree with as much momentum as he could generate. Then they were falling, hitting the ground hard, covering their heads.

But there was no explosion.

They stared at each other in shock for a brief second, then scrambled up and ran. Grabbing their rucksacks and gear, they continued their retreat.

"What the hell?" she muttered, brushing away the dirt as

they kept moving. "Why didn't it blow?"

"Whoever rigged it might not have had a clue. Or the rain got to it. Who knows?"

When he stopped and turned, she did as well. "I don't know what it says when the bastards in the Middle East can build better bombs than our own insurgents can."

"We're offshoring everything nowadays," Cait replied.

They grinned in unison, but her grin quickly faded.

"That was too damned close," he said, touching her cheek. "You didn't know it wouldn't explode. You risked your life for me."

"You would have done the same."

"Yeah, I would have."

"Which means we might still get our time together at a fancy hotel on the beach."

"You really liked last night, didn't you?" she said.

"Oh hell, yes. Eager for more, sweetheart. In fact, let's add in some time at my cabin up in Kentucky. You'll like it up there. It's really quiet."

Suddenly, she grabbed onto Brannon and planted a scorching kiss on his lips, pulling him tight against her, molding her body to his as she plundered his mouth. When they stepped back, they were both breathless.

"Damn, Caitlyn. I will happily save your cute ass anytime you need if that's what happens when I do."

"You can get a kiss like that without risking your life."

His breathing gradually evened out as they set off toward Ellers's compound again.

"That's the *second* time I've had an IED not explode," Cait said.

As he was about to ask about the first time, a dull explosion came from behind them. They turned as one and watched as the dirt and debris settled back down to the ground in a muddy cloud. The sharp crack of the oak tree heralded its demise, and it toppled over.

"Make that only *one* unexploded IED," she muttered.

"Let's get some distance from here in case Ellers gets nosy.

Then I'll call Veritas so they can tell the feds about the booby traps."

Cait took point. As he trailed in her wake, watching her move through the brush, he murmured a short prayer of thanks under his breath. How he'd keep the tough Marine alive from this point on, he didn't know. All he hoped was that at the end of this mission, they'd still be together.

The compound's mess hall was filled with long trestle tables and benches, like a kids' summer camp, and mosquito netting covered the windows, a precaution that would be vital during the hotter months. Susan and Patti worked at one of the tables, sitting opposite of each other, a mound of unpeeled potatoes between them. Maudie was farther down the same table, working pie dough on a pastry cloth. The faint squeak of the rolling pin reminded Susan of home and her mom's peach cobbler. She missed them both so much.

As she pushed aside another peeled potato, the rolling pin kept moving, flattening the dough with practiced movements. Four pies sat nearby, all ready for the oven. The ones already baking smelled heavenly, the homey scent at odds with their situation. Patti's hands still trembled as she shot nervous glances toward the older woman. Susan touched her arm, and the girl blinked over at her.

"We'll get out of here," she whispered. "I promise."

Patti gave a short nod, glanced at Maudie again, then went back to her peeling.

"So who are you, young lady?" Maudie asked. "Because you barely flinched when Ellers killed that man."

Susan realized she was talking to her. "I grew up in a bad neighborhood." It sounded like a lie, and she knew it.

So did Maudie. "No, I'm not buying that." The woman set aside her rolling pin. "One thing Ellers didn't allow for: If you kill a federal agent, they're going to send more. Maybe you."

"Why would you think I'm one of them?"

"Because you're not like the others. You got that look in your eyes, the kind that tells me you're a lot more dangerous than you appear."

Susan held her breath. Was this woman going to rat her out?

Maudie shook her head. "If you're here to take down the commander, God help you." She hesitated, then continued. "He's stoked up on his own ego. He'll kill us all before it's over." Scooting the finished pie aside, the woman swept the bits of dough into a pile.

"There're enough of you to stop him if you wanted to," Susan said.

Maudie shook her head again. "The ones with the most guns are loyal to him. What they don't understand is that he'll make them die for the cause and never allow his own blood to be shed. I see that now."

A low rumble echoed in the distance and the ground shook.

"What was that?" Patti asked, her head popping up.

"One of the mines. The swamp is full of booby traps. Ellers thinks it'll keep the feds from overrunning the place." Her eyes were back on Susan now.

"I'm sure the feds would let you surrender if you don't fight them."

The woman huffed. "Ellers will never allow that to happen."

How forgiving would her fellow agents be if some of them were maimed or killed as they closed in on the compound?

Maudie had just begun to roll out another crust when the door to the mess hall opened and a young man hurried in. He looked all of eighteen, if that.

"You gotta come quick. Carlin got snake bit. The commander said you gotta take care of him."

She dropped the rolling pin, then wiped her hands on her apron. "What kind of snake?"

"Pygmy rattler. The little bastard was hiding in the woodpile."

"That's exactly where it'd be." She shifted her attention

back to them. After a brief hesitation, Maudie took off her apron, placing it on the table next to Susan.

"You, girl?" she said. Patti's head popped up. "You come with me. You need to learn how to handle this kind of thing."

Susan suspected what the woman was about to do.

"Me?" Patti began. "But—"

"Go on with her," Susan urged. "It'll be okay. I'll stay here and work."

"Really? A snakebite? I don't know a thing about that."

"But you'll learn. It could come in handy down the line," Susan replied.

With a classic teen huff, the girl rose and headed for the door. Maudie leaned down and deftly slid something out of her pocket, hiding it under the apron.

"I'm giving you a chance to go," she whispered, "but you have to tell your people that not all of us are like Ellers. You have to give us a chance."

"I will."

"If you hurt this young man and you get caught, I'll tell Ellers who you are. You won't die easy. The last one sure didn't."

Their eyes met. "Understood."

With a jerk of her head, the older woman turned and swept out the door, leaving only the guard behind. He looked at Susan nervously, and then his eyes fell on the unbaked pies. He licked his lips without realizing it. Food appeared to be his weakness, and given how skinny he was, Susan guessed he didn't get near enough of it. Funny how Ellers didn't seem to have the same problem.

"There's a couple of pies about to come out of the oven," she said.

"You don't think she'd mind if I had some?"

"I doubt it. Maudie's okay. You're helping her out by keeping an eye on me."

Still, he didn't move from his post near the door, though his nostrils flared as the cooking timer dutifully counted down the last few minutes. Susan slid her hand under the apron, moving the pocketknife off the table and tucking it into her jeans. In the distance, another explosion shook the ground. It was up to her now: She could stay here and play tag with a madman, or she could run straight into a minefield.

I'll take the bombs any day.

Chapter Twenty-Three

The instant the second explosion occurred, Brannon lowered into a crouch. Cait was in the same position in front of him.

"See anyone?" she asked.

"No. You'd think Ellers would send someone out to check."

"Or maybe he's an overconfident prick who believes he's all secure in his big bad fortress."

"You're getting your second wind. Or is it your third or fourth?"

"What I'm getting is pissed," she replied. "I take it personally when some SOB tries to kill me. Doesn't matter if he's an Afghani warlord or some homegrown militia asshole."

They were about to return to their feet when she raised her hand for silence. The sound of something crashing through the brush came from their left, followed by a pair of white-tailed deer.

"Maybe one of their buddies set off the explosion," Cait said.

"Might be why Ellers doesn't send out a patrol every time. Between the wildlife and malfunctions, this might happen pretty often. If so, that's a blessing for us."

They slowly rose and continued on. A short time later, Cait's hand went up again.

"To our right, about twenty yards," she murmured, her hearing more acute than his. "We got movement and it's not a deer."

Crouching down, he waited, then spied a woman moving through the brush. She wasn't running, but proceeding with a caution that said she knew about the booby traps.

"It's Susan," Brannon said. "She found a way to escape. Do we catch up with her, or let her go?"

"We need everyone on our team we can get. But she might not be willing to accept that you're one of the good guys."

"Hopefully she's got an open mind."

They split apart. While Cait circled in from behind to keep an eye on pursuers, Brannon set off on a path to intercept the FBI agent. It wouldn't be long before Ellers realized one of his hostages had taken off, so their window of opportunity was closing fast.

Moving in tandem with Susan, he slipped ahead of her, remaining hidden. When he found an open space about forty feet in front of her, he stopped and waited. The instant she saw him, Susan came to a halt, her only weapon the pocketknife in her hand.

"So you're not dead. I wondered about that."

"I'm hard to kill, Special Agent Driscoll."

"Apparently." Her eyes widened. "How do you know who I am?" Her stance didn't change, but her focus on him kept her from realizing that Cait was slowly approaching from her rear.

"I work for Veritas. You heard of them?" A curt nod told him that she had. "I've been undercover, trying to track where the money was going from the armored-car robberies."

"So you decided to participate in one to find out?"

"Not my plan, but that's the way it happened. I was bringing the money to Ellers. Why was I double-crossed? Did they figure out I wasn't on the level?"

"Not that I can tell," she replied. "James told his uncle you took off with some of the money, and with you not around to dispute the claim . . . But now Ellers knows the truth."

"How?"

"The missing money was found in someone's backpack. James promptly lied his ass off, claiming he knew nothing about that."

"The rotten apple doesn't fall far from the tree," Cait said.

Susan whirled around, backing away so she could keep an

eye on both of them. Brannon could see her trying to decide: Trust them? Don't trust them?

Finally, she said, "Please tell me one of you has a phone."

Brannon nodded, his shoulders relaxing. "Sure do."

"How'd you get free?" Cait asked, leaning against a tree.

"One of the women helped me escape. She warned me about the mines." The agent studied each of them in turn, then closed the knife and stuck it in a pocket. "I'm taking a huge risk, trusting you."

"Roger that," Brannon said. "I'd argue that I'm in the same position. I suggest we head west of the compound, get us some cover so you can make your call. We'll fill you in on what we found during recon."

"Lead on," Susan gestured.

"I'll take point," Cait said, setting off.

The agent pointedly waited for Brannon to be next in line. Apparently, her trust only went so far.

They'd circled around to the area west of the compound and discovered it had fewer mines and pit traps, a mistake that Cait remarked upon. Perimeter defense was only as strong as the weakest area.

"I'll let my people know about that," Susan said. She was still working through the discovery that these two were alive. Nothing had indicated they were working for Ellers, and in fact, they'd readily shared what information they'd gathered.

In return, she'd explained how one big piece of apple pie had earned her freedom. She'd waited until her young, obviously hungry guard had dug into that pie, and then she'd carefully banged him on the head with a skillet. She'd left him tied up and gagged in the storage closet off the main kitchen.

Then, as if God Himself was looking out for her, she'd made it to the north fence where it attached to one of the buildings without anyone spotting her. Using brute force and the knife, she'd managed to peel enough of the wire back to wiggle through, scraping herself up good as she did.

"I'm worried Ellers will execute the kid just to make a point to the rest of his people," she said. "He's volatile, got a hair trigger."

"There's another tiger trap straight ahead of us," Cait advised. "Watch where you walk."

"You with Veritas too?" Susan asked as they skirted around the danger.

"No, just filling in on the tour for my friend. Mike was worried something hinky might happen."

"So it did, in spades."

"Is Patti okay?"

"So far. We're trying to guard her, keep her away from James." Which she hoped would happen now that she wasn't at the girl's side. Somehow, she suspected that Maudie might step up if needed.

"Any clue what Ellers's plan is?" Brannon asked.

"No. Other than ranting about liberty and traitors, and executing one of his own people, he hasn't said a word about what's on the wind."

Cait halted, turning back to Brannon. "What do you think about this location?"

"Looks good to me. We can hunker down in those bushes if need be." He removed his rucksack, dug inside, and handed over the sat phone. "Caitlyn and I will take guard duty while you contact your office. Warn them that if they come in like they did at Waco, it'll be a bloodbath."

"Believe it or not, we learned that lesson," Susan replied sharply, snatching the phone from him.

"Not dissing you folks, just pointing out the reality. Sometimes the higher ups can get a case of the stupids."

That, she couldn't argue. Susan took a deep breath and tried to calm her nerves. Settling on the still-damp ground, she turned on the phone, waited for the signal, then dialed up her fellow agent in Brunswick. Once her boss in Atlanta found out what she'd been up to, the shit was going to hit the fan, and she wasn't ready for that just yet.

The moment she thought that, Susan shook her head at how silly that sounded. She was stuck in a swamp with two former soldiers and virtually no weapons, up against a fully armed anarchist who had delusions of godhood.

It didn't get any shittier than that.

"Special Agent Wiseman."

"Wiseman, it's Susan. I need your help."

"You want to do *what?*" Cait said, frowning, as they stood some distance away from the FBI agent.

"I want to go into the compound, join up with Ellers," Brannon said.

"Are you nuts? He'll put a bullet in your skull the moment he sees you."

"I'm betting he won't. I have ten grand of his money. That's my ticket in."

Cait shook her head, her eyes not on him but on the swamp around them.

"You heard Susan: Ellers knows he was ripped off and thinks I'm dead because of it. If I show up with the missing cash, demanding to know what the hell is going on, he'll respect that."

This time, her eyes did swing in his direction. "Or he'll just kill you."

Before he could reply, her hand came up for silence. Then she pointed toward the compound. He caught the faint sound of someone moving through the brush far in the distance.

"One tango," Cait said. "Bless his little butt, he has no clue how not to make a ton of noise."

They returned to where Susan sat with the phone against her ear.

Brannon knelt down in front of her, catching her attention. "We got company."

She nodded. "Gotta go, Wiseman. They've figured out I escaped." He said something in return. "I will. Thanks." Then she shut down the phone and offered it to Brannon.

"You keep it," he said.

"Okay. It's going to take some time before our reinforcements arrive," Susan explained.

"Well, while that's happening, I'm going inside the compound," Brannon said. "Reporting for duty, just like a good little soldier."

"I told him it was a crap idea," Cait grumbled.

"It is, but it just might work," Susan replied. "Besides, he's probably going in whether we agree to this or not."

"Yeah, I can see that. And they say women are stubborn."

Susan turned back toward him. "Ellers is a lot closer to the edge than you realize. His word is law in that camp. If he decides you're the enemy, or no longer useful, you're dead."

"I know that. I also know that I'd take a few of them with me when I go."

Cait averted her eyes, as if somehow seeing his death. He gently touched her arm. "I'll be careful, I promise."

"Damn you, Bran," she whispered. "Don't you see? I lost Jeremy. I can't lose . . . you, too."

In those few words, he realized how much she cared. He walked her a short distance away, gaining them some privacy, then he placed his forehead against hers, wrapping his arms around her.

"I swear, Caitlyn, I'll do what I can to stay alive for you. You have to promise to do the same for me."

She blinked back tears, then nodded. "Then go, before I totally lose it here and ruin my badass rep."

He kissed her, a long, deep kiss. When it ended, he hugged her tight, then stepped away. Cait offered him the rifle.

"No. You keep it. I'll get my own inside."

He gave Susan a thumbs-up, then walked into the woods. It took only a couple of minutes to put himself along the path of Ellers's scout. He crouched down and waited until the guy walked right past him, making so much noise they could probably hear him in Atlanta.

"Stupid-ass woman," the man complained. "Probably got herself lost. If she had any brains, she'd have headed for the damned boats."

A few more steps, then he huffed. "I'm wasting my time out here."

"No, you're not," Bannon said, rising from his hiding place.

The guy whirled, his gun leveled at him. "Who the hell are you?"

"Brannon Hardegree. I'm here to see Commander Ellers."

The man stared. "But you're dead."

"Not today. Let's go show the commander just how good you are at finding people."

The guy brightened up at that. "Yeah, let's do that." He pointed. "The compound's this way."

Really? I never would have guessed.

"You and Hardegree, huh?" Susan said softly.

There was no way to hide it now, not after what the agent had witnessed. "Yeah, it came out of nowhere. Now, it's like he's always been part of my life. It spooks the hell out of me, you know?"

"Haven't had that feeling yet. Maybe someday."

Cait forced herself back into warrior mode. There, she felt secure, less confused. "Let's figure out the best way to get the cavalry in here without too many casualties. They'll probably want to come in by water."

"Or helicopter?"

Cait shook her head. "No LZ . . . no landing zone. So unless they're going to fast-rope from the chopper, it'll have to be by boat."

"I don't know how fate arranged to have both a Ranger and a Marine on this trip, but I'm definitely headed to shul to say thanks the moment I get back to Atlanta." Susan thumbed the sat phone. "I'll let them know about the lack of a landing zone. Oh, got a voicemail. Maybe it's good news."

As Cait waited, she watched Susan's expression go from hopeful to sincerely pissed off. Apparently, whoever had left the message hadn't said the right things. After she sent a text, the agent turned the phone off, swearing under her breath.

"And?" Cait asked, keeping her attention on the area

around them as they walked deeper into the woods.

"That was my boss, who just had to chew me out for my 'reckless and irresponsible' behavior. Said we'd be having 'a talk' once I get back to the office."

"Does this desk jockey not realize that you might not get back to your office if he doesn't help you out?"

"The desk jockey is a she, and I'm her problem child, as she puts it."

Cait ground her teeth. "We put up with enough of that bullshit from guys, but when it comes from a woman, that really rags me. So what is she going to do for us?"

"It sounds like the various offices are weighing their options. My boss is urging restraint, that the situation might not be as dire as I painted it."

Cait looked back over the swamp in the direction of the compound. "Yeah, I can see that. You're totally overplaying this whole goat rope. I mean, it's only an armed militia and a few IEDs. What could possibly go wrong?"

Susan rolled her neck around, apparently trying to reduce her tension. From the glower on her face, the maneuver failed. "I swear to God, if the state of Georgia didn't have the death penalty, my boss would be a rotting corpse."

Cait grinned. "I'll help you dispose of the body. I know a few tricks." That earned her a thoughtful smile. "How's about we go prove that your boss is an idiot and earn you a nice commendation?"

Susan's smile dimmed. "I'd be happy just to get out of this alive."

"Right there with you, sister."

Chapter Twenty-Four

There had been a few moments in Brannon's life when he knew he was pushing his luck. That night in the mountains of Afghanistan, when he'd tracked a group of insurgents on his own so he could call in an air strike. That day in Fallujah. Now here in the swamp.

The rational, "you thought this was a good idea?" portion of his brain was bitching at him that this plan sucked. That it was stupid and suicidal, especially when he had Cait and Susan counting on him.

Still, he hoped that the majority of Ellers's people were tired of being holed up out in the swamp, and sick of the man's bullying dictatorship. Or at least that's what he was telling himself.

Larry, Brannon's escort, was a guy who loved to talk and he'd done that all the way to the compound. By the time they approached the gates, Brannon had heard that one of the hostages had escaped—someone he'd claimed not to have seen—that Commander Ellers was pissed off at everyone, and that the food rations had been cut again. Also that no one understood exactly why the hostages had been taken in the first place, except for the writer guy and the photographer. And that Larry was thinking it was time to head back to Arkansas. He'd had his fill of Ellers and his crew.

When they reached the compound, one of the guards in the tower called down to Larry and told them to stay put. Time passed, but he didn't move. He made note that there was one man in both of the guard towers and each held a sniper rifle, though that didn't mean they had any skill with those weapons. Brannon did, and if he could get his hands on one of those, his chance of survival would improve dramatically.

"It's him," a man called out, his face peering through the fencing at the front gates. "Let him in."

The gates opened and Brannon marched inside. He was immediately surrounded, his rucksack and knife confiscated. Then he was patted down. He had to act the outraged party here, that Ellers owed him for the betrayal. That he was a loyal soldier to their unholy cause.

"No other weapons," one of the guards said.

Brannon stared at the guy who'd identified him. "How'd you know who I was?"

"I saw you that night."

"You one of the assholes who tried to kill me?"

"No, I'm not. My name's Rafferty," he said.

"Then it's good to meet you, Rafferty."

"By coming here you're putting your head in the noose."

"Says the man who lives inside an armed compound."

Rafferty glanced over at him. "Then it appears neither of us is that smart."

The open area in front of the cedar house was primarily white sand. A single flagpole sat in the center, but Old Glory wasn't flying proud today, hanging wet and limp on the pole. Rafferty told Brannon to wait there, and he did as ordered, feeling the guns trained on his back. Hopefully, if Ellers wanted him dead, he'd do the deed himself. That way Brannon wouldn't die alone; a single snap of the anarchist's neck would ensure he had company when he stood in front of St. Peter. But this wasn't just about him anymore. He had someone who cared for him. Someone who needed him.

The door to the house swung open and Ellers walked out, down the stairs, right up to him. His weapon went up against Brannon's forehead in a fluid motion.

"I was told you were dead."

Brannon made sure not to flinch. "You were told wrong."

"How did you find this place?"

"Once a Ranger, always a Ranger."

"How?" Ellers insisted, pushing harder with the gun.

"The tour guide had maps in her ruck. I've been checking islands for the last couple of days. When I heard 'Reveille' this morning, I knew I'd hit pay dirt."

"Just how did you do that when the canoes were wrecked?" Rafferty asked.

"Fixed one up. Wasn't about to be stranded just because someone felt the need to fuck me over."

Ellers chewed on that bit of news for a time. "What about the guide?"

"Dead. Took a round in her skull." Brannon pointed toward his rucksack. "The rest of your money is in there. Whoever tried to kill me was in a hurry."

"Why bring it to me?"

"Because I want to settle the score with the bastard who tried to kill me and I wanted to meet you. So here I am."

There was a very long pause as the commander sized him up. "The traitor was executed earlier today. He's no longer a problem."

Brannon gave a brisk nod, waiting to see if the same fate awaited him. Ellers took a step backward. At least the gun wasn't poking a hole in his forehead any longer.

"The FBI is looking for you," the commander announced.

"That, I wouldn't doubt. Doesn't mean they're going to find me."

"I've got a friend in the Army. He did some checking on you. He says you'd never be the type to join up with me. That if you're here, you're working for the enemy. So which one of you do I trust?"

Shit. Brannon hadn't expected that.

"Did your friend rob an armored truck and risk time in federal prison? Did he haul the loot all the way into some goddamned swamp to bring it to you, even after one of your people tried to kill him? No, he did not. But I did. So your friend is wrong."

Ellers cocked his head. Brannon felt sweat trickle down his

back and into his cargo pants, like it was summer in the desert.

The gun went back into the holster. "Come on," the man said, gesturing. "We need to talk."

Somehow Brannon had passed the first test, but he knew there would be many more.

The interior of Ellers's office was stark in its simplicity. There was a jerry-rigged desk, a rusty fold-up chair behind it. Papers sat on that "desk" in no discernable order. On the wall behind it was a framed black-and-white photograph of Ellers with a group of men, all in camo. From his time in the Army? Or maybe later?

There was no chair for Brannon, so he adopted the parade-rest position, moving his left foot out and interlocking his thumbs behind his back. This telegraphed that he viewed Ellers as his superior, massaging the man's ego.

"At ease, soldier," Ellers said, after sitting in the lone chair. He pulled his gun out of the holster and placed it in front of him, within easy reach. "What did you do in the Rangers?"

"Usual stuff. Explosives, hostage rescue."

"Sniper?"

"Yes."

"How good?"

"Good," he replied. "I'm better with explosives."

"So if I gave you a rifle, you could kill anyone I wanted you to?"

"Yes, but I don't kill women or kids. Unless they're trying to kill me."

The cunning look in Ellers's eyes made Brannon wonder if that comment had been a mistake. "Even if I ordered you to do so?" the man asked.

"Even then. I have some lines I don't cross."

"Huh. But you could kill anyone else?"

"Yes, but optimum results require a military-grade sniper rifle and proper site planning. It's not a point-and-shoot kind of thing, like in some damned arcade."

Ellers leaned back in his chair, sending an ominous creak throughout the room. "Why do you want to join us?"

Time for the sales pitch. "Because I went to war for this country and now it's not the one I fought for." In many ways, that was true, though not how Ellers imagined.

"Do you know the best way to kill a snake?"

"Take off its head?"

"Yes. And the best way to start a war?"

Brannon knew where this was headed. He'd read too much of Ellers's online rants not to. "By ensuring that the world understands the sacrifices required for liberty."

The commander slammed his palm down on the planks. "That's it exactly. When I get done, everyone will know why I struck the blow for freedom. They'll see the bloated bodies, they'll know the government is corrupt. There will be no way Washington can spin this to be our fault."

"Sounds like you got it all worked out."

"I do. Question is, do you want to be part of it?"

Brannon took a deep breath. "Yes, sir, I do, sir."

Ellers rose, jamming the Glock back into his holster. "Time for you to get settled in, Hardegree."

Well, hell. He seemed to have made the cut. Something told him that it shouldn't have been that simple.

Ellers escorted him to Rafferty, who was in the mess tent with a woman and two children. Most likely his family. The two little boys were about five and seven, wide eyed and curious at the newcomer. One had a wooden truck and was running it along the table, executing a tight course between a staggered line of salt shakers.

"You stick with Rafferty from now on," Ellers said. Then, as he turned away from the table, he added under his breath. "See that woman and those kids? You try to fuck me over, and they'll be the first to die. You got a line in the sand? So do I, asshole. You've been warned."

Ellers exited the building, leaving Brannon to stare at the boys and their mom, chilled by the threat.

"Something wrong?" Rafferty asked, unaware of what his boss had just said.

"Just your commander warning me to be on my best

behavior."

"Huh. Well, sit and have some coffee."

The fellow's wife rose, gave a nod to her husband, and herded the kids away. Before Brannon could say a word, a tin cup full of coffee arrived in front of him, courtesy of an older woman.

"Thanks, Maudie," Rafferty said.

This was the one who'd helped Susan escape.

"Thank you, ma'am," Brannon said, and he didn't mean just for the coffee.

She studied him for a moment, then returned to the kitchen.

"Are the hostages okay?" Brannon asked.

"They're good. The photographer and the writer are working on Ellers's book."

"Really?" he replied, trying to sound surprised since Susan had already given him that bit of information.

"Yeah. He's having them compile some of his writings. Says they need to be ready for when he isn't here anymore."

"Isn't here, as in dead?"

Rafferty shrugged his shoulders. "You can never tell with him," he said quietly.

"Is his nephew leaving that young girl alone?"

The man's eyebrows rose. "He is for now. He kept trying to sneak in to see her, claiming she was 'his.' His uncle got so pissed, he sent him off the island about an hour ago."

"Why do I think he didn't go quietly?"

Rafferty shook his head. "Not that kid. I don't know why Ellers puts up with him. Probably only because he's a relative."

"How long have you folks been here?" Brannon asked, then took a long sip of the black coffee. It was better than he'd expected.

"Been here about five months. I was one of the original few who came out here with the commander. Once we got the place livable, we brought in our wives and families." Rafferty rose. "Come on, I'll give you the tour."

As they walked through the compound, he pointed out certain buildings and introduced Brannon to various people. It was a community on edge. People's eyes weren't meeting his and they weighed each word as if it might prove to be their last. The one thing that was clear: They respected Rafferty.

"How far do you trust the commander?" Brannon asked, playing a hunch.

"Why do you ask?"

"Because he told me that if I fucked him over, he'd kill your wife and kids."

Rafferty stumbled to a halt. "You serious?"

"Absolutely."

The man's expression hardened. "Then you better not fuck up and betray us, because if you do, I'll kill you first."

"That's exactly what I'd do in your shoes."

Rafferty grunted and continued the tour, but his demeanor had changed now, and Brannon didn't think that it was in regard to him.

He knows Ellers is a threat. All of them do.

Hours later, by the time they'd completed the full reconnaissance and mapped out as many of the IEDs and traps as they could find, Susan was exhausted. She did field work, which involved long hours interviewing people, collecting evidence, then going back to interview the same people who'd lied to you the first time around. In contrast, Cait's skillset included forced marches, living on a single protein bar and some sips of water, and not issuing one complaint.

I feel like a damned wimp.

"Why do you think that?" her companion asked.

Apparently, she'd voiced her thoughts.

"You just keep going and going. Me? I'm exhausted, I ache, and I would kill for a hot bath, a massage, and a steak dinner. Yeah, that's me whining."

"You do remember Patti, right? That girl had whining down to an art form. Yours isn't anywhere near that level."

Susan chuckled at the memory. "So how'd you get so

tough?"

"I learned early on not to complain in front of the guys, because they might see it as a weakness."

"So you couldn't be a woman?"

"I couldn't act like a *weak* woman. There's a difference," Cait said. "Once they got to know me, I could joke about stuff like that, but not until then."

"I can understand that. It's like breaking in a new partner at the Bureau." She sighed. "So are we going to stop tromping around eventually? I have a hot date with a few blisters, and I can't wait to see just how big those puppies are."

"Here is as good a place as any to park it for the night. Hopefully, come morning, your crew will be moving in."

She heard the worry in Cait's voice, and she knew it wasn't all for them. "Brannon will be okay. He strikes me as the 'I can survive anything' kind of dude."

Cait did not reply as she laid out a ground cloth between two bushes. Only when she was done did she look back at Susan. "Trust me, even those kinds of dudes can die. If he does . . ."

"Then we won't be needing to put Ellers on trial, right?"

"You got it."

"If it goes down like that, I'll make sure the official report uses the phrase 'in self-defense,'" Susan said.

She blinked up at her. "I thought you FBI folks were all by the rulebook."

"I'm not and that's why my boss hates my guts."

Cait held up a protein bar, waggling it at her. "Split it with you."

"I'm all over that. I know, I'm easy."

Cait actually laughed, and it sounded as if she didn't do that very often. "You keep it up, and we'll be picking out china patterns in a few weeks."

It was Susan's turn to laugh. "My mother will be ecstatic. She's given up on me ever getting married."

"Mine too—or remarried, that is."

"What about Brannon? You two looked good together."

Cait's eyes shuttered, the mirth gone in an instant. "He's not the problem. It's me. I'm not the marrying kind."

"You sure about that?"

"Yeah. Ellers's mines and I have a lot in common. We're unstable and can destroy anyone who comes too near." She handed Susan half the bar, then rose. "I'll take first watch." Before she could reply, the former Marine vanished into the night.

Shaking her head, Susan fired up the satellite phone to deliver her report. Hopefully, her fellow agents would have a plan. If not, it'd be up to her, Cait, and Brannon to rescue the hostages and stop the bad guy. Only in Hollywood would that plot have a happy ending.

Chapter Twenty-Five

Brannon ended up bunking with ten other guys in a small hut. Since all the beds were filled, he took a thin sleeping bag to a corner and curled up. His gear hadn't been returned to him yet and neither had his knife, so he had only his hands to protect him if someone decided to get rough. That was enough.

His sleep was light, each new noise registered, evaluated, and then eventually discarded as a threat. Which is why he overheard the whispered conversation a few hours after lights-out.

"Commander says we're to be ready during 'Reveille,'" a thick voice said.

"So it's actually gonna happen. I'm not sure exactly what I think about this."

"Just do what you're told and it'll go fine."

"For us, maybe, but not for the others."

"You chicken out, and you know what will happen to you."

"Yeah, I know," the second man said. "Us or them."

"It's all part of the plan. Now get some sleep. We gotta be up before dawn."

Silence fell after that, leaving Brannon to parse through the conversation. Ellers's people weren't giving him trouble, so why was there an "us versus them" mentality? What did the man have planned for his people?

Rolling over, he stared at the roof of the hut for a time, wondering if Cait missed him as much as he missed her. He swore he could feel her skin under his fingers, what it was like to make love to her; feel her take her pleasure from him. He hardened at the thought, and barely kept the groan silent.

Mission first.

He let his eyes drift shut. Dawn would bring the answers to his questions. Hopefully, it would also bring him closer to freeing the hostages and returning to the woman he was beginning to love.

Cait watched the FBI agent sleep, wondering how long it had been since she'd slept that soundly.

Last night with Brannon in the cabin.

Was he still alive? She hadn't heard any gunshots, but that didn't mean Ellers hadn't cut his throat. Or tortured him.

Don't go there. You're just freaking yourself out.

With her gentle shake of Susan's shoulder, the woman woke. After blinking open her eyes, her companion frowned.

"You didn't wake me," she said, sitting up. From the way she moved, she was stiff in places that didn't appreciate that kind of discomfort.

"You needed the rest."

"And you didn't?" Susan asked, running her hands through her tangled hair.

"I'm used to running on little or no sleep. You're not. I managed to catch a power nap for a couple of hours since it's been quiet."

"I wanted to stay awake until you got back, but my brain just shut down." Susan yawned, then stretched. "I got a call right before I crashed. Our reinforcements will be here this afternoon about three. They have all the details worked out, and I gave them everything we know. They're aware of what they're walking into."

"What about Brannon? Do they know he's here?"

"Yes. And I told them he's trying to help us out. That met with a great deal of skepticism."

Cait gave a nod. "When you're ready, I'd like to check out that structure we saw last night." They'd seen it in the distance but had decided not to do a recon in the dark, in case the hut, or the area around it, was booby trapped.

"You got it. Give me a couple minutes and I'll be moveable."

She handed over a bottle of water. "This will taste different. I used the iodine tabs to purify it."

"Oh, yum. You got eggs Benedict in that backpack of yours?"

"Dream on. I could grill you some alligator, if you want."

"No, I'll pass."

"What are the chances that the FBI won't arrest Brannon for the robbery?" Cait asked.

"The truth? Slim to none. But if we can pull this off without anyone dying, that'll give me leverage to try to talk them out of it."

"And if you don't?"

"He's going down for some seriously hard time."

"Jesus."

"I know. But it sounds like he knew the risks," Susan replied.

"Yeah, but that won't make it easier."

When Cait tossed her a small packet of tissues, Susan nodded her thanks.

"I deserve a damned raise for this." With a groan, she rose to her feet and headed off into the woods.

Folding up the ground cloth, Cait packed it into the rucksack. Scanning the area, she ensured that they'd left no trace other than the flattened earth. A glance at her watch told her they were about an hour from dawn. If they were lucky, by this afternoon, all of this would be over.

They were nearing the location of the hut when Cait heard voices. She held up her hand for her companion to stop, then realized that Susan wouldn't know the hand signals.

She turned and whispered, "We got someone coming this

way." Susan didn't reply, but followed her into deeper brush, where they crouched down and waited. A short time later, two men crossed not ten feet away from them. Between them was a five-gallon carboy hanging from a thick wooden pole, filled with what looked to be water.

"This shit is heavy," one man said.

"Duh," the other guy replied. "Forty pounds, what did you expect?"

"Why the hell are we doing this?"

"Don't know. I just do what Ellers tells me, okay? He says we fetch this water, we fetch it."

They staggered on, heading for the compound.

"We could have mugged them for that. Had to taste better than the stuff you have," Susan said.

Cait didn't reply. Something wasn't right about what they'd just seen.

"What's wrong?" her companion asked.

She looked in the direction of the compound, then back at Susan. "So you're Ellers, and you've made your own little country in the middle of the swamp. You're dead sure that the ratbag feds are going to attack you, so what do you do?"

"Build an armed compound, which he did. I'll ignore the ratbag fed comment for now."

"Probably best. Let's take it a step further: How do you withstand a long siege? With food and water, right?"

"He's got that covered. I saw dried food and there's a cistern. With the way it rains here, he and his camp can hold out for a very long time." Then, slowly, it seemed to dawn on her where Cait was headed with her questions. "But if he has all that water, why are they carrying more into the compound?"

"Why, indeed?"

Brannon was up before dawn, tired of listening to the others snore. With his years in the Rangers, the sounds shouldn't have bugged him, but somehow they did. He was more on edge than usual, and with that twitchy feeling crawling up the back of his neck, he knew something was going down soon.

After making a quick stop at the latrine, then washing his face and smoothing back his hair, he headed toward the front of the compound. People were taking care of their chores, even the children; he passed one little kid feeding the chickens, another one milking a nanny goat. Yesterday, when he'd been given the tour he noticed there were no dogs here. When he'd asked why, Rafferty had told him the commander didn't like them, thought them a waste of time. Apparently the IEDs were deterrent enough.

Curious eyes followed his every step, all because he was the new guy in town, the man who'd stolen for them and still brought the cash to their commander after being double-crossed. Some of the others' expressions held respect; most looked at him like he was a sucker. Once again, he checked the security arrangements and found that they were unchanged this morning. A quick look up at the towers proved nothing was different there, either. So why was he on edge?

Rafferty joined him as he headed toward the parade ground. "Good morning."

"Morning," Brannon replied.

"You sleep good?"

"Pretty fair."

When they reached the flagpole, there were groups of men chatting among themselves.

A man walked up to the front, then called out for silence. When the crowd obeyed, he said, "Okay, guys, time to get those weapons inspected. Bring 'em up!"

"Again?" someone called out.

"Yeah, again."

"But why?"

"Don't know. I just follow orders. Come on, let's get it done," the man snapped, pointing at the long table in front of him. "Firearms on the right, knives on the left. You know the drill."

Men began to file up now, discarding their weapons as

ordered.

"What's happening?" Brannon asked, puzzled. It was an odd request and he didn't know how to read it.

"Once a month, we turn in all our weapons so they can be inspected," Rafferty replied. "That way Ellers can ensure that we're taking proper care of them. Makes no damned sense to me, but that's the way the commander wants it done."

"And if someone isn't keeping their weapon properly?"

"There're penalties. Trust me, you don't want to find out what they are."

Rafferty walked up, removed his firearm, and added it to the pile. His knife went into the other stack and then he returned to Brannon's side.

"Don't know why we're doing this again," he added. "We already went through the inspection earlier this month."

"Reveille" sounded and the men lined up in rows. Once it ended, someone coughed behind them. There were barely stifled yawns as well.

"Now what?" Brannon asked.

"Next will be the morning pep talk," Rafferty said. "Sometimes it's short. Sometimes it's long. I'm hoping it's a short one today. I'm hungry and we don't eat until he's done talking."

Minutes passed. The men didn't break ranks, but they began to chat with one another. Meanwhile, nothing was happening with the weapons on the table.

"Usually he's out here by now," Rafferty said.

Brannon studied the guards again and found that the ones in the towers were still in place, but the others were not where they'd been the day before.

"Your perimeter guards are inside the wire now," Brannon said. "Is that normal?"

"What?" Rafferty said, looking around. "No, it's not." Then he frowned. "Where are the women and kids? They always join us for 'Reveille.'"

The twitching was getting to Brannon, growing in intensity. His heart rate kicked up, his muscles tightening. A battle was coming, and he wasn't sure it was going to be survivable.

He did the math. "You have six guys still armed. Wouldn't they turn in their weapons as well?"

Rafferty paid more attention now. "Yeah, they should have. What the hell is going on?"

From the looks of it, Brannon wasn't the only one who'd read the situation. Some of the others began shooting anxious glances toward the main house.

"If this goes bad, don't charge the table. Go lateral, work around from the back."

"Are all you Rangers this paranoid?"

"Only the ones who are still alive."

Chapter Twenty-Six

Cait and Susan's progress to the hut had been halted by IEDs, the first of which involved a pressure plate. Since her companion seemed genuinely interested in explosives that had led to Cait patiently explaining the difference between a VI, or victim-initiated IED, and a command-detonated one, those that required human assistance to explode. How some in the military called them IEDs, others called them mines. There seemed to be a lot of gray area in the terminology.

"So what do you call them?" Susan asked.

"Shit that can totally ruin my day."

The agent laughed. "You know way too much about this stuff. I'm guessing that learning didn't come out of a book."

"You would be right."

"If I haven't said it already, thank you for what you did for us over there, in the service."

"You're welcome," Cait replied, sensing that the sentiment was sincere. "Thank you for keeping the streets safe back at home."

"Yeah, well, sometimes we have mixed success with that."

"Same on our end," she said.

The hut stood about fifty feet in front of them. She was guessing that there were multiple IEDs around it, carefully placed to make it damned hard to figure out where they were located. If the hut had been used regularly, there would have been a discernable path to follow, but the constant rain had made the grass grow too quickly.

"How do those guys get in here without blowing their asses

up?" Susan asked, frowning.

"Probably had a map," Cait said. "I'll go in, you stay back here."

"I'm willing to take the risk."

"Won't argue with that, but Brannon will need you alive to call in updates, coordinate things with the FBI. We both go in and we both get dead, he's without backup."

Susan grumbled under her breath, then gave in. Cait stripped off her rucksack and dropped it near the woman's feet, then handed her the rifle.

"Sometimes I think you have a death wish," Susan said.

Cait stopped breathing for a brief moment, then turned her back so Susan couldn't see how close she'd hit home. There was no way the fed could know that the dark voice in her head kept guilting her, telling her that it should have been her who'd gotten the flag-draped coffin, the rifle volley, the grieving relatives. Jeremy had died, not her, and she had a job to do, so she tried to hush that dark voice, if just for now.

As she moved forward, one cautious step at a time, she smiled. Once again, the rain had been her friend. Now that she knew what to look for, faint depressions marked where the earth had sunk after the recent heavy downpours, and they formed a discernable pattern.

With a final glance toward Susan, she began to thread her way through the minefield. Sweat formed on her forehead, then ran down her face. Cait wiped it away, swatting at a mosquito who'd come to call. When she reached the door, she knelt to study the lock, but found no sign of it being booby trapped. The padlock was solid, but the hasp in which it was slotted was anchored in wood that had seen better days. With only a few solid kicks, the door swung open, trembling on its rusty hinges. Cait wasn't sure what she expected, but a room full of wooden racks wasn't it.

"What's in there?" Susan called out, wisely keeping her distance.

"Not sure yet. Hold on."

The five racks were homemade, with five shelves to a rack.

On each of those shelves were three cookie sheets, the cheap kind you'd buy at Walmart, seventy-five of them in total. A small worktable sat nearby with empty bottles of acetone, a grungy blender, tweezers, and a stack of newspapers. A heavy-duty electrical cord lay curled on the floor, but since there was no electricity, that meant someone had to have brought in a portable generator at some point. Judging from the dust patterns on the table, there'd been other equipment, perhaps too valuable to leave behind.

"What the hell were they making?" she muttered.

"Cait? What have you got?"

She stepped to the door and listed off what she'd found inside. As she did, Susan's frown grew deeper.

"Sorry, but I need to see this stuff. I insist."

"Okay, I'll guide you in. Go slow."

It took another gut-knotting five minutes for Susan to reach the hut without getting herself blown to bits. The moment the FBI agent cleared the door, she froze.

"Is it like a meth lab or something?" Cait asked.

Susan didn't reply, but did a quick inventory of the equipment on the table. Then she dropped to her knees and began peering under the racks. Reaching far under one, she retrieved something. When she regained her feet, she displayed the item on her palm, a large seed or nut of some kind.

"This is a castor bean," she announced.

"Okay," Cait replied, not understanding the significance.

"Castor beans, when properly processed, make ricin."

She felt the bottom fall out of her stomach.

"Yeah, our wingnut commander has managed to create one of the deadliest poisons in the world, right in his own backyard." Susan gestured. "That's what the racks are for. You process it out, then let it dry, which would have taken some doing given the humidity out here."

"So the water those guys were carrying contained ricin?"

"Probably." The agent rolled the bean around her palm a few times, then jammed it into her pants pocket. "After I phone this in, let's get closer to the compound, see what's happening. We can't have Ellers leaving with this stuff. There's no antidote."

Cait pulled the door closed behind them, then studied the open ground in front of her. "'Once more unto the breach, dear friends, once more,'" she murmured, then walked out into the minefield.

"A Marine quoting Shakespeare? Now I've heard it all," Susan said, following her.

"Wait until I break out the Dylan Thomas."

The FBI agent's laughter filled the air once again and brought Cait a smile. The smile continued as they walked out of the minefield, into the clear.

"Everything ready?" Ellers asked. Both men standing in front of his desk nodded. He could sense their tension, like smoke in the air.

Jason was one of his more loyal men, and recently, Cyrus had taken up the call. Both should be proud of the service they were about to perform.

"The boats loaded?" he asked.

This time only Jason nodded.

"Then go on outside and wait for me."

"Sir—" the other one began. Cyrus wasn't much more than nineteen.

"Go on," Ellers barked.

"Just wonderin' if it has to be this way. We've worked so hard buildin' up this camp and—"

"Do you want our enemies to win this war? Is that what you're telling me?"

Cyrus shook his head. "It's just that those folks are friends of mine, and I don't . . . "

Ellers shifted his eyes to Jason. "Do it."

The man's arm was around Cyrus's neck before the kid could react. It took a while for the hold to kill him, and all that time, the boy fought for his life, kicking, struggling as the smell of urine filled the air. When he finally slumped to the ground, Jason picked up the boy's gun and stuck it into his jeans, then dragged the body out of sight of the door, propping it in the corner.

"Go on, I'll be out in a moment," Ellers said.

"Yes, sir," Jason replied.

When the door closed behind him, his eyes moved back to the body in the corner. "Coward," he muttered.

He'd planned this moment for almost a year, once he'd realized what it would take. Only a bold move, something no one anticipated, would bring this country to glory. He knew some would fault him down the line, but the rewards would nullify the sacrifices.

Ellers would ignite a conflagration that would roar through the country like a fire through dry timber, cleansing every state, every city. At the very end, once the blood had stopped flowing and the bodies had been buried, America would be free, and they would know that he'd been right. That he, Quinton Ellers, had shown them the way forward, all because he wasn't afraid.

"God Bless America," he said, smiling to himself as he shouldered his pack and headed for the door, and his destiny.

The door to the house finally opened and Commander Ellers took a position at the top of the stairs. It was the perfect location—everyone could see him—and Brannon knew he did it on purpose. The man was as much showman as tyrant. The commander wore camo, like the day before, and had his gun in hand. He raised it into the air and fired twice. All movement ceased.

"Good morning, patriots!" he called out, holstering his weapon.

"Good morning, Commander!" the men shouted back.

Ellers's eyes sought out Brannon, and he felt his hackles rise. "Twenty years ago tomorrow, on April nineteenth, 1995, a true patriot struck a blow that was heard round the world. He taught the traitors that one man could paint the sky red with the blood of his oppressors. That one man could bring a nation to its knees."

April nineteenth, 1995.

Brannon's twelfth birthday. He'd been so wired for the party his parents had planned for him, time with his best friends at a paintball range, then pizza, cake, the whole works. Then his father said something bad had happened and it was all cancelled.

Brannon couldn't believe it. Demanded to know exactly why. His parents had left him in the kitchen, went into their room for a private discussion. No voices were raised, but when they came back out his mother was crying.

"I'm so damned sorry this had to happen today," his father said, clicking on the television. "Or any day, for that matter."

On his twelfth birthday, a white supremacist named Timothy McVeigh had detonated a Ryder truck full of ANFO, ammonium nitrate, outside the Murrah Building in Oklahoma City. He'd parked in the drop-off zone for the day-care center.

As Brannon had watched the news reports, he'd been just as stunned as the rest of the world. 168 people dead, many of whom were children, and over 600 wounded. The blast had been felt over fifty miles away.

It was the day Brannon learned that not all of America's enemies were overseas, that some of them lived right next door. They shared the same restaurants, the same churches, schools and bars. Even if it was homegrown, their hatred was no less fanatic than their counterparts in the Middle East.

He'd never forgotten that day, and every year on his birthday he'd say a prayer for those who'd lost their lives to a cause that was more butchery than liberty.

Now, listening to this asshole laud McVeigh's "blow for freedom" made him furious. He bit the inside of his lip, drawing blood, trying to keep from launching himself at Ellers and ripping him apart.

"But today will be just as important as tomorrow. For today, you people will be remembered for your bravery, for your love of your country, for the sacrifice you will be making."

"What's he talkin' about?" someone whispered.

"Today, our enemies will come to this place in an attempt to roust us from our chosen home, but we will not let that happen. For this is New America and here, we are free!"

There were a few cheers, but for the most part the onlookers were confused.

"Is this the way he usually is?" Brannon asked Rafferty.

"Not really. I don't know what he's talking about."

"You must guard your liberties, your families, your freedom," Ellers continued, pacing now. "Tomorrow the world will see the truth. I'll make sure they count you among the most loyal patriots this country has ever known."

Then Ellers hefted his backpack onto his shoulder and marched right down the center of them. He shook hands with those closest to him, slapping some on the back.

"I don't get it. What's he doing?" Rafferty asked.

Once the commander was free of the group, he walked to the front gates and waited as two of his men opened them. He marched out, turned smartly on a heel, and saluted Old Glory. Then he took off down the path, double time, his escorts right behind.

"What the fuck was that?" one man asked.

"Damned if I know," another responded.

The gates swung closed and then bars were engaged, locking down the compound. Ellers's message had a finality to it, one that made Brannon shift uncomfortably. As if by instinct, his eyes rose to the towers again. This time they were manned, but the guards were facing *inward*. As were their weapons.

Now he understood what Ellers had meant.

The bloodbath would start here, but the FBI would have nothing to do with it.

"Oh hell, no!" he said.

Chapter Twenty-Seven

Brannon was already on the move, even as the first bullets were fired. The realization that Ellers had turned on them came quickly to the others, and they spread out, desperately seeking cover. The few that headed toward the table were cut down after only a couple steps.

Working his way around, he drew closer to one of the armed men, then launched himself across the open space. After a throat punch, he claimed the man's weapons as the assailant writhed on the ground, trying to breathe. When another turned to fire at him, Brannon dropped and rolled out of the way, bullets pelting the ground next to him. A round went into the side of the building near his ear, scattering splinters. When he found one of the attackers with his back exposed, a single shot to the head ended that threat. He collected the man's weapon and moved on.

Some of the other men had always confiscated weapons and were fighting back. There were bodies were strewn across the parade now. A few of the braver souls pulled the wounded out of the line of fire, risking death to help their comrades.

Rafferty joined him, blood on the side of his face, and Brannon passed him one of the guns.

"I'm going to check on the women and kids," Rafferty said breathlessly. "They aren't armed."

"Take some men with you. I'll hold them as long as I can."

With a nod, Rafferty sprinted in toward the rear of the compound, grabbing a couple men along the way. Brannon turned his attention to the killers, and continued his hunt.

At the first sounds of gunfire, Susan and Cait had headed toward the compound as fast as the terrain and mines would allow.

"Is this FBI?" Cait asked as they ran.

"No. They wouldn't be that stupid." But Susan dialed her office anyway. "We got a battle going on here. Please tell me it's not us or some other federal agency."

"Negative. We're not onsite yet."

"Then something has gone massively wrong," she said, ending the call.

They were some distance from the compound when the north gate burst open and a woman ran toward them. She'd made it only a short distance before a man stepped into the opening and shot her in the back. She fell into the dirt, then tried to crawl away, hand over hand, even as her assailant continued to stalk her. Cait took the kill shot and the man went down.

As they hurried toward the gate, Susan knelt to check on the injured woman. But in that short space of time, the woman's face had grown slack, her eyes staring at nothing.

"Dammit," Susan murmured. "What is going on here?"

"How is she?" Cait called out.

She shook her head, rising to her feet. Just inside the gate was chaos, people running in all directions. Screams and gunshots filled the air.

"Ah, hell. How can we tell who's the enemy, and who isn't?" Susan asked.

"Welcome to the Middle East, my friend," Cait said.

They edged inside the gate, trying to make sense of the battle. A man fired at another woman, one shielding a child in her arms. After Cait shot him, Susan claimed his gun.

A quick check proved that the guard who was usually in front of the jail was missing. "I'll check on the others. You find Brannon."

Cait nodded. "Watch your back."

But Susan was already sprinting across the compound, fearing what she'd find inside that building. To her relief, she made it to the jail unscathed and threw the bolt, pulling open the door.

"Preston?" she called out. Hopefully he'd have the good sense not to come outside. "It's Susan."

"Susan?" Patti called out.

"Stay inside! Is everyone okay?"

"Yeah, we're fine," Preston said. She took a quick peek to ensure that was the case, then entered. Four confused pairs of eyes watched her every move. They hadn't been idle; one of the bunks had been disassembled and each hostage held a piece of cypress bed slat for a weapon. The table had been overturned and was being used as a barricade, the commander's notes spread all over the floor now.

"What the hell is going on?" Keith asked, rising. "Is it the FBI?"

"No," she said. "Not yet." Waving Preston forward, she handed over the spare weapon she'd confiscated. "I'll guard the door. We don't want them to lock you in."

A scream reached her just as she stepped outside; Maudie and three other women were trapped against the side of one of the small huts with a handful of kids. One woman was frantically trying to dig a hole so they could escape under the fence. Coming closer to them was one of the armed men.

"John Lawson, why are you doing this?" Maudie asked, positioning herself in front of the others.

"It's the commander's plan, Maudie. Nothin' personal."

"Dead is damned personal, John. You can't kill your neighbors."

He raised his weapon, proving he had no problem with that issue.

"Hey!" Susan shouted. As he turned, she shot him, twice, watching as the blood bloomed on his chest. He took a few hesitant steps backward, as if his brain hadn't quite processed the fact that he was dying. Then he collapsed.

"Come on, over here," Susan beckoned. "Quickly!"

Maudie herded the frightened children toward her, and once they were inside the jail, Susan took up guard again. When Preston and Keith joined her, she gave them an encouraging nod.

"Brannon and Cait are still alive. Or at least, they were a while back. We'll get through this," she said.

"I should have just signed the damned divorce papers," Keith grumbled.

"What?" she asked, confused.

"Wife wanted a divorce. I wouldn't give her one, thought maybe we could patch things up. If I had signed the papers, I'd be in Constantinople now. Instead I used that voucher for the tour just to buy time, and now I'm in just another damned war zone."

"Yeah, except this one is on American soil."

Cait's progress had been difficult, and dangerous. Since almost no one knew her, that made her a target for all of them. To keep out of sight, she skirted around the backside of a building, crawling along in the mud, trying to keep from being snagged by the fencing and barbed wire. Eventually she reached a clear view of the flagpole—and what was a killing ground. There were at least ten casualties, most of whom weren't moving.

Good God, what is Ellers doing?

When she saw Brannon alive and tracking tangos, Cait smiled in relief. As if someone had recognized that this was a mistake, a barrage of bullets came his way from the guard towers, pinning him in place. Edging away from the building, she sprinted for the nearest cover: a raised flower bed made out of cypress timbers. Belatedly, the guard in the right tower saw her and turned his sights in her direction. She actually felt the bullet whiz by her head and threw herself flat on the ground.

"About time, Marine," Brannon called out. "Thought I was going to have to win this war all on my own."

Cait snorted and resisted the temptation to flip him off.

He pointed at her, then the right tower. She nodded her understanding. Ensuring that she was as unexposed as possible, she began firing on that location. The left tower's guard immediately responded, slamming bullets into the cypress timbers.

Brannon lined up his shot, took a deep breath, let it out, and then fired the rifle. The sniper's head exploded, and in near slow motion the body pitched over the side of the left tower and dropped to the ground. When the guard in the other tower reacted, shooting at him, Cait rose and dealt with him. She sent Brannon a thumbs-up and he matched it.

Only a few sporadic shots came now as the battle died down. He waited as she worked her way over to him, covering her as she did. Finally, Cait crouched next to him. Her clothes were muddy, but her eyes were bright.

"It's good to see you're in one piece." He reached over, pulled her closer, and kissed her.

When it ended, she studied him for a moment, no doubt checking for injuries. "Good to see you, too." Then she looked out at the carnage, the light in her eyes dimming. "What happened here?"

"Ellers went after his own. He made sure they were unarmed, then turned his killers loose."

"Why?"

"Not sure yet."

"All clear!" someone shouted. "All clear!"

Brannon cautiously stood, eyes moving across the open area. It was bad, but not as bad as he'd feared. One by one, people came out of hiding. It was then that someone noticed Cait.

"Who the hell are you?" he demanded as guns turned in her direction. "You with the feds?"

"She's with me," Brannon said. "She was leading the swamp tour. She's here to get her people."

"Thought you said she was dead."

"I said what it took to get inside this compound. You have a problem with that?"

The man gave a gruff shake of the head and slowly lowered his rifle.

Rafferty approached them now and his eyes held a haunted expression that Brannon knew all too well. He'd seen it countless times when he looked in a mirror.

"How's your family?" he asked.

"Alive, thank God," the man replied. "Not everyone was so lucky. I still can't believe Ellers did this. What kind of goddamned madman is he?"

"The motivated kind," Brannon said. "Most of them are."

He handed Cait the rifle. "I'm going to make a run down to the water, see if he's still there. If he is, I'll be bringing him back."

"Naw, he'll be gone," Rafferty said. "He gave his orders and bailed on us. Damned bastard." He hesitated. "That other woman from the tour, the one named Susan. She's contacting someone to get us help."

"Good. She has . . . resources."

The man lowered his voice. "I know she's FBI. I found her badge in her backpack. I just didn't tell Ellers that."

Brannon patted the man's shoulder. "That was a good call. She'll make sure your people are well taken care of."

"God, I hope so."

Brannon headed out the front gates and down the path toward the water at a quick jog. In his wake he left the dead, the wounded, and the betrayed.

Cait watched him go, knowing that what he was doing was probably a futile gesture.

"Anyone with medical experience, front and center," Rafferty called out. "Bring the wounded here, even if it's minor!"

The men and women slowly complied, moving like dazed zombies, their world imploded by the man they'd trusted with their lives. The injured were carried to the front of the compound, laid out in two lines near the flagpole, their blood staining the ground beneath them. Cait, Rafferty, and a man who said he'd been an Army medic worked that line. Some wounds were minor; others were likely to be mortal given the compound's remote location.

Women slowly reappeared from where they'd been hiding, bringing hot water for cleaning the wounds, bandages, and plenty of tears. Cait held the hand of a young man as he died, remembering a different place and a different young man who had lost his life in the sands of Afghanistan. She shut her eyes, fighting ears. Fighting a darkness that told her it wasn't worth the struggle.

"Rest in peace," she whispered, the weight pressing down on her again.

Now she understood why soldiers chose to remain in the battle. It wasn't only a matter of supporting your team, but often it was the easiest way to let death to stake its claim. Let fate make the next move. In so many ways, she'd been waiting for that moment when the decision was no longer hers.

When it looked as if her first aid skills were no longer needed, Cait moved to the house's front stairs. As if magically summoned, Brannon strode through the front gates. His annoyed expression told her their quarry was long gone. He took in the makeshift field hospital, then headed directly toward her.

"No luck?" she called out.

He shook his head. Pausing long enough to give her shoulder a squeeze, he moved on up the stairs and into the house. Cait followed him. Their first discovery was the body of a young man propped in the corner, head slumped.

"Poor kid," Brannon said. "Probably didn't want to be part of Ellers's massacre."

As he hunted around, Cait checked the desk but found only duty rosters, supply lists, other mundane items. Nothing to indicate Ellers's plans.

"Found our phones," Brannon said, removing them from the top of an old wooden cabinet. She claimed hers.

While he talked to someone from Veritas, she went back

outside and found five voicemails waiting for her, all from Mike. Each one was increasingly worried, until the final one was primarily one swear word after another.

She sent her friend a quick text to let him know she was alive, and that the FBI would be arriving to take them home soon. That his hunch had been too damned correct.

Brannon joined her, thumbing off his phone as she did hers. "The money is headed south."

"Then we should be too."

He looked away for a moment, then back. "Roger that. Let's talk to Susan first. I want her to still have a job when this is over."

Chapter Twenty-Eight

As the pair of them approached her, Susan read the expression on Brannon's face: He was falling in love with Cait Landry. Might already be there. Whether that was good news or not, she didn't know. If she couldn't convince her superiors that Hardegree deserved a pass, he was bound for prison.

"Guys," she said.

"Everyone okay?" Cait asked.

She meant the campers. "Yeah, they're good. Two of the attackers survived. I'm about to question them. I don't want to wait since they might not be alive for much longer."

"They're injured?" Brannon asked.

"No, but they will be if this crowd turns on them."

He nodded his understanding. "Veritas says the money is headed south, probably accompanied by Ellers."

"Okay, let's find out where he's going and what he's got planned."

It took some effort to push through the crowd that had encircled the two prisoners where they sat up against one of the buildings, the side of which was riddled with bullet holes. The mood was ugly, one step away from a lynch mob. Susan couldn't blame them.

The prisoners were a mismatched pair. One of the men glared back at her, the other trembled in fear. She recognized the angry man—he'd been one of the two toting the carboy. Someone had said his name was Jason.

"You'll need this," Rafferty said, opening his palm. In it was the wallet that held her FBI badge and ID.

"Thank you," she said. "I mean it. But why did you take the risk?"

"I think, deep down, I knew that Ellers didn't care about us, that we were as expendable as anyone else. I wasn't here when he killed that FBI agent, but when I found out he'd done it, I knew it was over."

"I'm so sorry. I never saw this coming, or I'd have tried to stop it. How many are dead?"

"Eleven. Four more might not make it. Two of those are kids."

"Good God," she whispered.

As Susan turned toward the prisoners, she pulled on her "don't jack with me" FBI face. She raised her voice so all could hear her. "So, what the hell was this all about?"

Jason spat at her. "Fuck off, bitch. I don't owe you any answers."

"Answer the woman, or we'll be stringing you up in the courtyard," Rafferty said.

"Always knew you were a pussy, Rafferty."

"At least I don't turn on my neighbors, unlike you."

"Give him over!" someone in the crowd called out. "We'll make him talk."

"There you go, Jason," Susan said. "You answer my questions, or I'll hand you over to those folks. What's it going to be?"

"Why the hell should I talk to you?"

She leaned down so he could see her better. "Because I'm the only one who will keep your ass alive."

"You're a fed," he said.

When she didn't deny it, his eyes widened, then gradually became cunning. "It was you! The FBI. They set this whole thing up."

"Try again, Jason. Because that's definitely a lie."

He spat at her again. "You're the one who's lying."

"Yeah, yeah. Same old bullshit," she said. She shifted her attention to the other prisoner. "Okay, what about you? What's your name?"

"R-r-rob."

"You keep your mouth shut," the other man warned.

Susan ignored him. "Rob, huh? Why were you killing these people?"

"I didn't! I didn't hurt anyone."

"He's right, he wasn't part of it," a woman said. "We found him tied up in one of the outbuildings."

"Then why is he a prisoner?" Susan asked, confused.

"He was talking with the others this morning," the woman replied. "We didn't want to take any chances, just in case he had something planned."

"Okay." She turned back to Rob. "Why did these guys do this?"

Tears rolled down the man's face. Now that Susan studied him, he didn't look to be much over seventeen. "They s-s-shot her. Linny. She's my girl and they shot her." His eyes sought out Rafferty's. "She's d-d-dead, isn't she?"

"No, she's going to be okay as long as she gets treatment. The bullet didn't do that much damage."

Rob bowed his head. "Oh, thank God, thank God."

There was increased murmuring behind them now.

"Help us, Rob," Susan said softly, putting her hand on his arm. "Tell us what you know."

"You shut the fuck up, kid! You tell them anything, and you're a damned traitor."

"Ignore him," Susan urged. "Just go on."

Rob blinked away the tears. "The c-c-commander told me to set up a couple video cameras. They're probably still going if they haven't run out of juice."

"When did you start filming?"

"Right before 'Reveille' this morning."

"Where are the cameras?" Brannon asked.

The young man had calmed considerably now, evidenced by less stuttering. "They're on the front of Ellers's house, up in the eaves, one on each side. I swear he never said anything about killing folks."

"Of course he didn't," Brannon said.

"You bastard. You're a traitor!" Jason growled.

In a single heartbeat, Brannon had the man's neck hyperextended and a knife at his throat. "So what was the plan? Why'd you turn on your own people?" he demanded.

"The FBI—"

The knife pressed harder against the man's windpipe, causing a trickle of blood to flow down his skin. "Can the bullshit. Tell us the truth!"

Jason slowly swallowed. "We were to kill everyone, make it look like the feds did it."

Brannon released his hold, but didn't sheath the knife. "Go on."

"We were going to keep a couple of the women alive, then execute them when everyone else was dead. We got an FBI jacket. One of us was gonna wear it in the video when we did the women."

"*That* was Ellers's plan?" Susan said, stunned.

"Yeah. He thought it all out. We were going to have Rob edit it, get it all ready, make it look like someone had smuggled out the video."

"How were you getting it to Ellers?"

"We were supposed to send it to him in an e-mail before we left the compound. Said we were supposed to break it into smaller chunks so it'd upload faster. Then he'd edit it and put it up on his YouTube channel. That way the whole world would know that the FBI is nothing but a bunch of fucking murderers."

The irony was as thick as the humidity.

"What were you supposed to do with Rob after he sent the video?" Susan asked.

"Kill him. We were to make sure there were no survivors."

"You mean like you?" Rafferty said.

Jason blinked. "No, we were supposed to go to the south camp, wait there until Ellers contacted us."

"South, huh?" Susan said, looking over at Brannon now. He gave a single nod in agreement. "What's at this camp?"

"It's a cabin on one of the hammocks, a couple hours from

here," Rafferty explained. "Nothing fancy, just a place to hunker down if things got bad. We had supplies delivered there sometimes."

"Yeah, that's it," Jason cut in. "Our boat's all loaded. Once we were done here, we'd take off."

"What's Ellers's final target?" she asked.

The man shook his head. Apparently they'd reached Jason's line in the sand, and Susan suspected that even the threat of the Ranger's blade wouldn't drag the truth out of him. Or the fool really didn't know.

"For God's sake, tell her," Rafferty said. "We got enough dead bodies on our conscience as it is."

"I'm no traitor. Ellers did right by me. I'm not going to rat him out."

Susan's mind returned to that damned carboy of water. It kept poking at her, like a splinter in her finger.

"That container you hauled out of the woods? Where did you get it?"

"You saw us?" Jason asked.

Obviously. "Did you get it from the hut, the one with the drying racks?" Jason nodded. "You know what Ellers used that place for?"

"No, he said it was off limits. Kinda surprised me when he told us to go there this morning. It was a bitch getting past those mines."

"What was in the container?"

"Water. Said to take some of it with us, not to use the well at the south camp, that it was contaminated."

"Why not fill it at the cistern inside the compound?" Susan asked.

"He said it might let people know we were up to something."

It was a lame answer, but this guy had bought it.

"There's nothing wrong with the water at the camp," Rafferty said, frowning. "I had some less than a week ago and it didn't bother me."

No witnesses. It finally clicked.

Susan zeroed back in on the prisoner. "Someone was making ricin in that hut. You heard of it?"

"Ricin?" Jason said, his eyes widening now. "The poison?"

"I always wondered what James was doing out there," Rafferty said.

She filed that information away for the future. "I'm willing to bet that if we tested that container, the water would be poisoned with that ricin. No witnesses, remember? That means you too."

"But—" he began.

"You would have gotten to your little hideaway, had a drink or two, and then fallen sick. It can take days to die from that stuff, did you know that? It's hellish agony."

Brannon rose to his feet, sheathing his knife. "No survivors. Ellers was clearing the decks."

For a second, Jason acted like he was going to argue with them, but instead his face turned crimson. "That son of a bitch! He would have killed us!"

Welcome to the crowd.

"He lied to us! He said we had to show the world what the government was really like, that a few dead women and kids would make the rest of the patriots stand up and fight."

"A few dead women and kids?" Rafferty shouted, lunging for him.

Brannon corralled the man. "Chill down. He'll get his, don't worry."

Rafferty shook himself free. "He damned well better. Because if he doesn't, I'll kill him myself." Angry voices came from behind them now, eager to settle scores.

The prisoner's bravado vanished. "Ellers said you'd be martyrs. That after the video was shown, folks would know why he was striking his blow for freedom."

"What's his plan?" Susan asked.

"Don't know. And I mean that. He never told us. All the commander said was that he was going to rain hell on Atlanta, and his name would never be forgotten."

Atlanta.

Susan groaned. Georgia's state capitol was a target-rich environment for a lunatic anarchist. It was home to the Centers for Disease Control, the world's busiest airport, the EPA, Homeland Security, and FBI, ATF, and IRS offices. So many places to hit. So many people to kill.

"How do you know about ricin, lady?" a man asked from the group around them. "Are you really a fed?"

She'd wondered when that question was going to be asked. Did she dare risk it? A glance at Brannon indicated that he was as unsure as she was. With a sigh, one that she hoped wouldn't be her last, Susan pulled her wallet out of her jeans, opened it, and then held it up so the group could see her badge and ID.

"I'm Special Agent Susan Driscoll from the Atlanta FBI office. I was on the swamp tour because I was checking into what Ellers was up to. I had *no* idea he planned to hurt you people. And I swear to God the government had nothing to do with this."

"Like we can trust you," someone called out. The mood began to shift again, and not in her favor. Brannon and Cait moved closer to her now.

Maudie pushed through the crowd, putting herself next to Susan. "Listen up! This woman saved my life and some of the children's as well. I don't care if she's FBI. She did the right thing today. Which is a helluva lot more than Ellers ever did."

The murmuring continued, but the anger began to subside.

"Your people coming here?" a voice called out.

"Yes," Susan replied. "I called them as soon as the shooting stopped. They're bringing in a medical team, boats, and a helicopter. That way we can evacuate the most seriously injured first, then move the rest of you. The wounded have priority, of course."

"What will they do with us?" Maudie asked.

"As I see it, you're as much victims of Ellers as the rest of us."

"Are your bosses going to believe that?"

Hell no. "Not sure, but I'll do my best to get them to see your situation. The common enemy is the commander; that's who we need to be focusing on. The more you folks can tell us, the more lives we can save. If you don't cooperate, you'll be considered accessories to whatever crimes he commits."

Profound silence surrounded them now.

Susan gestured toward the prisoners. "Can you make sure nothing happens to these guys? Especially the asshole."

"Yeah, I will," Rafferty replied. "They'll both be breathing when the feds arrive."

Susan knew hard it been for him to say that. "Thank you. You saved lives today. That's all that matters."

"Some might not see it that way."

As she walked away from the group, Brannon by her side, she realized that someone was missing. "Where's Cait?"

"Looking for our rucksacks." Brannon hesitated, then continued. "Ellers will know something's up when that video doesn't land in his inbox. He'll go underground, pick another day, another target."

"We certainly can't release that video footage. That could set off any number of the patriot groups, and they'll strike even before we know what they're up to."

"Damned if you do, damned if you don't."

"Isn't that always the case?" she said. *Thank God it's not my call.*

They'd reached the front of the compound now. She could feel eyes tracking her, knowing the word had been passed: *There's a fed here. Can we trust her?*

The satellite phone rang. "Driscoll."

"It's Wiseman. Two choppers are headed your way, along with boats. Should be there in a couple hours. We have park rangers on standby, if we need them. The fire is out, so they have people to spare."

"Good. We got some serious casualties here. The bad news is that Ellers is long gone, headed for Atlanta. We need to issue the appropriate warnings, because we don't know what his target is, but it's definitely in the city."

"Damn," Wiseman grumbled. "Did you find Hardegree?"

She looked over at the Ranger. "Yeah, he's here."

"Good. The Jacksonville office is really eager to lay their hands on him."

"Understood," she replied. "Anything else I need to know?"

"Yeah, your boss is a consummate bitch," he added.

Susan laughed. "Like I didn't know that. Next time we meet, you owe me a few beers."

"You got it. Later, Driscoll."

"Bye, Wiseman."

She stared up at the front of Ellers's house. There were two video cameras tucked in the eaves, just as Rob had said, and Keith was currently retrieving them for her, preserving the evidence.

She waved Brannon away and they halted in front of the "hospital." Cait was there, rucksacks at her feet.

"How many dead?" Susan asked.

"Thirteen," Cait replied.

She could see them now, each covered with a blanket. In a split second, she made the decision. "I need someone to check out that site down south. You two up for that?"

She could see that both of them knew there was more behind the request than just needing to find Ellers.

"We can do that," he said evenly. "One way or another, we'll stop him, no matter what it takes."

"From your lips to God's ears," Susan murmured. As the pair walked away, she took a deep breath and slowly released it.

Make this count, guys. Because I'm not throwing away my career for nothing.

Cait and Brannon had only been on the path a short time when she felt them being watched. "We got company," she said quietly. "Fifteen or so yards to our left, moving parallel."

"That's our backup, one of my buddies from Veritas. Used to be a SEAL."

"Why the hell wasn't he helping us during the firefight?"

"Iceman just got here. He had the pilot fly him in the moment I sent him the message about the shootings."

"Iceman?" she asked.

"Once you meet him, it'll make sense."

As they approached the shoreline, their escort cut across to meet them. He was as tall as Brannon, built much like him, probably close in age. He had the same intense gaze, the same quiet strength. Curiously, he had a flat silver disk in his right earlobe. She bet there was a story behind that.

"Iceman," Brannon said. "Good to see you."

The man nodded, his eyes on Cait, assessing her in a calculating way.

"Caitlyn, this is Neil MacFayden."

He gave her a curt nod, dismissive, as if she was just dead weight. Why had he dissed her? No matter why, it certainly didn't sit well.

"You're *Neil the SEAL?* What is this, a damned Dr. Seuss book?"

An dark eyebrow rose. "A mouthy female Marine. Now there's something new," he replied, the sarcasm thick. His attention moved back to Brannon. "Sit rep?"

Situation report. This guy was all business.

"Intel says that Ellers might have a staging area south of here. He needed someplace to store the C-4. We think his target is Atlanta."

Neil grunted, then headed toward one of the Jon boats and began readying it for departure.

"Short on manners, isn't he?" Cait said.

"He can be. He suspects there's something between us."

"How could he know that?"

"Neil can suss out that kind of thing, and it makes him nervous."

"Why?" she asked.

"Just does. It's the way he is."

"Well, as long he's not in my face, I don't care. But I won't tolerate disrespect, not even from a friend of yours."

Brannon smiled at her now. "Didn't expect you would, Sergeant."

"You two going to stand there all damned day?" Neil called out.

"Yeah, that's the Iceman for you," Brannon said, chuckling.

"As long as he watches our six . . . " Cait replied.

"*That* we can always count on."

Chapter Twenty-Nine

The trip south went smoothly, and fortunately they'd encountered no one else along the way. Neil sat in the front of the boat, a sniper rifle resting on his lap. Cait was in the rear, while Brannon sat in the middle, navigating. None of them was in the mood for conversation, each getting into the zone.

As agreed, they disembarked on the northern end of the hammock where Rafferty had said the camp was located, and hiked in.

"I'll take point," Cait said from a good thirty feet in front of them. Brannon suspected it was her way of putting distance between her and Iceman.

Fifteen minutes into the hike, Neil asked in a low voice, "You two hooked up?"

Brannon nodded. "Didn't see it coming, that's for sure. She's . . . amazing. One helluva woman."

His friend shook his head in despair. "First Morgan takes a round to her heart because of the White Knight, and now you? What the hell is going on? And *please* don't tell me it's love, because that's just bullshit."

"Cynical as always, my friend."

"No, that's reality."

Brannon could say he was falling for a woman who had more personal demons than he did, but he wouldn't bother. Neil wouldn't get it. Or if he did, he wouldn't admit it. Cait was everything Brannon had ever wanted. Everything he'd hoped to find and thought he never would.

When he didn't answer, Neil muttered under his breath,

"Come on, buddy, she's just messing with your head."

Brannon frowned. "Your Iceman armor is getting a little too thick, bro. Dial it down a few notches, okay?"

"I'm just saying that you have to watch yourself."

"Oh, like you and Alex's sister? I heard you gave Miri a kitten, and she even *named* it after you. That true?"

Neil's sour expression told him he'd hit home. "Yeah. What of it?"

"She's a hottie. Can't argue that."

The look in his friend's eyes changed from annoyed to possessive. That was rare. Unheard of, even.

"We have nothing in common," his friend hissed. "I haven't seen her since . . . the New Orleans mission. Plan to keep it that way."

Nothing in common except a cat, and that Miri seemed to be a very easy button to push.

Well, I'll be damned. Who's messing with whose head now?

Cait had stopped. She pointed upward. "Copter."

"I don't hear anything," Neil said.

"Wait for it."

It was another five seconds before the sound reached Brannon's ears.

"Damn," Neil muttered. "She's got good hearing."

Which meant it was likely she'd heard every word of his conversation with Iceman, and that didn't trouble Brannon at all.

"It's coming from behind us," she said, hunkering down. He and Neil did the same and a short time later, the helicopter flew past.

"Park Service," she said, rising. "Running lower than you'd expect."

"Rafferty said there was a clearing near the cabin. But why would it head there?" Brannon asked.

"Maybe the pilot doesn't have a choice," Neil replied.

They traded looks and then all three took off at a trot.

✦ ❖ ✦

It was almost a quarter of an hour later when they reached the clearing. Once there, Neil insisted on reconnoitering the location on his own.

"Is he always like that?" Cait asked.

"Yeah, that's Iceman for you." Brannon leaned over and placed a kiss on Cait's cheek.

"Why did you do that?" she asked, puzzled.

"Because I wanted to remind myself that there's more in life besides battles." To his dismay, her eyes grew sad. "Hey, what's wrong?"

"Not sure. Seeing those people die, it stirred up some stuff. Bad stuff."

He lightly brushed a finger down her cheek. "Don't give that bastard inside your head any more real estate. He's got enough as it is." She shrugged. "Just hang in there. When this is done, it'll be just you and me."

Her frown began even before he'd finished. "When this is done, if we're not dead, you're headed to jail. For a very long time. Did you forget that part?"

He sighed. "Maybe. Maybe not. We'll see. Don't give up on us just yet."

Cait began to protest, but Neil's return, near silent as it was, ended the conversation. He studied them both, then shook his head.

"What did you find?" Brannon asked, not in the mood for his friend's judgmental behavior.

"Four tangos and a chopper pilot in a Park Service uniform. Sounds like he's a hostage, not a true believer. Both Ellers and his nephew are here. I recognized them from the photos. They're loading weapons from a cabin near the clearing."

"Okay," Brannon said. "Caitlyn, can you secure the cabin?"

"Roger that."

"Iceman? We need a diversion, something that will pull them down our way," he said. "That way the sergeant will have a fairly clear field near the chopper."

"You want me to blow the cache if we can't bag Ellers?" she asked.

He raised an eyebrow at Neil. The man nodded in response.

"That's a go, but make sure we all have time to get clear. No matter what, this asshole does not leave the swamp with those weapons."

"Then let's make that a reality," she replied.

While Brannon remained in place closer to the water, Neil and Cait headed north, skirting along the eastern edge of the clearing. Voices reached them: Ellers issuing orders, grumbles from some of the men. James seemed to be helping with the loading, but only because his uncle insisted. He kept looking inside the copter, probably keeping an eye on the pilot.

As they ghosted through the woods, he'd remained taciturn, which didn't bother her. He had his head in the game. When she and the former SEAL reached the point at which she would continue on alone, he shot her a look.

"Don't fuck this up, *wook*," he said, his voice cold.

She glowered at him, instantly angry. Wook stood for Wookiee Monster, a play on WM, Woman Marine. He was dissing her again, and she'd had it with the jerk.

Don't fuck this up? She shoved him back with a hand. "Same to you, *guppy*."

Neil's eyes grew round at the insult. Before he could reply, Cait moved away. She wasn't sure if the attitude was because she was a female Marine, or because of Brannon. It would be easy to believe it was the former, but she suspected it was because of his buddy.

Pushing the encounter to the back of her mind, Cait took the long way around, moving quietly through the woods, careful not to step on anything that would make noise. The helicopter sat in the center of the open space, engine off. Some twenty yards away was the ramshackle cabin, its door open. Two men carried out a wooden crate and judging from the way they struggled, it was heavy. Probably the C-4. As she scoped out the site, she saw three more crates stacked near the copter. A terse conversation was going on between the copter pilot and Ellers. The park ranger was pale and sweaty, just what you'd expect if he'd been hijacked.

"Look, I don't know what you guys are up to, but you can't just kidnap a park ranger. We're federal employees."

"I don't acknowledge your government. All you need to know is that you're here for one purpose: to fly this bird wherever I tell you. Or I will shoot you and leave your body for the gators. Understand?"

The ranger shook his head in despair. "What's in those crates?"

"Explosives."

Now the man went ashen. "Are you crazy?"

Ellers laughed. "I've been told that." He waved at his men. "Get it all loaded." The closest carton was hefted up and carried inside the chopper.

"What? No," the pilot protested. "That's too much weight. This isn't a damned Sikorsky!"

"James?" The commander's nephew stepped out of the copter. "Explain to this fool what he's going to do. If he gives you any shit, kill him. I'm done wasting my time on him."

The pilot stepped back, shaking.

"Come on," James said, grabbing the guy's arm. "Let's go look at all those pretty instruments."

"Get the Tannerite loaded next," the commander ordered. "Move it! We need to get out of here."

Tannerite and *C-4?* This guy knew how to throw a party.

Once she was sure she was in the clear, Cait sprinted to the side of the cabin. Edging up on her toes, she took a quick peek through the window, whatever glass had been there long gone. Three 55-gallon drums sat near the door, the Tannerite

The explosive was designed for firearms practice, in particular for long-range shooting, allowing the shooter to know whether they'd hit the target. But in sufficient quantities it made a very nasty bomb, one that could easily be detonated with a single high-velocity bullet.

Cait ducked down as men entered the cabin and removed the barrels. That left the place empty. She leveraged herself up and inside. Well, not quite empty. Right beneath her was a wooden crate, its lid open, and inside were M67 grenades. Ellers could do a lot of damage with these beauties.

So can I. She picked up a grenade and carefully tucked it into a cargo pocket, only needing one for what she had in mind. After a quick look outside, Cait positioned herself to the left of the open door, out of sight. The location gave her a good view of the rear of the copter.

Get on with it, SEAL.

As if in response, there was the sound of rapid gunfire. Cait stepped into the doorway, in case any of them retreated to the cabin. Instead, Ellers ordered all of his men, except James, into the woods to deal with the attackers.

In the distance, she saw a grim figure stalk one of the militiamen, then Brannon rammed his knife into the base of the tango's neck. The man was dead before he hit the ground. Another fell, cut down by Iceman's sniper fire.

"Spin this bird up!" Ellers shouted. "James, get in the copter!"

As his nephew ducked around the side and into the chopper, two of the commander's men retreated, firing wildly behind them. One went down, but the other kept shooting. As he drew closer, Ellers leaned out and put a bullet in him. Stunned, the man staggered for a few steps, then crashed into the dirt.

"That's one way to lighten the load," she muttered.

Knowing she had little time, Cait sprinted out of the cabin, then crept around to the other side of the cockpit. Just as the engine kicked in and the rotors slowly began to turn, she yanked open the door. The pilot glanced over at her, his eyes wide.

"Out!" she ordered. After cutting the engine, the ranger scrambled across the equipment. The instant he reached the ground, he took off into the woods. Cait trotted behind him, smiling to herself. Unless Ellers could fly one of those things, he was stuck.

The park ranger abruptly stopped, and she nearly barreled into him. "Keep going!"

"No, you've got to get the girl out of the copter."

"What girl?"

"The younger guy had her all tied up. She was scared out of her mind."

"Blond hair with a blue streak?" He nodded.

Patti.

Brannon and Neil had rejoined forces after efficiently neutralizing Ellers's men. Now they only needed the commander and his nephew, either alive, or in body bags.

"Can you take the shot?" Brannon asked.

"Negative on tango one," Neil said, his sniper rifle positioned on the tripod in front of him. "Ellers knows how to keep hidden. Where the hell is your Marine?"

"Don't worry, *my Marine* is out there. She'll move when she's ready."

Neil huffed, his attention not moving from the scope.

Brannon repositioned his field glasses. "Pilot is no longer in the cockpit." Which meant Cait must have found a way to pull him out of danger.

"Still no go on tango one."

The rotors picked up speed now. Puzzled, Brannon rechecked the cockpit. Someone had climbed in from the back. "We've got a new pilot, Ellers's nephew."

Why the hell didn't Veritas know he could fly a chopper?

"You want me to take him out?"

Brannon was just about to give the order when Ellers moved to the side door. In front of him was a terrified Patti, his gun to her head.

"Back off, or I'll kill her!" the man shouted.

"Dammit! What the hell is she doing here?" Brannon hesitated. "You got a clean shot?"

"Negative," Neil replied.

The rotors picked up speed, jostling both Ellers and his hostage as the chopper lurched up from the ground.

"Brannon?" Iceman said quietly.

This was on his head. Did they kill James and hope Patti survived the crash? Would that crash set off the explosives, in which case almost all of them would die?

But if he let Ellers go to spare the girl . . .

Where the hell are you, Caitlyn?

As the copter began to rise, Cait ran toward the craft at top speed. It'd already cleared the ground when she launched herself at the far landing skid. One hand got hold of it, and she dangled for a moment until her other hand found purchase. As the copter picked up speed, the rotor wash slashed across her, eager to toss her aside like a stray leaf.

Above her, Ellers stood behind Patti, using her as a shield, which meant that James must be the pilot. A gag hung loose around Patti's neck, and it appeared that she'd managed to loosen the ropes at her wrists. The wind wiped her hair in all directions and there was stark terror in her eyes. Fortunately, the commander was too focused on Neil and Brannon to notice his extra passenger. Now, it wasn't just a matter of stopping Ellers: She had to get the girl to safety.

The helicopter had barely passed over the shoreline when it lurched like a drunk at a frat party. Ellers lost his balance and fell backward, as Patti grabbed onto the doorway. Something inside broke free. The commander shouted as one of the barrels of Tannerite rolled toward the door and plummeted out of sight, barely missing her and Patti.

The copter lurched sideways again. The park ranger's warning had come true: The thing was overloaded. Cait looked down and found that they were over open water now, maybe fifty feet from the shore. It was time to get the girl out of here.

"Patti!" she shouted. "Patti!"

From her place at the open door, the teen finally saw her, her eyes widening in surprise.

"Go!" she shouted, pointing down. The girl shook her head. "Jump!"

Patti looked over her shoulder, then back. In what had to be the hardest decision of her life, she reached out a shaking hand. Sidling along the landing skid, Cait grabbed onto it and helped her down to the first skid, then the second.

"Go!" Cait commanded.

To her relief, she jumped, tucking into a ball as she headed for the water below. If the guys got to her quick, before any alligators had a chance to sniff her out, she'd probably be okay. Once Patti's head reappeared above the water and she began swimming for shore, Cait turned back to the problem at hand.

The SEAL wouldn't make the shot as long as she was on board. Brannon wouldn't let him. If the sniper missed, Ellers would be taking his war to Atlanta. There was only one sure way . . .

The grenade's explosive range was adequate to destroy the copter, and the murderers inside. It took some effort to free the grenade from her pocket and flick off the safety clip. Once she pulled the pin and released the "spoon," she'd have four or five seconds, tops, to hit the water before the thing exploded.

As Cait turned to lob the grenade inside the copter, Ellers regained his feet. He stared at her in confusion for a split second, and then it registered what she held in her hand. Even before she could pull the pin, he fired at her. The round barely grazed the top of her left shoulder, making her lose hold of the grenade in her bid to keep from falling. She cursed as it tumbled out of sight.

A sudden burst of speed pitched her enemy onto his knees and forced her to cling to the skid with both hands. Her way forward was clear now, and somehow, Cait had always known it would end like this, that fate would stack the deck against her. Once it was over, the darkness would no longer stalk her. No more nightmares, no more hoarse screams in the dead of night, no more Jeremy forever dying in her arms.

The microseconds ticked down, agonizingly slow. She knew Brannon was on the shoreline now, even if she couldn't see him, and she knew he was watching her through his field glasses, caught in a hell from which there was no escape. Would her death haunt him for the rest of his days? Would he see her in his dreams, fragmenting into a bloody cloud?

The darkness licked at her again, tasting her indecision, making her hand cramp around the Glock. One shot into the barrel of Tannerite and it would all be over.

Looking toward the man on the shore, she mouthed. "I love you." It was a pity he'd never hear it from her in person.

NO! It was as if he'd shouted in her ear.

NO! Suddenly, that became *her* word. She didn't want to die. She craved Brannon's love, his endless light, and to have it she needed to live.

As Ellers came to his feet, sighting down at her with his weapon, she arched up, sending a single bullet into the center of his forehead. As he fell, his Glock barked once, then twice.

On instinct, Cait threw herself backward into the air, tucking into a cannonball. As she plummeted toward the dark water, she prayed she'd been given a little more time.

Chapter Thirty

Brannon's field glasses tracked the copter from the shoreline as it headed across the water. Someone jumped. He followed the body and when it surfaced, reported, "The girl, Patti, she's in the water. Caitlyn's still on the landing skid."

"I can disable the copter, but time is running out," Neil warned.

Brannon swore. "Get the hell off that copter. Jump, damn you, jump!"

But he knew she wasn't thinking of life, only of stopping the enemy. She turned toward him now, wind blowing her hair in all directions. He saw her lips move, and though he wasn't sure what she said, he knew what it meant.

"No!" Brannon shouted.

A gunshot, then more, followed by a sharp, primary explosion that rent the air.

"Get down!" Neil cried. They sprawled on the shoreline, covering their heads. The secondary explosion was deeper, nearly deafening, as the C-4's concussion wave rolled outward from the copter, spraying them with dirt, branches, and other debris. Closer to the site, trees splintered and uprooted, their trunks falling with solid thumps as they fell.

Brannon pulled up the field glasses with quaking hands, watching as the helicopter disintegrated into hundreds of flaming metal shards, roaring outward like an exploding star. The rotors sheared off and sliced through the air like scythes. He was on his knees even before the wreckage plunged into the water.

"No, Caitlyn! No!" He pounded the dirt with his fists, furious. How could she do this to him? Why hadn't she given them a chance?

Neil's hand gently touched his shoulder. "Jesus, man," he said. "I can't believe she did that."

His breath heaving, Brannon shook his head. "She said she was afraid of living."

"Too many of us are," his friend replied. He looked out onto the water. "We gotta get the girl before some gator does. If she's still alive. That was one hell of an explosion."

Iceman was right, and the realization forced Brannon to his feet. No more bright smiles, no more touching her face, holding her, loving her. He knew what it took to go on, hiding the grief, saving it for later. But this time, it was Caitlyn. Her loss might be more than he could bear.

Neil took the field glasses from him and searched through the thick smoke in the distance. "The girl looks uninjured." He hesitated. "At least one of them made it."

"Yeah, at least one."

There was a loud splash. Brannon jerked his gaze toward the water. "Gator?" he said, his hand reaching for his weapon.

"No," he said, a smile appearing. "Something much better."

Another splash.

"Ooh-rah!" a voice shouted, followed by a hearty round of coughing.

"Caitlyn?" He desperately tried to find her through the smoke and burning patches of aviation fuel on the water.

"There!" Neil said, handing him the field glasses.

Brannon scanned the water and found her. She treaded water, then flipped onto her back, floating and kicking her feet as if she were on vacation at the beach. He knew what she was feeling: the joy of life.

They were in a boat and crossing the water before Brannon could even catch his breath. First, Patti came on board, and then they headed toward Cait's location.

"Is she okay?" the girl asked. She sat near Neil, a sizable bruise on her right cheek and her hair plastered to her face.

"We'll find out. What about you?"

"I'm good. Did you see her? She blew them right out of the air. Take that, you assholes!" she said, executing a fist pump.

The rare sound of laughter came from his friend and Brannon couldn't help but join in. Then, as they came closer to the woman he loved, his eyes filled with tears. He could probably blame it on the burning fuel later, but in his heart he knew the truth. She'd chosen life. Now it was up to him to make sure she'd never regret that.

Despite the burning fuel nearby, it was oddly peaceful on the water. Cait hadn't expected to survive the blast, but luckily the water had shielded her from the worst of the explosion. Even then, the concussion wave had rammed into her, churning up mud and other debris.

Once it had ended, it'd taken time to determine where the surface was, since it wasn't clearly visible. A civilian would have panicked, but the Marines had trained her for this, in full gear no less. Cait readily fell back on that training—and survived.

She relished each breath, each ache, each lap of the water against her body. It all meant she was alive. The dark voice inside her head was oddly silent now, cowed into submission. She made a vow to try to keep it that way.

The sound of a boat engine intruded on her tranquility. When it abruptly cut out, hands pulled at her and she let them do whatever they wished. As she was helped inside the boat, she caught sight of Patti. They'd both made it. Cait's rucksack was removed and then she was cradled by arms she knew as well as her own.

"Sit rep?" Neil called out.

She coughed. "Wet, sore, but Oscar Mike." *Operationally mobile.*

"You got a death wish, Marine?" he asked, eyeing her closely.

This time there was no derision, only respect. Though Neil had asked the question, she looked up into Brannon's deep brown eyes. "No, not anymore."

With that admission came a curiously light feeling, like shaking off a heavy pack at the end of a thirty-mile forced march.

"Damn glad to hear it," her lover whispered in her ear.

"Cait?" Patti said. She turned so she could see the girl. "Thanks for saving my life."

"Sure thing." Other than a large bruise on her cheek and being soaking wet, Patti didn't look any worse for the wear. But sometimes outward signs didn't tell the whole story. "You okay?"

"Yeah."

"Honest? He didn't hurt you, did he?"

"No," she said, even as she touched her face. "Not like that."

"Thank God."

"That was an impressive jump, young lady," Brannon said.

Patti shrugged as if it'd been no big deal. "I'm on my high-school swim team. I'm really good at diving."

"That was still one helluva jump," Cait replied. "How'd James get you out of the camp?"

"It was right after the shooting stopped. I was helping one of the women who'd been hurt, and he put a gun in my back. Told me if I didn't go with him, he'd kill me and the poor lady. I believed him."

"Why didn't she tell us he took you?"

"He hit her on the head. I hope she's all right."

"I thought he left before Ellers did," Brannon said.

"The dickwad came back for me. He seemed to think I was his personal possession. His uncle was way pissed, but James refused to leave me behind." She sighed. "You know, I'm not the least bit upset he got his ass blown up."

"You're not going to find anyone in this boat who'd argue with you on that," Brannon replied.

They fell silent for a time as they returned to the landing. The debris in the water made it difficult to keep from fouling the prop, but Neil had it handled.

"You didn't give up," Brannon whispered in Cait's ear. He hugged her tightly. "Thank you. You gave us a chance. I promise not to screw it up."

Hopefully she could do the same.

Unaware of their private conversation, Neil asked, "Any chance Ellers survived that blast?"

Cait eyed the former SEAL. "Not with a bullet in the center of his forehead." Neil frowned. "Surprise! The gyrene didn't fuck it up."

This time he grimaced. "Sometimes, I don't know what the hell I'm talking about."

"Already figured that one out. But apology accepted anyway."

He huffed, then ignored her.

Cait wondered what had caused him to retreat behind those walls of his, and if anything, or anyone, would ever break them down.

Once on shore, Brannon stepped away from the others and phoned Veritas, knowing it might not be wise to call Susan directly. He didn't want to generate any more flak for the agent; she'd risked enough on his behalf.

"That's damned fine news," Morgan said, relief coming through every word. "You guys okay?"

"We're good." His eyes tracked the billowing smoke. "The park rangers are going to be majorly pissed, though. We made a big mess down here."

"Far better than having Ellers get to Atlanta. God knows what he had planned."

"Thanks for sending the Iceman as backup. He made all the difference."

"Good. What are you going to do about the FBI?"

"I'll turn myself in. I don't have much of a choice."

"Actually, you do." A lengthy pause followed. "Crispin will ensure that you get a new identity and sufficient funds to start over wherever you want."

Jesus. The man always had their backs.

"That's too dangerous for him, and for Veritas. I don't want this to compromise what we do. It's too important."

"He told me you'd say that. Then you'll get the best legal support we can find."

"That works." He stepped away from the others. "There's another thing you could do for me."

"Name it."

He explained what he'd like done for Cait.

"I'll take care of it personally."

"Thank you. That means so much to me," Brannon said, his heart heavy with unspoken emotion. "She's very important to me."

"Sounds like it, Bran. You stay safe."

"See you soon, Valkyrie."

Or at least, he hoped so.

Brannon returned to the others and was greeted by curious expressions. Patti was sucking down a bottle of water and Cait had her boots off, wringing out her socks.

"The FBI should be arriving at the compound right about now," he announced. "Morgan will call our favorite FBI agent, so she knows that the tangos are neutralized and Patti is safe. And she'll call the Park Service about the helicopter crash so they know about the fire."

Neil looked up at the cloud of dense black smoke ascending into the air. "Like they could miss it."

"Hey, 'mess with the best, die like the rest,'" Cait said.

"Right, but 'Rangers lead the way,'" Brannon replied, egging her on.

"Ha! Only after a Marine shows them how to read the damned map."

Neil snorted and slapped Brannon on the back. "You are screwed, my friend. So screwed." He quickly shifted back to business. "I'll hang here, find our missing pilot, make sure he's okay."

"There's a case of grenades in the cabin," Cait said. "Might be best if they don't go wandering off."

"Roger that."

Brannon removed his rucksack, stored his sheathed knife inside, then offered it to Neil. "Keep it for me, will you? I'll need it down the line."

Iceman hesitated, then hefted it onto a shoulder. "I take it this means you're turning yourself in."

"Have to. I'm not going on the run. I just hope the boss man is able to work out a miracle."

"You're not the only one."

"Thanks, man. I owe you."

"Yes, you do." Neil gave a nod to the women, then walked off into the woods.

Once he was out of earshot, Patti gasped. "Ohmigod! Is he cute or what? I didn't know guys like that were for real. Now there're two of you. Just. Wow. Nobody is going to believe me when I tell them about all this."

Brannon smiled at the compliment, but couldn't help but notice that Cait's eyes had saddened.

"Veritas will do everything they can to keep me out of jail," he said as they loaded back into the boat.

"They damned well better," she said tersely. "If not, it'll be up to me."

Chapter Thirty-One

From the moment they'd heard the blast, felt the ground shudder underneath them, Susan had feared she'd lost them all. It'd been even worse after she'd learned that Patti had vanished. She knew the girl hadn't taken off on her own, and eventually that had been confirmed when one of the wounded women told them what had happened to the teen.

Now, as she ended the call with someone named Morgan at Veritas, Susan sagged in relief, far closer to tears than she had been in a long time. Ellers was dead and so was his nephew. Patti had been rescued and the explosives were history. Cait and Brannon were unharmed and Atlanta was safe.

"Susan?" Preston asked. "What's happened? What was that explosion?"

She smiled at those crowded around her. Her eyes sought out Rafferty, the man who'd taken a huge gamble on their behalf. "That was the sound of true freedom," she murmured.

Then she told them what had happened, and there were cheers—at least from the tourists. For some of those in the compound, the news was sobering.

"Now what?" Rafferty asked.

"Now we pick up the pieces and start over," she said.

Susan took a deep breath, issued a silent prayer, and waited as the advance team walked up the path toward the compound. Behind her were Ellers's people, and they were still armed. She hadn't expected to go any other way: Their leader had taught them that trust came at a high price, often one involving the death of a loved one. Now it was Susan's job to convince the FBI to treat them like victims, not enemies.

She walked out the front gates of the compound, holding up her badge, trying not to shake. The lives of so many people depended on her, and that scared the hell out of her. One wrong word, one wrong move, and this place could descend into a war zone. The advance team halted as she approached. They were all in tactical gear, except for one. A familiar face smiled back at her.

"Britelli," she said, nodding at her partner.

"Driscoll. Good to see you in one piece."

Joseph Britelli was a second-generation Italian and the best partner she'd ever had. The fact that he was here gave her hope.

An older Black man stepped forward. "I'm Special Agent McDonald from the D.C. office. What's the situation here?"

"You know about the shootings?" The man nodded. "And that Ellers is dead?" Another nod. "The current situation is volatile. We have multiple wounded, some dead. These people were ambushed by their own leader. Right now, they wouldn't trust God Himself if He came down in a flaming chariot."

The agent blinked.

"So this can go bad in a heartbeat," she continued, "as in Waco or Ruby Ridge bad, if you get my meaning."

The agent nodded curtly. "So what do you suggest?"

"We send in the medical team first so they can treat the wounded, evacuate them. While they're doing that, you, Britelli, and I will talk to the folks who are in charge of this group. I think that if we do this carefully no one else has to die."

McDonald raised an eyebrow. "How do I know they won't come down on us the moment we're in there?"

"The fact that they have wounded family members. I'm not saying we shouldn't stay vigilant, because there might be one hothead in there somewhere, but the rest of them are scared out of their minds. They've watched their husbands, their wives, their kids die. They just want to get out of here."

McDonald heaved a sigh. "What else did you promise them?"

She couldn't stop the grin. "How do you know I did?"

"We're not being shot at . . . yet."

"I promised them I would do everything I could to ensure that they aren't treated as felons. They got caught up in one man's insane vision and they regret it."

"They've broken a ton of federal laws," one of the other agents grumbled.

"Yeah, they have. We've all been in a situation that went bad and had no idea how it got that way. I certainly have. These guys have too. They want a chance to start over."

"They'll have to be interviewed, and if there are any outstanding warrants—"

"They know that," she cut in, though it was rude. She was too keyed up to be polite. "We have a chance to prove we are fair minded, not the brownshirts the militias keep claiming we are."

McDonald ran a beefy hand through his cropped hair, thinking. "Okay, you got it. One shot and this is going Wild West, you understand?"

"Yes. I'll go tell them."

Susan walked back to the compound, her heart pounding and her throat dry. As she entered the front gates, she found every eye on her. She stopped in front of the group, raising her voice so she could be heard.

"They're bringing in the medical team. You people keep it cool, they will do the same. If not, there's going to be more blood spilled today. None of us want that." She looked at Rafferty now and beckoned him to join her as she walked toward the makeshift hospital. "If there is anyone you think might want to start a war, corral them now."

"Already done," the man said.

She realized how much she owed this guy. "Thank you."

As he walked back to join his people, she gave a thumbs-up to McDonald. He made a call on his radio and within a few minutes, the medical team descended on the compound. He and the others followed in their wake, on edge.

"Welcome to New America," Susan said, eyeing the agent. "One man's dream is another man's nightmare."

"Hell, isn't that the truth. So where's Hardegree? We've got a warrant for his arrest."

Before she could tell him that she wasn't exactly sure where the former Ranger was at the moment, McDonald's phone rang. He answered, frowned, then gave an order. When he'd ended the call, he zeroed in on Susan.

"Seems our fugitive has just turned himself in down by the boats. Care to explain why he's not inside the compound, under lock and key?"

"Because he and Caitlyn Landry were hunting Ellers. Since he was an Army Ranger, and she was a Marine, they had the best chance of stopping that bastard. And they did."

The frown on McDonald's face deepened. "You're damned lucky Hardegree turned himself in."

"I was willing to risk losing him if it kept those explosives away from Atlanta."

He snorted. "So what we've heard about you is true—you don't play by the rules."

"Only when I have to," Susan said, turning away.

As Cait and Brannon were escorted toward the compound, they met stretchers headed to the shoreline. It took three people to handle each stretcher—two to carry the victim, and one for the IV bags. At the waterline, the victim was raised into a hovering chopper via a Stokes basket to be treated by emergency personnel onboard. Once the chopper was loaded, it would fly off and another would move in.

"Gotta give them one thing, they know how to handle mass casualties," Cait said.

"Probably learned it from us. We're the experts," Brannon said. He walked just ahead of them, handcuffed and flanked by two agents.

Patti nudged Cait. "They have to let him go. Right?"

The optimism of the young. The teen hadn't yet learned that bureaucracy had its own brand of cynicism that often crushed the good along with the bad. "We'll see," Cait replied.

As they entered the compound, the area in front of them was full of people. Some had a few possessions at their feet, awaiting relocation, others had gathered near their wounded, watching as they received medical treatment. One young woman wept as she cradled a man, most likely her husband. From the stark grief on her face, she was now a widow.

Susan stood in the middle of a group of heavily armed men. She looked exhausted, which was pretty much the norm for all of them. Rafferty was next to her, arguing with one of the agents about something.

Susan turned toward them as they approached. "Special Agent McDonald," she said, gesturing at Cait and Brannon now. "These are the folks who took Ellers down."

Five sets of solemn eyes studied them.

"You sure he's dead?" McDonald asked. He didn't look like he put up with any shit.

"Very dead," Cait replied.

"I hear he stole a Park Service helicopter. Pilot dead, too?"

"No, it was Ellers's nephew flying the chopper when it blew."

"And just why did it blow up?"

"A bullet just happened to hit a barrel of Tannerite."

"Your bullet?" the man asked.

She smiled. "Nope, it was Ellers's. Which proves that karma really does work."

That remark seemed to confuse the agent. "We'll get into that later. Lock Hardegree up," he said to the two agents holding Brannon. "I don't want him wandering off again."

Somehow, Susan kept her face neutral, though clearly that had been a slap in her direction.

Brannon looked back at Cait. "Keep those home fires burning, okay?"

"Always."

As he was led away, Susan pulled Cait away from the others. "I'll make sure my report details everything he did for us."

"Will it make any difference?"

"I don't know. Veritas has a lot of clout. I'm hoping it's enough in this case."

And if not . . . "How hard is it to break someone out of federal prison?" Cait asked.

The agent started at the question. "Please promise me you're joking."

Cait walked away without replying. She knew better than to make a promise she might not keep.

She found the other campers in the mess hall, drinking coffee, listening to Patti tell them about Ellers and James and the helicopter explosion. Patti had just gotten to the crucial part where everything was about to blow up when the others noticed Cait. They descended on her in a flood, sharing backslaps and smiles. Even Keith hugged her.

She sat between Bill and Patti. Preston and Keith were on the other side of the table.

"When we heard that explosion, I was afraid I'd never see you guys again," Bill said.

"We got lucky. And we had some help." *From a hardass named Neil.*

"What are they going to do with Brannon?" Keith asked. "I saw them hauling him off in cuffs."

"I have no idea," she admitted.

"He was really undercover?" Preston asked.

"Yes. Had me fooled for a while," Cait said.

Without asking, Patti brought her coffee and a slice of pie. It was apple. Realizing it'd been some time since she'd eaten, Cait demolished it in a few bites.

"Another slice?"

"No, that's okay. Thanks." She looked over at the others now. "Brannon will need all the support he can get."

"He's got it," Keith said. Nods came from the rest. "We'll

make sure to tell the FBI everything that happened, what he did for all of us."

It was good to hear that they were on the Ranger's side. He'd taken tremendous personal risks and never fallen short of his duty. He deserved his freedom and the recognition that came with such a dangerous mission.

But more than that, she knew he'd rescued her. Now it was time for her to do the same for him.

It was late in the afternoon when the moment that Brannon had been dreading finally arrived. Transportation to Jacksonville had been arranged so he could face charges related to the armed robbery. Cait and the others were being sent to Atlanta for a "debriefing."

This might be the last time he'd ever see her, at least until his trial. He didn't know how she did it, but Susan made sure they had some time with each other right before he left. Even though they weren't somewhere private, he hooked his arms around Cait, pulling her close, the handcuffs still in place.

"Don't let the darkness gain any ground," he whispered. "You beat it back and keep it there. You're too special to lose, Caitlyn."

She looked up at him, her rust-brown eyes damp. "I owe you my life," she whispered. "You saved me."

"That saving went both ways, honey."

"Not from where I'm standing."

"Trust me, I know what I'm talking about."

Brannon kissed her, savoring the moment, fearing he'd never do this again. Then he reluctantly let her go.

Looking over at the disgruntled FBI agent, who clearly saw this emotional display as a waste of time, he gave a nod.

"Let's get this done."

As he walked out of the gates, he looked back over his shoulder. The other campers were lined up. Patti was crying. Susan looked resigned. He didn't fault her, she'd done her best for him.

"Rangers lead the way!" Cait shouted, giving him a crisp salute.

"*Semper Fi!*" he called back.

Then he saw the tears on her cheeks and he knew his heart would always belong to her.

Chapter Thirty-Two

Monday, April 20th
Eastern Kentucky

It had been over two days since she'd last seen Brannon, last been kissed by him. During that time Cait had slept, eaten a few meals, downed a lot of Advil, and endured endless "debriefings." The others on the tour had been questioned and sent home, but not her. To her surprise, she'd heard that Brannon had been transferred to Atlanta, so for all she knew, he could even be in the same building as her. She knew better than to ask to see him.

His transfer meant that she now had a lawyer sitting in the meetings with her, a woman from Veritas. Morgan Blake was formerly with the FBI, but that didn't seem to help in this case. Cait liked her instantly—she was solidly in Brannon's corner and that meant she was good people.

The problem was Special Agent in Charge Maxine Rhodes, the head of the Atlanta FBI office. A woman in her early fifties with graying hair and no sense of humor, she came at Cait like a pissed-off hornet. Rhodes kept picking at Cait's testimony like a small kid worries a bandage, apparently hoping to find something to use against Brannon. That put her on Cait's enemy list.

Rhodes's attitude hadn't improved with all the increased pressure. Not only was Veritas pushing for Brannon's release, but it also seemed that Cait's call to her dad had led to certain Army brass expressing their "concerns." Loudly. Brass was always good at that. First Lieutenant Brannon Hardegree had a lot of admirers, and they were all trying to free him.

Cait's latest session with the FBI included not only Morgan, who'd informed her she was licensed to practice law in Georgia, but Agent Britelli. Susan had been nowhere to be seen, apparently on some sort of "leave." The way Britelli had said the word, it sounded like only one step down from being sent to a Gulag.

"How do we know it wasn't you who disabled Montgomery's car instead of James Gray? That way you could lead the tour group instead of him," Rhodes said. She was in one of her usual power suits and looked as tired as the rest of them.

This was a new tactic, directly implicating Cait in Ellers's activities, and she knew it was pure bull. "Why would I try to harm my former commanding officer, a man I deeply respect?"

"For a share of the robbery money and a chance to meet Quinton Ellers."

Morgan rolled her eyes. "My client had no contact with Hardegree before the tour. Neither has she had contact with any of the domestic militias."

Cait appreciated the backup, but she didn't really need it. Rhodes was blowing smoke and they all knew it. Luckily, she was The Major's daughter, and he'd taught her the skills needed to deal with prickly bureaucrats, whether civilian or military.

Leaning forward, she frowned. "I've given you everything I know about Ellers's operation and Brannon's role in bringing him down. I'm sorry you didn't get a chance to have Ellers do a perp walk in front of the news cameras, but it was either kill him or let him blow up a bunch of innocent folks *in your city*. So which of those do you think is more important: your resume, or the fact that Atlanta isn't a war zone?"

Agent Britelli made a strangled noise.

Her face crimson, Rhodes waved at Morgan. "Get her out of here. I have Hardegree. He's all I need. But if I find your stories don't match *exactly*, you're coming back and we'll be charging you with obstruction."

"Understood. Brannon and I are *not* the enemy, ma'am. You need to remember that."

Once she and Morgan were at the exit leading to the parking lot, Cait swore, fearing she'd pushed too hard. "Damn, maybe I shouldn't have said that."

"Maybe, maybe not." Morgan tossed her a set of keys. They were to her Jeep. "Your ride is in the parking lot. We had it driven up for you."

"Thanks, I appreciate that. I'll get a hotel room somewhere. I don't want to leave Bran, have him think I walked out on him."

"He won't. He asked me to make arrangements for you. In your car, you'll find the directions to his cabin in Kentucky, along with the house keys and the alarm code. He wants you to wait for him there."

"But—"

Morgan was already shaking her head. "Brannon will worry less if he knows you're somewhere safe. And *quiet*."

Just how much had he told this woman about her PTSD? Maybe more than Cait would have wished. She looked up at the ceiling, trying to decide.

The lawyer pressed her advantage. "He's worried about you. If he knows you're okay, it'll help him stay focused through this hell."

The guilt worked. "All right. Remind him that he promised me a weekend in a fancy hotel."

"I'll do that. Now go on before Rhodes changes her mind. Oh, and text me when you're settled up there. Brannon will want to know you're safe. He'll plague me until I tell him that."

That brought a faint smile, as it sounded like him. "I'll let you know. Send my thanks to your boss. I owe him one."

"I will," Morgan replied. "Who knows, maybe someday he'll need to collect on that gratitude."

"Just let me know when and where. I'll be there."

As the doors closed behind her, Cait breathed in the warm

April air, but still shivered. Leaving Brannon behind felt wrong, but she would do what he asked, if only for his peace of mind. She prayed it wasn't a mistake that she'd regret for the rest of her life.

Wednesday, April 22nd
FBI Atlanta Field Office

Brannon shifted his weight in the chair. He was about to endure yet another round of questioning. The transfers back and forth from lockup to the FBI office were getting old, especially sometimes when they made sure the handcuffs were a little too tight. Messing with his head, hoping to get him to crack. It wasn't working. After what he'd endured to become a Ranger, this was kindergarten stuff. But he knew that thirty years in prison wouldn't be.

Morgan took a seat next to him. His friend had been there for every interrogation, no matter how long it took. She'd remained positive, but not ceded any ground to the FBI. They'd found Valkyrie a tough opponent.

"Any news from Caitlyn?" he asked.

"She said to tell you she loves the cabin, and she's going to stay put until you show up," she replied. "She's been calling folks, as well. Her dad has rattled some cages at the Pentagon, no less."

"I can imagine. I've heard The Major is pretty formidable. Like our boss." He laid his hands on the table, still in handcuffs. "I'm glad she went to the cabin. It'll be good for her. She can recharge there, not lose any ground."

Something in his tone made Morgan look up. "How bad was she?"

"She planned on dying along with Ellers. Something stopped her from taking that final step."

"That something being you," his friend replied. It hadn't been a question.

"Yes. I almost lost her. You know what that's like."

Morgan nodded. "But you didn't. Now we just need to get you out of here."

"What are our chances?"

"The longer it goes, the better."

That was just the opposite than what he'd figured. In fact, Brannon's hope had dimmed with each passing day. His birthday had been celebrated in jail. One of the agents in Jacksonville had found it amusing to give him a dry donut out of the vending machine, minus a candle. His parents were freaking out, but so far his father hadn't made the trip up from Florida.

Apparently, Morgan had talked to him and assured him that his son's legal needs were being met. Crispin had called them too, and that had made all the difference. There was no doubt that he trusted Morgan and Veritas, but Brannon's nerves were starting to wear thin. This felt more like a personal vendetta than anything.

The door to the room opened, but this time it was just Britelli, no sign of the office's head honcho. Brannon tried not to read anything into that. The agent laid out his notes, then looked up from them. His tie was loosened and he looked as tired as they were.

"Based on some of your information," he began, "this afternoon we arrested Ellers's Atlanta contact, a Mr. Wiley Davis. The raid on the man's apartment got us the commander's *detailed* plans, including maps of each of the proposed bomb sites."

"What was he going to hit?" Brannon asked.

"One of our federal buildings, to start with. Apparently that was to have been Ellers's homage to the McVeigh bombing." Britelli grimaced. "The barrels of Tannerite and the grenades were headed for a downtown music festival. There would have been upwards of twenty thousand people there, so God knows how many deaths and injuries he would have caused."

"And the ricin?" Morgan asked.

"It was to be put in the iced tea at a Women in Law

Enforcement Conference luncheon. I'm sure all two hundred of the attendees would have just loved that."

"Oh my God," Brannon murmured.

"Yeah. We dodged a massive bullet here." Britelli grinned at this point, which made Brannon wonder what the guy knew that he wasn't sharing.

"About an hour ago, my boss received a call from the deputy director himself. We've been advised that we are to drop all charges against you." Britelli's grin widened now. "It seems our office was unaware that you were working undercover for the D.C. office. But since you had been instructed *not to tell anyone* of your involvement, it wasn't surprising that we were out of the loop."

It took a moment for the agent's words to sink in.

The charges were dropped?

Crispin Wilder must have called in a megaton of favors on Brannon's behalf. How would he ever repay the man? After a quick glance at Morgan, Brannon made sure not to smile, as if this was exactly how it'd been planned.

"I see. Good that got cleared up then," he said. Beside him, his friend nearly levitated with joy.

"Yes, I thought so too," the agent replied, smirking. "My partner was particularly happy to hear the news. Our boss? Not so much."

Morgan stifled a laugh.

"What's happening with Agent Driscoll?"

Britelli's grin vanished. "She's on leave right now. There're some internal issues to work out. I'm hoping they get resolved soon."

"She made all the right calls. If she hadn't, the FBI would be facing a congressional investigation as to why they were involved in a firefight in the swamp. And why they let a terrorist go free."

"I know that. D.C. knows that. Other people are not so . . . understanding."

Brannon growled. "They need to be. She's one helluva agent."

"Amen to that," her partner replied. He pushed the handcuff keys across the table to Morgan so she could do the honors.

"Since you're no longer under arrest, we'd like whatever else you can tell us about Ellers's organization," the man continued. "The contacts you made while you were undercover and on the militia boards. We'd like to track down the rest of his crew and get them behind bars before they decide to blow something up in retaliation for their leader's fiery demise." He looked up. "A fiery demise that I totally applaud, by the way."

Nodding his understanding, Brannon shoved the key and the handcuffs in the agent's direction. "What do you guys need to know?"

Chapter Thirty-Three

The cabin had almost everything Cait needed. If Brannon were here with her, it would be perfect. Though a classic log-cabin design, the inside was modern, with a cozy kitchen, a large living room, and a woodstove. Sliding glass doors led to a wide screened porch, which offered an unobstructed view of the forest beyond. Various bird feeders hung from branches, and a cedar picnic table sat under a broad oak tree near a fire pit.

She could easily imagine Bran out here in the early morning, still in his briefs, coffee in hand as the day began. Or at night, as the sun set behind the trees. This was a place for healing. A place to begin anew. He'd been right to send her here. He knew her better than she did herself.

Cait most loved the evening hours, with the hoots of owls, the foraging of raccoons and other creatures. Deer regularly visited the backyard, and one time she'd seen a fox.

After she'd slept in Brannon's bed, listened to the music on his stereo, read his books, she knew they were kindred spirits. So much alike, it was uncanny. She missed him every second, every minute, every hour. This was love, and she didn't bother to deny it. She'd fled from those emotions before, nearly let them be lost to the darkness inside her.

Never again.

Now, as she ran the five-mile circuit from the cabin to the lake and back along a road bordered by old-growth trees, she thought of him. Morgan had told her to be patient, but that patience was long gone.

Her father had been helping, calling his buddies, putting in a good word. He'd been happy to do so, especially after she'd told The Major what had happened on the tour, and the aftermath. How close she'd come to letting her past kill her and why she'd decided it didn't have that power over her any longer. When she'd finished her story, it was the only time she'd heard him weep.

As Cait entered the final mile back to the cabin, she was in the zone, muscles warm, heart thumping. Behind her came the sound of a car's engine, not a frequent occurrence out here. Unless it was Brannon, she didn't care.

The debriefing had gone on until well past midnight. Britelli had called another agent in and they'd recorded everything Brannon could give them about Ellers and his contacts. Calls had been made so that the Jacksonville and Brunswick offices could lob in their questions, now that he was no longer considered a suspect. Hopefully all that intel would be of value.

Once he was done, he'd asked Britelli to send his best to Susan, then left the FBI behind, his mind only on going home to *her*. He'd intended to call Cait with the good news, but then he had held off. He'd wanted to see her face when she realized he was free. See her smile. Wipe away her tears. After a quick combat nap in Morgan's hotel room, a shower, and some food at an all-night diner at the Tennessee/Kentucky border, he'd completed the drive.

Now, he slowed his car, watching the lithe woman running along the side of the road, her honey-colored hair swinging with each step. She was in a USMC T-shirt and green running shorts, her tanned legs chewing up the pavement. His Caitlyn was beautiful in so many ways.

He drew up alongside her, rolled down the passenger window, and issued a sharp wolf whistle. Cait's head snapped toward him, frown in place, ready to give him a dressing down. Then her eyes registered who it was. As he stopped the car, she leapt at the door.

"Brannon?!" She pulled it open, pushed his rucksack out of the way, and launched herself at him. Her lips were on his, the kiss urgent, heated. He pulled her tight to him, wondering if they dared make love on the spot.

"Oh my God! You're really here," she said, pulling away from him too soon. The frown returned. "Why the hell didn't you call me?"

"I didn't get out of Atlanta until way late. I figured I'd surprise you."

"You should have let me know!"

"You needed your sleep," he said. "The charges were all dropped. I'm a free man again."

With a half sob, she was back in his arms. This time there were no kisses, just tears. Finally, she shut the car door, the tears still rolling down her cheeks. She wiped them away, but more came. Knowing she needed time to regain her composure, he put the car in gear again.

"This morning, the D.C. FBI office will be telling the world how they had an undercover agent in place, one who delivered vital information that prevented a domestic terrorist attack on Atlanta."

Her frown returned yet again. "But that's total BS. You weren't working for them."

"That's the way they'll spin it. It's a win-win for everyone. I don't do hard time, they get the good press, and the rest of the country rests easy. Our names won't be mentioned, so we won't have crazies coming after us."

Cait wiped away the tears again, apparently working through that convoluted bit of fiction. "What about Susan?"

"I'm not sure how that's going to play out. With me out of the way, I'm afraid she's going to take a lot of the heat." When she didn't reply, he added, "I missed you."

That softened her expression. "I missed you, too."

They pulled into the driveway and he turned off the car. He

took her hand. "Do you like the cabin?" he asked.

"It's great. So quiet. No explosions or anything. I could get used to that."

He sobered now. "This whole thing with us happened pretty fast."

She blinked over at him. "If you're saying you want to back away—"

"No! I don't. But I'm not sure where you are in all this. You've had a lot of things happen in a very short period of time."

Cait looked away, and his heart sank. "I need a shower," she said. And then she was out of the car, headed toward the cabin before he could reply.

He watched her unlock the door, then deal with the alarm panel. He wasn't naïve—feelings changed. They'd forged their relationship in fire, but sometimes that kind of attraction cooled very rapidly. Did she want him to be part of her life now? Or was it already over before it'd barely begun?

Brannon retrieved his rucksack and duffle bag from the back of the car, along with a bouquet of flowers he'd picked up along the way. Cait was in the bedroom, so he dropped his gear, locked the door, and found a vase his mom had left behind during one of her visits. The flowers fit nicely. Knowing nowhere else to put it, he set the vase in the middle of the kitchen table. He looked up to see Cait watching him.

"Are those for me?" He nodded. "They're very pretty."

"Like you, then."

"I know this thing between us went really fast. I know I'm a handful and I come with a lot of negatives. But I don't want to lose you," she said.

"Everything you said applies to me too."

"Not as much, Bran." She held out her hand. "Let's start with a shower. I'm a mess after the run."

Clothes seemed to melt off once they were inside the bathroom. He was sure one of his socks ended up in the sink, but he didn't care. His hands roamed over her body, reclaiming, remembering. Hers did the same to him. When she dug her nails into his butt, he almost lost it.

He managed to get the shower going, and then they were under the water, kissing, stroking. When she moaned as he suckled a breast, he knew he was done waiting. Hoisting her up, he pushed her against the tile wall, and then swore.

She reached over into the soap tray and retrieved a foil package. "Thought you Rangers were always prepared."

With a laugh, he took care of business, then returned to her.

It went down fast and hard, both of them crying out as they reached their peaks. Slowly they broke apart, and he kissed her.

"You're mine," he said as the water sluiced over them.

"Claiming me, are you?"

"Do you mind?"

"Not at all."

He leaned his forehead against hers. "Then it was worth it."

A few hours later, they'd finally left his bed and retreated to the porch. Cait's sleeping bag was out there and they settled on it, watching the forest beyond.

She tucked herself up against him. "You slept out here?" he asked.

"Yeah. Your bed's comfortable, but I was here last night. It was so peaceful. I saw a mama bear, with a cub. She was checking out your bird feeders."

In that moment, Brannon saw her with a child in her arms. His child. He'd been thinking long term, *but marriage?* That was beyond him. Wasn't it?

"You okay? You look spooked," she said, gazing up at him.

He saw the worry in her eyes. "I'm just coming to terms with what's happening between us, what it might mean. I want us to be together as long as its good for both of us." He hesitated, wanting to get the words right. "God, Caitlyn, you've come to mean so much to me so quickly, I'm . . . hell, I'm scared."

She looked down at the floor now. "Me too."

He tipped her chin up, then kissed her forehead. "I love you."

Her breath caught. "Well, that's a big deal."

Now it was his turn to worry because she wasn't saying those words back to him.

"I've . . . made some decisions and . . . " she began.

"Am I going to like these decisions?"

"I'm not sure."

Cait moved, settling between his legs, her back to him. He wrapped his arms around her, tucking her up against his chest, his chin on top of her head.

"Tell me what you're thinking."

Please don't walk away. Give us a chance.

"I spent the last few days working through everything. I looked at my life, I looked at what I've done. I cried, I mourned, I did a lot of soul searching," she said, pulling his hand close and kissing it. "I looked at where I want to be in a few years."

"And?" he said, his voice suddenly thick.

"I want a home. I want . . . stability. I want something I haven't had since I was really little. My parents love me, that's not the problem. But I was moving so often I barely had the chance to make friends."

Brannon still had a family home, one that he still visited. She'd been packed all over the globe, following her father's career. "Okay. Go on." He felt her tense, as if she thought he wasn't going to like what she was about to reveal. "When I said I love you, it was for real. So tell me what would make you happy."

"Besides you?" she said, looking at him now.

His heart went molten. "Besides me."

"I found an organization that would teach me how to train service dogs. It's a significant time commitment of at least a year, and then there's more training for the PTSD portion."

And with him bouncing all over the planet . . . Brannon's breath hitched.

"I checked the place out, and it's highly respected. It's only a few hours from here."

He closed his eyes, realizing she'd kept him in mind even as she'd planned her future. It made him love her even more.

"Sounds good. How soon would you need to start?"

That seemed to catch her off guard. "Ah, in a month. Until then, I thought I'd spend some time with this hot guy I know. Do some hiking, some camping, make love all night. That work for you?"

She meant him. "Oh, sweetheart," he whispered, kissing her neck. "Count me in."

Cait laughed. "You're so easy." She stretched her neck up so he could get even closer. "I need to visit my folks. I told them what happened in the swamp and they're worried about me. Well, not so much now that you're on the scene. My dad wants to meet you. You've done the impossible already, you've impressed The Major."

"Then we'll go see them together."

"You'd be okay with that?"

"He can't be any worse than my commanding officer in the 75th. That man ate corporals for breakfast." He paused. "But you have to come visit my folks, too. They're pretty mellow, at least until my dad gets in attorney mode."

Cait laughed. "I'll love them."

"How do you know that?" he asked.

"Because I love their son."

As his mind took in the words, Brannon felt his world change. He gently turned her in his arms. "You love me?"

She nodded. "I don't jump from exploding helicopters for just anyone, bud."

The kiss they shared was like a pact between them, one that promised more than either had ever thought they'd have. The silence that followed felt right, precious somehow.

"If you want, you can live here while you're going to school," he offered.

"I'd like that. Classes run until Friday at noon. I can drive back up here for the weekend, keep an eye on the place. And if the owner is here . . . even better."

"I'll try to be here as much as I can, but my job sends me all over the place, sometimes for long periods."

"I know. I'm going to check out the VA in Lexington. I need to see a counselor every now and then, work through some stuff."

"I think that's a good idea. I'm all for anything that helps you grow stronger."

"Your parents are in Florida, right?" she asked, and he nodded. "Then when we go to visit them, I should drop by the swamp and empty out that cabin. I won't be staying there on my own any longer."

Because she'll be here with me. "I'll help you. We can rent a boat and it'll go a lot faster."

"I need to visit Mike and Kia. And I . . . need to see Jeremy's girl and his son. That'll be rough."

"Count me in for that. Unless you don't want me there."

"I do. You make me feel whole again, give me a reason to go on."

He ran his fingers through her hair, caressing it gently. "When I saw you on that copter, I was so afraid you'd given up, you'd leave me behind."

"I thought I might too. But then I knew I had something to live for."

"Thank God you did."

She looked up at him now. "We'll make it, Bran. I don't doubt it. We're too stubborn to let this go."

He heard the certainty in her voice, and took it inside of himself as gospel.

Cait pulled him up and ushered him back into the cabin, made him sit at the table. A few moments later, a frosted cupcake appeared in front of him, with a single lighted candle.

"Happy belated birthday," she said. "Go on, make a wish."

So he made his wish, because it never hurt to ask the universe for a little help.

Let her stay with me forever.

THE END

Mission Notes

Before Veritas undertakes a mission, a comprehensive background dossier is compiled to assess the potential for success or failure of that mission. Here are some of the more interesting items gleaned from the mission code-named KILLNG GAME:

Returning veterans face many complex issues: finding jobs, reintegrating into society and dealing with physical and mental health problems. Post-Traumatic Stress Disorder occurs in anywhere from 11-22% of returning Afghanistan and Iraq war vets, and is even higher for those who served in the Vietnam War. Not all vets can find their way out of the darkness: Nearly eight thousand commit suicide each year, an average of 22 per day.

In 2015 it was estimated that nearly *fifty thousand* vets were homeless. The vast majority were male (over 90%), and nearly half of those had mental or physical health disabilities. Women are not excluded from the homeless ranks, often dealing with mental health issues secondary to sexual trauma sustained during their service.

Where women were not allowed in combat, they could be "attached" to a Special Ops, thereby skirting the ban. Working within that "loophole", the Marine's Female Engagement Teams (FET) were utilized primarily during the Iraq and Afghan wars.

In 2012 they were phased out. The Army also had a similar program (Cultural Support Teams) which interacted with village women. The book ASHLEY'S WAR talks about being part of a CST, and the ultimate cost of 1st Lt. White's service to her country.

Where much attention has been focused on threats from overseas terrorists post 9/11, homegrown threats have continued to grow, and, in many ways, have begun to eclipse those from outside the country. According to the Southern Poverty Law Center, over three hundred thousand people are involved in various separatist movements, including white supremacist groups such as Aryan Nations, as well as Stormfront, League of the South, Posse Comitatus, and numerous Christian Identity groups (to name a few).

One common thread running throughout these groups is the belief that the federal government is corrupt and does not legally hold power over American citizens. That revolution is often the only solution, rather than then ballot box. The sovereign citizen movements began in the late 1960's and gained traction in the 1980s. With the standoffs at Waco and Ruby Ridge, their numbers increased dramatically. That increase continued after the inauguration of a Black president in 2008.

Over the years, militia members have stockpiled weapons and resorted to extreme violence to make their cause known. The most notable of these was Timothy McVeigh's bombing of the Murrah Federal Building in Oklahoma (1995). Other targets have included synagogues, Black churches, federal marshals, local law enforcement and other government personnel. In essence, anyone they deem "the enemy."

In the end, KILLING GAME's mission came down to the tenacity and skills of two of America's finest warriors against those who would destroy what it is that makes our country free. Fortunately, Hardegree and Landry were up to the task.

Or as Cait would say, "Mess with the best, die like the rest."

About the Author

Jana Oliver never planned to become an author. In fact, she told her sixth grade teacher she wanted to be an international spy, which sounded very cool at the time.

That so didn't happen.

After pursuing various careers (registered nurse, disc jockey, travel agent, copywriter) someone flipped a switch in her brain and stories began to pour out. There were so many stories she decided to write them down and publish them. Then someone else published them, in the U.S. and then all over the world.

She's still surprised by all that.

A few years down the line Jana's an international bestselling author with over twenty books to her credit, and has won over a dozen major writing awards, including the Maggie Award of Excellence, the Daphne du Maurier, National Readers Choice and the Prism Award.

Nowadays she can be found writing her tales in Portugal when not sharing time with her very patient husband and their cranky (ghost) Feline Overlord, Ms. Dali.

www.JanaOliver.com

Also by Jana Oliver

DEMON TRAPPERS® SERIES
Forsaken (formerly The Demon Trapper's Daughter)
Forbidden (formerly Soul Thief)
Forgiven
Foretold
Grave Matters
Mind Games
Valiant Light
Lost Souls
Bitter Magic

TIME ROVERS® SERIES
Sojourn
Virtual Evil
Madman's Dance

VERITAS SERIES
Cat's Paw
Killing Game
Broken Dreams

DRAGONFIRE SERIES
The Circle of the Swan
The Healer's Path
The Summoning Stone
The Lore of Dragons

STANDALONE NOVELS & NON-FICTION
Briar Rose
Dead Easy
Tangled Souls
Socially Engaged: The Author's Guide to Social Media
(co-authored with Tyra Burton)